INDIAN SUMMER

www.transworldbooks.co.uk

Also by Marcia Willett

FORGOTTEN LAUGHTER

A WEEK IN WINTER

WINNING THROUGH

HOLDING ON

LOOKING FORWARD

SECOND TIME AROUND

STARTING OVER

HATTIE'S MILL

THE COURTYARD

THEA'S PARROT

THOSE WHO SERVE

THE DIPPER

THE CHILDREN'S HOUR

THE BIRDCAGE

THE GOLDEN CUP

ECHOES OF THE DANCE

MEMORIES OF THE STORM

THE WAY WE WERE

THE PRODIGAL WIFE

THE SUMMER HOUSE

THE CHRISTMAS ANGEL

THE SEA GARDEN

POSTCARDS FROM THE PAST

For more information on Marcia Willett and her books,
see her website at www.marciawillett.co.uk

INDIAN SUMMER

MARCIA WILLETT

BANTAM PRESS

LONDON · TORONTO · SYDNEY · AUCKLAND · JOHANNESBURG

TRANSWORLD PUBLISHERS
61–63 Uxbridge Road, London W5 5SA
A Random House Group Company
www.transworldbooks.co.uk

First published in Great Britain
in 2014 by Bantam Press
an imprint of Transworld Publishers

A CIP catalogue record for this book
is available from the British Library.

ISBN 9780593071533 (cased)

Addresses for Random House Group Ltd companies outside the UK
can be found at: www.randomhouse.co.uk
The Random House Group Ltd Reg. No. 954009

The Random House Group Limited supports the Forest Stewardship
Council® (FSC®), the leading international forest-certification organisation.
Our books carrying the FSC label are printed on FSC®-certified paper. FSC is the
only forest-certification scheme supported by the leading environmental organisations,
including Greenpeace. Our paper procurement policy can be found at
www.randomhouse.co.uk/environment

Typeset in 13½/16½pt Fournier by
Kestrel Data, Exeter, Devon
Printed and bound by
CPI Group (UK) Ltd, Croydon, CR0 4YY

2 4 6 8 10 9 7 5 3 1

To Peter Kingsman

CHAPTER ONE

The old Herm stands at the crossroads, looking west, guarding the secrets of a thousand years. He was known as Mercury or Hermes, the small god of travellers who kept company with those other gods of woods and streams. These Old Ones are forgotten now; those who worshipped at their shrines, poured a libation, left offerings of food, are long gone. But the old Herm remains, though his plinth is smashed and his body is crumbling away. The blank eyes, the faintly smiling lips and the rim of beard are still visible to anyone who stoops to look, pushing aside the wild flowers and fading grasses that hang like dreadlocks around his stony brow. He watches over this ancient way and those who travel it.

The dogs appear first around the bend in the lane, tails waving, still eager and energetic despite their walk. Their liver and white coats are sleek and shining, wet from their splashings in the stream, and the larger spaniel carries a ball in his mouth. Mungo follows more slowly with his elderly mutt, Mopsa, pottering along behind him. The August sunshine is hot and Mungo has slung his jersey around his waist, tying the sleeves in a loose knot. He stands for a moment, stretching in the warm dry air, snuffing up the scents of new-cut grass and honeysuckle. The dogs come racing back to him. Boz drops the ball at his feet and Sammy makes a grab for it but Mungo is quicker. He seizes the ball and throws it as far as he can. They skitter after it, jostling and barging each other, and he laughs out loud as he watches them. As usual, he is aware of the past all around him: the ghosts of Roman soldiers marching to the long-vanished fort; a line of laden packhorses plodding down to the Horse Brook, where the original granite clapper bridge still crosses the narrow stream.

Way back, when his name was beginning to be on everyone's lips, he'd acted in and directed a film that rocked the British box offices and became an international hit. This was its location: this valley, these crossways, the ford at the horse bridge. The vanished wooden fort had risen again and the air was once more riven with the clash of swords and the shouts of soldiers. The camera crew spent many rainy hours drinking coffee in Mungo's kitchen in the long-since converted smithy whilst the older members of the cast retired to their trailers in the paddock at Home Farm.

Isobel Trent was cast in the role of the wayward local beauty opposite his tough Roman general. They'd become cult figures; his films always successful, their partnership so magical. The media treated them like royalty; photographed them, gossiped about them, conjectured at the depth of their relationship.

'Let them talk,' Izzy said. 'Much the best way, Mungo darling. Puts them right off the scent.'

Her secret, stormy affair with Ralph was over by then.

He'd disappeared out of their lives for ever, after that final, terrible argument in Mungo's kitchen. How young they'd been; how serious and intense their emotions: his own rage and helplessness, Izzy's tears, and her despair, and Ralph's cruel indifference.

Mungo pauses at the crossroads, makes his obeisance to the old Herm, and follows the dogs up the steps, through the gate and into the cobbled courtyard. In the lane silence gathers again, shadows creep beneath twisty boughs of ash and thorn. The old Herm remains, watching the pathways, guarding his secrets.

Mungo towels down the dogs, pours them fresh water and leaves them to lie panting in the courtyard. He pushes the kettle on to the hotplate, pulls it off again as the telephone rings.

'Mungo. It's Kit.'

Kit Chadwick. Her voice is warm and eager and he sees her vividly in his mind's eye: ashy brown hair, smoky blue eyes, slender, restless.

'I hope this is to tell me you're coming down,' he says. 'God, it'd be good to see you, sweetie.'

'Well, it is, if you'll have me. London's sweltering, and something a bit weird has happened.' Her voice is suddenly uncertain. 'Honestly, Mungo. I really need to talk to you.'

'Then get the next train out.' He is alert, interested, but knows it's best not to question her now. 'Or will you drive?'

'I'd rather. You know me. I'd like to stay for a few days, if that's OK, and I might need to be a bit independent.'

'Fine,' he says easily. 'So when?'

'Later, when it's cooler. I'll be with you, say, nine-ish. Not too late?'

'Of course not.'

'And listen. I remembered earlier. It's Izzy's birthday.'

A tiny pause. 'So it is. We'll have a delicious little birthday supper. Gnocchi suit you? And I've got a bottle of Villa Masetti chilling in the fridge.'

'Sounds like heaven.'

'Go and pack then. And drive carefully.'

Suddenly he can't be bothered to make tea. He goes to stand at the stable door, looking out across the recumbent forms of the dogs into the cobbled courtyard. The big kitchen, where a long line of smiths once plied their trade, has blackened beams supporting its ceiling, and a slate floor and it is still the heart of the house which – over the years – has been extended to include the adjoining barn and converted into a very comfortable home.

'Camilla and I want you to have the smithy and the barn,' Archie said to him, forty years before. 'We think it's unfair that Dad's left it all to me just because he didn't approve of you being an actor.'

Mungo was very touched but not surprised: the gesture was typical of his older brother's sense of fair play. Archie, a partner in their late father's law practice in Exeter, still had the house, Home Farm and two small cottages, but he was welcome to them. Mungo loved the smithy. It was a perfect place to keep as a bolt-hole from London; coming down on the train from Paddington with his friends, giving parties. Camilla aided and abetted him. She loved his theatre friends, filled his fridge, asked them all up to the house for dinner.

Pretty Camilla: fair hair, fair skin inclining to freckles, generous, practical. She managed Archie, their children and the dogs with cheerful competence. His friends adored her, brought her presents, played with the boys, whilst Archie watched with contented tolerance. Archie and Camilla were his still centre. They'd get a babysitter so as to dash up to London to watch him perform on each first night, going backstage to congratulate him, and camping overnight in his tiny flat. And when he became famous they revelled in his success, shared in his good fortune and celebrated on a grander scale.

Leaning on the stable door in the sunshine, Mungo reflects on the glory days. It was good, back then, to return to his bolt-hole; sometimes alone, more often with a few special friends. He'd never much liked being alone. In those early days Izzy had been his most constant companion: Izzy – and a little later, Ralph.

Izzy's birthday. He hadn't needed the reminder.

Darling Izzy: sexy, complicated, highly strung. She'd started in musical theatre: Ado Annie in *Oklahoma!*, Adelaide in *Guys and Dolls*, Lois Lane in *Kiss Me, Kate*. He saw the potential actress, masked by low self-esteem and dramatic mood swings, and he persuaded her to audition for Puck in *The Dream* at the RSC, and later for Ariel in *The Tempest*. These roles brought her the attention of the critics, and acclaim – and, later, her partnership with him brought her great fame – but her heart remained faithful to those early days.

'I'm just a song-and-dance man,' she'd say. 'I'm terrified that suddenly everyone will realize I'm a fraud.'

They were in rep in Birmingham just beginning rehearsals

for *Twelfth Night* when she first met Ralph Stead. Izzy was cast as Maria, Ralph as Sebastian, Mungo as Feste. They shared gloomy digs and rehearsed in draughty church halls, but they were happy, the three of them. Izzy taught Mungo how to project his voice, singing with him to encourage his light tenor voice: 'Come away, come away, death' and 'When that I was and a little tiny boy'. They practised alone in the hall when everyone else had gone home, Izzy picking out the tune on the ancient piano. One evening she stopped suddenly, looked up at him as he leaned beside her.

'Oh, darling, isn't it hell? I think I'm in love with Ralph.'

Mungo remembers the mix of anxiety and excitement in her brown eyes, the odd clutch of fear in his gut; a brief, sharp foreshadowing of disaster.

'So what, sweetie?' he said lightly. 'So am I. Everyone is in love with Ralph.'

'Are you jealous?' she asked him much later, when she and Ralph became lovers. 'Don't be, Mungo. I need to know you're on my side.'

'I'm always on your side,' he answered. And it was true.

As he leans on the stable door it seems that he can hear her voice, singing somewhere from the lane below him near the old Herm: 'A foolish thing was but a toy, For the rain it raineth every day.'

When he finished singing that, on the first night, alone on the stage at the end of the play, there was a moment's hush in the theatre before the audience exploded into ecstatic applause. Even now his eyes fill with tears as he remembers it; remembers the warm congratulations of the young cast, Ralph's slap on the back, and Izzy's hug, her voice breathing in his ear: 'Oh, well done, well done, darling. That was just perfect.'

Just perfect until terrible old love spoiled it all so disastrously.

'Damn and blast!' says Mungo violently, surprising himself. After all, why should the past disturb him so much today? Because it's Izzy's birthday?

The dogs stir. Silent and alert, they stare towards the gate and then jump up, tails wagging. The gate opens and Camilla comes into the courtyard. She's wearing an old denim skirt with a faded cotton shirt and flip-flops; her fair hair is tucked behind her ears and she looks youthful: the Camilla of those old, happy days. For a moment the past is vivid with him again, then she moves out of the shadows and he sees her clearly.

'Hi,' she says. 'I've come to collect the dogs. Have they been good?'

Mungo is glad that she is here. It is difficult to imagine a ghost in Camilla's calm, sensible presence.

'Good boys, then. Good fellows.' Praising the dogs, who leap about her, she bends to receive their welcome, stoops to stroke Mopsa, who beats her tail briefly on the cobbles, rolls an eye, but doesn't stir. 'Come on then. Time to go home.' She looks at Mungo hopefully. 'Coming up for a cup of tea? Archie's not back yet. Come and keep me company.'

He hesitates, but he doesn't want to be alone; not just at the moment, with Izzy's shade hovering in the lane by the old Herm.

'Yes,' he says. 'Only I've just had a phone call from Kit asking if she can come down tonight so I mustn't be too long.'

'Oh, that's great!' Her face is bright with the expectation

of seeing Kit. 'What time? Do you want to bring her up to supper?'

'Not this evening.' He doesn't want to share Kit on her first night. 'She's not arriving till about nine. Tomorrow, perhaps? She's staying for a few days.'

Camilla nods. 'Fine. Archie'll be thrilled. Any special reason for the visit? Seems a bit sudden.'

'She says London's sweltering,' he answers evasively as they marshal the dogs. He can't imagine what Kit's problem might be but he has no intention of mentioning that she has one until he's found out a bit more. 'She said that she won't be leaving until it's cooler but I want to be quite ready for her.'

'I hope it's not another drama,' Camilla says as they walk together up the lane. 'I shall never forget the trouble with that man she met on the internet dating site last year. All the excitement, and then finding out he was married.'

'He was such good company, though. From that point of view he was a huge improvement on the Awful Michael.'

'Oh my God! The Awful Michael.' Camilla bursts out laughing, clutching Mungo's arm. 'He could bore for England, that man. Whatever did she see in him?'

'Well, to begin with, I think she saw him as a rather dear old dog. You know, a noble golden retriever or a kindly Labrador. Wonderful to look at but no brain. I could see the attraction. You wanted to stroke his head and give him a cuddle. Take him for a walk. The trouble was, she mistook his utter lack of character and imagination for stability. And, of course, the naval connection encouraged her to think that her family would approve. The Establishment and so on.'

'You were rather brutal, though, in the end.'

'What else could I do, Millie? He was ruining her. Wearing her down. She was becoming as boring as he was. Well, you saw that for yourself. An elderly widower with however many children and grandchildren. He wanted her to become staid and sensible and wear terrible shoes. I was kind to begin with, admit.'

Camilla can't stop laughing. 'I think we all hoped that if he came to stay often enough she'd see him in his true light, but my heart used to sink every time you phoned to say, "The Awful Michael's coming down with us this weekend." Archie would groan and complain that Kit was being turned into a stranger and that he'd have to invite Michael out sailing. And then he'd take him on the river and Michael would tell him how to sail the boat. Archie would be fuming by the time he got back home. Even Izzy couldn't work her magic on the Awful Michael.'

'We were all terribly patient, Millie, but I had to act once there was talk of selling up her flat and moving to his house in the country. He didn't want her to work, of course, and he disapproved of me and Izzy. Kit would have simply died of boredom. Anyway, we needed her.'

'But how did you actually do it, in the end? She told me you said brutal things to her.'

Mungo snorts contemptuously. 'Rubbish. It's simply that the truth hurts. I told her quite firmly that once they were living together she would see that the Awful Michael was not a handsome, darling old dog but a narrow-minded, intransigent old bore. I explained that her friends were already growing tired of the stories of his mind-numbing experiences in the Falklands War droning out over their dinner tables and that if she moved to Kent or Surrey, or wherever, that would be the end. She would wither and grow old trying to learn bridge and listening to *The Archers* with only the Awful Michael for company.'

'There's nothing wrong with *The Archers*,' says Camilla indignantly. 'I love *The Archers*.'

'But there is if it's your sole form of entertainment, Millie. There is more to life than *The Archers*. Kit loves the theatre, she loves going to exhibitions. Did you know that she's got the most delightful collection of small original paintings by practically unknown modern artists? She adores little jolly supper parties where everyone gossips too much, drinks too much, and we diss our friends. The Awful Michael was slowly annihilating her. It was like watching a candle being put out very, very slowly. Agony. She knew it really, of course, and she was in two minds anyway, so I just told her very firmly what was best for her.'

'Dear old Kit. She's so trusting. There's a naïvety as if she's never quite grown up. That's why she's so much fun. But the internet man was a bit of a downer for her and then her mother dying last year really knocked her sideways, though it was hardly unexpected. She was over ninety, after all.'

Mungo remembers Kit telephoning: 'Guess what? My old ma died this morning. I'm an orphan, Mungo. The funeral's on Friday. May I come on to you afterwards on Saturday?'

She mourned, drank too much, had Mopsa on her bed at night. They sat together on his sofa, heaped about with dogs borrowed for the occasion – 'I need the dogs,' Kit explained to Camilla, who totally understood and brought Bozzy and

Sam straight down to the smithy – and she talked and wept in turn.

'There's something timeless about her,' Camilla is saying. 'You never think about Kit in terms of age. You're the same, Mungo. Perhaps it's because neither of you has had the wear and tear of marriage and children.'

'You just try working with actors, sweetie,' he says. 'Plenty of wear and tear, I promise you.'

She laughs. 'But at the end of the day you say good-night and walk out,' she says. 'Anyway, I'm glad. It means I have you to myself.' She links her arm in his as they turn in through the gateway from the lane. 'Do you ever regret anyone, Mungo?'

'I regret Ralph,' he says without thinking – and she looks up at him, surprised.

'Ralph? Gosh, that was a long time ago. Was he . . . ? Did you . . . ? I thought he was mad about Izzy. She was certainly crazy about him.'

'Ralph was . . . versatile,' he answers. 'Anyway, much too long ago to be regretting at this late date.'

'He went to the States, didn't he? I remember Izzy was devastated.'

Mungo nods. 'So was I. We were in the middle of rehearsals for *Journey's End* and he simply walked out. He was invited to audition for a small film part but I never heard if he got it. By the time the dust settled he'd moved on. "He had softly and silently vanished away – For the Snark *was* a Boojum, you see." He was good at the young British gentleman roles but he wasn't very talented beyond his youth and spectacularly good looks. Sorry. That sounds bitchy, doesn't it?'

Camilla frowns, trying to remember. 'I didn't care for him much. Rather too pleased with himself.'

The meadow below the house is being cut and they pause to watch the tractor as it wheels around the edge of the field. Tall grasses fall in golden clouds of pollen and dust; a shimmer of midges hangs and sways in the hot blue air, breaking and reforming in its endless dance. The dogs hurry on towards the house; a pretty, white-painted stone house set amongst camellia bushes and azaleas. The wooden frames of the sash windows are painted dark green to match the front door. Coming upon it here, at the edge of the moor in this wild ancient setting, one might think it like a house in a fairy story.

Mungo is comforted by its familiarity, glad that Archie and Camilla have been able to keep it much as it was through his and Archie's childhood. Camilla is watching him.

'Are you OK?' she asks.

'Yes,' he answers quickly. 'Yes, of course,' and then adds: 'It was just Kit reminding me that it's Izzy's birthday.'

'That's why you were thinking about Ralph.' She sounds almost relieved, as if some puzzle has been solved.

The dogs have disappeared in search of cold water to drink and cool slates to lie upon, and the house is full of sunshine.

'Yes,' he says. 'That's it. Izzy and Ralph,' and he changes the subject as they go into the house together.

After Mungo has gone, Camilla goes out to fetch the washing from the line slung between the plum trees in the orchard. In the long grass wasps crawl stickily in the rotten fruit, drunk on the sweet fermenting juice, and down in the woods a pigeon is cooing its lazy summer song. The sheets are hot and crisp and she folds them carefully into the old wicker basket, thinking all the while about Mungo and Ralph and Izzy. If she's honest she has to admit that she never really liked Izzy all that much: she was too mercurial, too needy. Of course, Archie adored her – and she played up to him.

'Poor little Izzy,' he'd say affectionately. 'She's had it tough, you know. Both parents killed in a car accident. Brought up by a strict old cousin. She's done jolly well for herself.'

Camilla had to bite her tongue sometimes; close her lips on a cool rejoinder. Izzy was so thin, so quick, so witty, that she, Camilla, felt ponderous beside her. Pregnant, slung about with small children, she felt it was an unequal contest. Yet those years were such happy ones.

Camilla folds the last sheet into the basket. She remembers what Mungo said about Ralph and wonders in what way he regrets him. Perhaps he sees Ralph simply as a symbol of their youth. The three of them were inseparable during those early years in rep; and afterwards when Mungo started his own company. Camilla hoists the basket on to her hip and takes it into the utility room. She can't be bothered to sort out the sheets; it's too hot. Instead she wanders back outside where the dogs are stretched in the shade, fast asleep.

It was Kit who named the dogs, litter brothers, when she saw them first as puppies. Camilla remembers how she and Archie argued over names, neither able to hit on the right ones. Then Kit came to stay with Mungo and was told of the dilemma. She walked up with Mungo to see the puppies, curled together in the big dog basket.

'Boswell and Johnson,' Kit said at once, going to kneel

beside them. 'Bozzy and Sam. Sammy and Boz. The big one's Bozzy and the little one's Sam. They are *so* cute.'

The names were so right for them that Camilla and Archie couldn't think why they hadn't thought of them first.

'It's a gift,' Kit said modestly, perching in the dog basket, lifting the warm, sleepy puppies on to her lap. 'Oh, why wasn't I born a dog! How simple life would be.'

Camilla is filled with affection as she remembers the scene; glad that Kit is coming to stay. She's been such a good friend to Mungo, and the whole family love her.

'She should have been married with children of her own,' Camilla has said at regular intervals through the years to Mungo, to Archie. 'I can't imagine why she hasn't. She's so much fun and she's very attractive.'

It's funny, Camilla thinks, that she's never minded Archie adoring Kit, flirting with her, making jokes. She's never scented the whiff of danger that was present with Izzy. There was an instability, a vulnerable neediness, about Izzy that has never been there with Kit despite her moments of crisis and sudden crazy whims. She's managed her interior design company with confidence and flair, and she has good friends. Izzy was always so grateful for attention, for love.

'She's an actor, Millie,' Mungo would say. He is the only person to call her Millie; she doesn't like the nickname from anyone else. 'That's what we actors are like. We crave approval. It's what it's all about.'

But Mungo was never like Izzy, thinks Camilla, though Ralph always needed to be the centre of attention, admired, fêted. Perhaps that's what drew him and Izzy together – and perhaps that was the reason for the break-up of their affair.

Camilla glances at her watch. Archie should be home soon. She might try to catch him on his mobile and suggest that he picks up a few things for her in Ashburton. It would be nice to make something special if Kit is coming to supper tomorrow.

Down on his mooring at Stoke Gabriel on the river Dart, Archie watches life on the water. It's been too hot to take the boat off her mooring, and there's no breath of wind anyway, but he likes to potter, check things out; to sit here on *The Wave*, feeling the lift of the tide beneath her keel. Here he can escape the responsibilities that worry at him at home: the cost of repairs to the properties, paying his tax, keeping things running. It's odd how being just those few yards away from dry land makes such a difference; gives that sense of escape and relaxation. He can hear the whistle of the old steam railway as it trundles through the valley on its way to Kingswear; such an evocative sound bringing memories of his childhood; trips on the paddle steamers coming down to Dartmouth from Totnes; sailing with friends from the naval college when he was older. On the river, out at sea, he feels free, detached from that other self who sees things with such a clear eye: who likes to dot the i's and cross the t's.

'Mungo's been in for tea,' Camilla says, phoning his mobile, interrupting this idyll, 'and he was a bit odd. Apparently it's Izzy's birthday so I think he was just feeling a bit nostalgic. Oh, and Kit's coming down later this evening. Isn't that great? He'll bring her up for supper tomorrow.'

Archie agrees that it is great, makes a note of the shopping list, says he'll be home soon. He continues to feel contented, idle, delighted that Kit will be arriving. His relationship with

Kit is uncomplicated and rewarding: she demands nothing from him except his complicity in her eccentricities. She loves to come sailing with him on the river as long as nothing too frightening is likely to happen and she is allowed to be a passenger. It's no good asking Kit to take the helm or haul on a sheet. She'd be gazing at something on the bank – 'Is that a heron?' – or waving at some fellow traveller just at the crucial moment. She likes it best when they moor up in quiet backwaters like Old Mill Creek to make a cup of coffee or tea. Even then he doesn't totally trust her with the gas – 'Which tap do I turn, Archie?' – so she sits in the sun, feeding the ducks with pieces of bread.

'Isn't it utter heaven?' she'll say, taking her mug, beaming up at him. 'I don't know why we don't all live on boats, do you?'

Camilla never minds him taking Kit out. 'It'll do you good,' she says. 'You don't need me along. Enjoy yourselves.' She's never been jealous of his closeness to Kit. Not like with Izzy – Archie makes a little rueful face – but then Izzy was very different. God, he'd lusted after her when they were all young together. She was so gorgeous in a waif-like Audrey Hepburn way and she made him feel tough and protective. He was sure that Camilla never knew how he really felt, and there had never been anything out of order, but he wondered if some feminine intuition made her suspicious. She was always just the tiniest bit on edge when Izzy was around and he had to be very careful to play it cool.

Izzy's birthday. She shall grow not old, as we that are left grow old, he thinks rather sentimentally. It's easy now to remember her as she was way back when they were all

young: the trips to Birmingham, when she and Mungo were
in rep, or to London, and weekends at the smithy. It was the
wretched Ralph who flung the spanner in the works. Archie
never much liked Ralph: too good-looking, too smooth.
He got poor darling Izzy into a crazy state where she didn't
know whether she was coming or going and then he'd simply
walked out on her – on them all – without a backward glance.
Izzy was devastated. Of course she became very successful,
Mungo made sure of that, but it was as if an era of their lives
was suddenly over: their youth had come to an abrupt end.

Archie empties the dregs of his tea over the side, rather
ashamed of his mawkishness. He wonders what happened to
Ralph, stands for a moment to salute Izzy on her birthday,
then goes below to close down. Maybe Kit will like a little
jaunt on the river. The others won't be interested. Camilla
will probably say it's too hot for her, and it's no good asking
poor old Mungo, who feels sick on the Dartmouth Ferry.
Archie shakes his head, amused, thinking of how Mungo
was named by their father for Mungo Park: nobody less like
the great explorer than his younger brother. At the same
time, Mungo was always a naughty child: making up stories,
persuading Billy Judd at Home Farm – who was old enough
to know better – to join in with his pranks. Their father
despaired of Mungo and he, Archie, had been detailed off to
look after this troublesome sibling, who broke every rule,
frightened the local children with his stories of ghosts and
vampires, and encouraged them in his games of make-believe
and dressing-up. It was almost a relief to go away to boarding
school so as to escape the responsibility. It changed when he
was older, met Camilla at a point-to-point and fell in love with

her. Camilla adored Mungo from the outset. She thought he was amusing, good value.

Archie wonders now why he never minded; was never jealous of their close relationship. Was it simply because he knew Mungo was gay and therefore no threat to him? Camilla softened his rather censorious attitude to his younger brother so that he was able to allow his natural affection for Mungo to surface. And then, when their father died and Archie inherited the whole shooting match, he was able to be generous, to give Mungo the old smithy and the support he needed in his early acting career.

Occasionally his own rather strict moral code is stretched by Mungo's laid-back approach to life, his ability to turn a blind eye and break the rules, but not just lately. Today on the river, tomorrow Kit coming to supper: life is good. Archie locks the cabin door, climbs into the dinghy, starts up the outboard engine and heads for the shore.

Mungo waits for Kit. He checks his watch, looks at his preparations for their supper, dashes upstairs to check her bedroom and shower room. All is ready. When the smithy, with its little barn, was converted Mungo decided that the barn should be self-contained, connected to the smithy not just by a door from the kitchen but also with a covered way and its own front door. It would be perfect for his guests with its two double bedrooms, bathroom and a kitchen-sitting-room: to give them a measure of independence so that they could stay up late to watch television or get up early without feeling they were being a nuisance. Anyway, he rather dislikes seeing women in a state of *déshabillé*: hair all over the place, pale faces, tatty dressing gowns. He prefers a little *maquillage*, a touch of artifice. Only Izzy, and, later, Kit ever had the privilege of staying with him in the smithy rather than in the barn.

Izzy simply took it for granted.

'Just in case I have bad dreams, darling,' she said. 'You know me!'

She'd appear unexpectedly at his bedside in the early hours, shivering, and he'd sleepily push the duvet aside and hold out his arms.

'Come on then,' he'd say. 'Just for the cuddle,' and he'd hold her and comfort her until the nightmares passed.

He guessed that it was losing her parents so suddenly and violently when she was barely nine that caused the night-mares. Her imagination was vivid and the terrible details of the car accident haunted her.

Very occasionally they'd make love.

'Just to be friendly,' she'd say, but it wasn't important to him. It was the companionship, the jokes, the gossip; these were the things he craved. They'd sit with a bottle of wine between them, laughing, shredding reputations or building them, praising or slandering, depending on whom they loved or disliked most.

'Why don't you invite Ralph down?' she asked him during those early days of rehearsal for *Twelfth Night*. 'He'd love it. You like him, don't you?'

'So long as he sleeps in the barn.'

She made a face at him. 'Don't you trust me?'

He shook his head. 'It's me I don't trust, sweetie.'

She'd sing to him while he prepared supper: 'I Cain't

Say No', '(When I Marry) Mister Snow', 'Why Can't You Behave?'. He'd hear her lines, give her some tips, encourage her. She'd listen to him sing, show him how to breathe, to project his voice.

As he waits for Kit he seems to hear Izzy's voice again: 'Come away, come away, death; And in sad cypress let me be laid'.

Hot tears sting his eyes. Mopsa leaps up, begins to bark, and Mungo hears the car engine in the lane. Kit is here. Filled with relief, casting away his sadness, he hurries out to meet her.

In one of the small farm cottages, further down the lane, James Hatton assembles his supper. Beans on toast, an apple and a mug of coffee. Sally wouldn't approve but Sally isn't here. She's comfortably tucked up in Oxford, in their little house in Jericho, with a glass of wine. Or she might be with friends. Anyway, she's not here, in this quiet valley surrounded by this wonderfully bucolic silence, and looking in horror at the pile of washing up to be done or at the unmade bed. They came on holiday to this cottage, quite a few years ago now, just after they were married, and loved it so much they returned several times. Perhaps it was those holidays that gave him the ideas for the location for the book that he is now researching. Back then the cottage was charmingly rustic; these days it wouldn't meet the health and safety regulations. Camilla warned him about it when he telephoned; explained that the cottage had been empty for a year and was about to be renovated but that he was welcome to it for a low rent for a month. He dashed down to see it and couldn't find much wrong with it. The kitchen and bathroom needed modernizing; so what? It was fine for his simple needs; perfect to get away from the daily round and let his mind roam out into the new novel.

'So long as you're quite sure,' Camilla said. 'No complaints, mind, once you're in. Loved the book, by the way. I think it was so clever how you mixed up the suspense with the romance and made it all so real. Now, don't worry, nobody will disturb you. We've got a new tenant coming into the other cottage next door – a young military wife with two small children – but we'll warn her that you like to be left alone. How exciting to think that you're setting the book around here. We'll have to be careful, won't we?'

He laughed with her. Impossible to imagine anything of great excitement happening to Camilla and Archie, or the two old boys at the farm. Of course, Sir Mungo was a rather different story but even he was well past his glory days. Still laughing, James went back to the house to have a drink with Archie and Camilla, paid a week's rent in advance, and the deal was done.

Now, James eats his supper with the door open. Just back from his weekend dash to Oxford, he is readjusting to the silence of the valley: no wail of police sirens, no traffic, no low-level quacking of neighbours' television or radio. He is beginning his second week at the cottage and he is pleased with his progress. This is his second book – the first one was self-published – and the big hope is that this new one will catch the attention of a London agent or a big publishing house and he'll become an overnight sensation. He'd like to be able to give up his teaching job at the local comprehensive and write full time; maybe even free up Sally from her nursing work so that they can start a family. He needs a lucky break of some sort, but he'll get it, he's sure of it, and at least he can take these few weeks during the summer holidays to check the location and rough out the first draft. He set his first book in Gloucester and it had received quite a lot of local hype. He'd seen, then, the value of using actual places – cafés, pubs, shops – and he was given support by the local bookshop and the local press, so now he's decided that the West Country tourist trail might bring even better results.

It was Sally who reminded him of the cottage, of how kind Camilla and Archie had been, and managed to dig out the telephone number. Sal's a great support; she wants him to succeed and she's prepared to put up with the separation to make it happen. Sal works hard at the Radcliffe – he glances at his watch, suddenly remembering that she's on nights this week – in fact she'll be on her way there now. He'll send an email instead of phoning her to tell her how the day has gone and she can pick it up later.

He finishes his beans on toast, cuts the apple into quarters and throws the core out into the hedge. Pushing the plate aside, opening his laptop, he starts to type his email.

Another good day. Very hot again and lots of tourists but I'm really finding my way around now. Not the new boy any more. I know where to park when the car parks are full, cafés off the tourist beat, etc. The cottage continues to work very well while I'm writing. I really like this big living space and being able to be untidy!! Not like our little box, is it? Nobody bothers me, which is wonderful, but everyone is friendly, they wave when I see them in the lane, etc. I thought we might give a little party at the end and invite them all. Archie and Camilla are very kind. I am tactfully issued invitations for coffee or a drink, and Archie has offered another day on the river. Very useful. So different seeing the land from the water and I think he likes an excuse to get out there. Sir Mungo is at his cottage, back from a week in Scotland with friends, apparently. He shouted a greeting when I drove past, very matey, and I'm tempted to see if he could give me a bit of a leg up. The thing is, I see my stuff definitely as television and he was always a theatre man, apart from those big epic dramas he did back in the sixties and seventies. I imagine he still has contacts, though Camilla says he's more or less retired now. Next door continues to be quiet, given there are two small children living there. They go to bed quite early and their mother – Emma, did I say her name was? – keeps herself to herself. I suspect that Camilla has warned them that I'm trying to work.

I did another recce around the little local towns this morning. Ashburton and Buckfastleigh. Little grey-stone moorland towns that, at first sight, are so attractive that I can't quite see my unsavoury characters inhabiting them. The other problem is their smallness. You can use big department stores to set scenes in and get away with it, like I did in Gloucester, but it's much more difficult in these very small shops where you'd know everyone by name after the first few weeks and I'd probably be done for slander or libel or whatever!! I shall have to be a bit more subtle. Of course there's Exeter just a few miles away, and Plymouth to the west, but I'm very much drawn to these smaller places. As

I was telling you at the weekend I've rather fallen in love with Totnes and the surprising mix of characters you see in the town. There's a good, relaxed vibe but something edgy, too, which makes it possible to allow my story to take place there. I just know that this is going to be my breakthrough book, Sal. I shall put Totnes on the map!! But not this valley! Nothing could ever happen here except the peaceful predictability of ages past stretching through another millennium. Great for working, though. What I really love is not having any timetables to work to, no homework to mark or lessons to plan. I feel a bit selfish being able to do this while you're working hard, Sal, but it'll be worth it when I'm at number one in the bestseller lists. I know you were worried that I'd stay in bed till midday but actually I get up quite early. I'm really enjoying just being out and about, soaking up the atmosphere and watching people, and then drafting out the novel in the evening. Which is what I'm about to do now. I've got a few new ideas, Sal, so I shall get down to some work. Hope it's quiet on the ward!

Lots of love J xx

An hour later he switches off his laptop and wanders out through the open door. The small front gardens, separated by a stone wall, are a tangle of fuchsia bushes and he leans on the wooden gate relishing the darkness and the silence. Out in the lane the shadows are black and dense beneath the ash trees, though there is still the faint gleam of gold where buttercups grow in the ditch. A bat flittering close to his head startles him and he lets out a smothered cry, ducking and beating it away, just as a brighter light shines out suddenly from an upstairs room next door. A shadow detaches itself from the darkness under the trees and James peers at it, the gate creaking under his weight, wondering if it is Sir Mungo taking a last walk with his little dog. There is no sound, the shadows merge again, and presently he hears the sound of a car engine starting up, growing fainter and dwindling away.

CHAPTER TWO

When Kit awakes in the morning she knows exactly where she is. There is no confusion between waking and sleeping: she is instantly alert to the pattern of the leaves of the tree outside the open window and the warmth of Mopsa curled behind her knees.

'She always deserts me when you're here,' Mungo said.

'That's because she knows my need is greater than yours,' she answered.

She reaches a hand down to stroke the rough warm coat, and Mopsa stirs and grumbles in her sleep. Kit sighs with the pleasure of being here with Mopsa and Mungo, knowing that Archie and Camilla and the dogs are just along the lane. Though she lives and works alone she needs these networks that support her. Her own family live barely fifteen miles away from the smithy: her twin brother, Hal, and his wife, Fliss, live at The Keep, which has been the family home for generations of Chadwicks. There are three generations still living at The Keep – there were four, until their mother died last year – and Kit loves the continuity, the sense of home-coming whenever she returns.

With Mungo, however, there is a different dynamic: she is not a sister, cousin, aunt or daughter. He is a mate, an old chum; no judgements are made, no standards required except the crucial one of loyalty. They sympathize with each other's weaknesses, rejoice in their respective strengths, commiserate when vicissitude strikes.

She saw him first years and years ago when she was working at the Old Vic in Bristol during her school holidays, running errands, making coffee, checking props. Oh, how she loved it: the sense of family, of seeing a new production building; Val May directing with such energy and inspiration. Watching from the back of the tiny auditorium, she was stage-struck; star-struck; in love with the whole young cast of actors.

When, years later, she was invited to provide some props for a play Mungo was directing, and she was introduced to him, she reminded him of that season in rep in Bristol and his face lit up with the memory of it.

'Richard Pasco as Henry V,' he said at once.

'Oh, yes!' she cried. 'I was totally in love with him. And with Michael Jayston. Both at once.'

'Oh, sweetie, me too,' he answered with such a heartfelt expression that they both burst out laughing.

'I felt so proud,' she told him, 'when you became really famous. I used to go round telling everyone I knew you. Just on the strength of making you an occasional cup of coffee or finding you a lost prop. I was very lowly.'

'So was I,' he said. 'Understudying, getting all the tiny parts. But it was a wonderful time being in rep. Let me introduce you to Izzy. I just know you'll get on so well.'

Izzy greeted her as if she was already an old friend; there was an immediate rapport. They were two single women, unconventional and creative, with a similar line in humour and experience. Mungo encouraged them, drew them closer, orchestrated a dazzling evening. Kit could hardly believe her luck: she was talking, laughing, drinking with Sir Mungo Kerslake and Dame Isobel Trent as if she had known them for ever.

So it began. They took her to their hearts, invited her to first nights, Sunday lunch parties, and, in turn, she introduced them to her friends and family. It was a delightful coincidence that the smithy should be only a few miles from The Keep. A supper party was arranged so that Camilla and Archie could meet Fliss and Hal, and so the bonds were strengthened even more.

Izzy took a particular interest in Kit's work. She relished a day out with Kit, going to an auction, to a reclamation yard; finding an unexpected bargain or choosing a particular object for a client. They had fun together; protected each other from occasional bouts of loneliness, joked about their mutual married friends' combined mission to propel them into a similar state of marital bliss. As she grew to know Izzy better, Kit began to see the bravery behind the laughter; the pain beneath the jollity. Later, she was able to support Mungo in his attempt to conceal Izzy's lapses from her fans and from the media. The drinking became more difficult to conceal; the suicidal depths of her depression impossible to alleviate.

Her death was tragic but, in the end, almost a relief to all three of them.

Kit misses her terribly but Mungo remains one of her dearest friends. It was wonderful, last evening, to arrive to such a welcome, to a delicious supper, to a comfortable exchange of news, of gossip; to discuss everything and everybody – except Jake.

'I don't want to talk tonight,' she said at once. 'Not tonight. The timing's got to be right, Mungo.' And he understood just as she knew he would; no irritation or impatience, just a calm acceptance. She didn't want to pick apart her affair with Jake all amongst the coffee cups and empty wine glasses and burned-out candles as if he were simply another item of gossip. Jake is far too important for that.

Kit pushes aside the duvet and sits on the edge of the bed. On the wall are four small watercolours by an almost un-known Suffolk artist that she found for Mungo in a gallery in Aldeburgh. She remembers that journey: the joy of her discovery of this artist, a shy, private woman with whom she still communicates by email. The watery evocation of marsh and estuary is so delicate, the pale tints so beautiful, that Kit can almost hear the lonely cry of the curlew. It was her first commission from Mungo but there had been others since: the old French farmhouse table in the kitchen; the hand-painted blinds for the dormer windows in the barn. One of her great joys is to travel to out-of-town salerooms and exhibitions in search of the unusual; to stay in a pub, meet the local people.

Kit is longing for a mug of coffee. The makings are all there on the oak chest but she feels a need to be outside, breath-ing the fresh air, experiencing a connection with the natural world. Mopsa raises her head, watching her with bright intelligent eyes. She jumps off the bed and runs to the door, tail wagging. Kit stands up, seizes her dressing gown from the chair and thrusts her feet into her sandals. She opens the door quietly and follows Mopsa down the stairs and into the kitchen. There is no sign of Mungo, though the kettle is hot to the touch, which means that he is awake. She pushes it back on the hotplate to boil and lets Mopsa out into the courtyard. Then she pulls on the dressing gown, makes coffee and takes the mug outside. How quiet it is, how warm. Honeysuckle loops and tangles over the high stone wall; red valerian and crowns of pink and white feverfew cling in its crevices. A tiny wren works the cobbles, flittering up to the wall and continuing its hunt for food amongst the stones.

Mopsa is at the gate. She whines impatiently and Kit opens it gently, quietly, and they go out together into the lane. Kit strolls slowly, the coffee mug clasped in both hands. She pauses to sip, to breathe deeply, to watch a rabbit long-legging it into the tall faded grasses in the ditch. Mopsa, busy with a scent, sees the flick of the scut out of the corner of her eye and is after the rabbit in a dash and a scatter of dry earth and tiny stones. Kit watches sympathetically as Mopsa scrapes and scrabbles at the hole down which the rabbit has vanished. She sips her coffee, wondering how she might begin her conversation about Jake with Mungo. She's mentioned him but never in great detail; it's still impossible, even after all these years, to talk lightly about Jake.

As she tries a few opening gambits she feels foolish. How to explain a love affair that drifted on for years, that was neglected occasionally in favour of new experiences, that she took so much for granted? For twelve years Jake was a part of her life. He proposed to her at intervals but she never took him too seriously. Jacques Villon: she nicknamed him Jake the Rake because he loved women. As well as being lovers they were such good friends that she feared they'd become too used to each other for it to be the real thing: how awful if she were to marry him and then fall madly in love with someone else. And then, when she realized how much she loved him, how much she had to lose, it was too late.

Wandering behind Mopsa in the lane, she remembers the shock when the depth of her love for Jake revealed itself. Suddenly she simply couldn't imagine life without him.

She went to his flat to see him. He'd been away in France on family business; his matriarchal paternal grandmother had died suddenly and there had been lots to sort out, loose ends to tie up. His father was dead and a great deal was now falling on Jake's shoulders. The Villons were a clannish family, staunch Roman Catholics, and even Jake had been under his grandmother's thumb. He'd also been extraordinarily fond of her.

'Was it hell?' Kit asked sympathetically. She'd met Jake's grandmother once at a family gathering but it had not proved an overwhelming success. 'I'm so sorry, honey. You'll miss her, won't you?'

Jake nodded, made an attempt at a smile and sighed instead, pushing his hands through his hair. Kit saw that there were a few grey hairs amongst the black and she felt a twinge of terror. The years had fled by so fast and she'd wasted so many of them. She opened her mouth to tell him so but he was already speaking.

'I'm moving to Paris,' he was saying abruptly. 'I've arranged a transfer with the bank. There's so much to look after and Uncle Jean-Claude is too old to take it all on.'

She stared at him. In his dark city suit, white shirt, sober tie, he looked frighteningly adult; not the familiar Jake of student days but a mature man with responsibilities and worries.

Kit thought: he's not far off forty. Nearly middle-aged. Thank God I realized before it was too late. Paris will be fun. I'll learn the language properly, settle down, have darling French babies. He's hating the thought of leaving, I can see that.

She said, 'Well, I can understand that. You're the only male of your generation, aren't you? You can't just abandon them.'

He looked at her then, eyebrows lifted quizzically, and she guessed that he was surprised that she should respond in such a calm manner. With an inner twist of bitterness, she realized that he would expect her to be far less adult; to protest or make light of it, refusing to take it seriously. Her heart gave a twinge of compassion, imagining his feelings at the thought of the separation that surely lay ahead.

'No, I can't just abandon them,' he agreed heavily, turning away, dragging off his jacket. 'But it'll be a hell of a wrench.'

She guessed at the reason for his misery: she had refused him so often that it was unlikely she would change her mind now that he was returning permanently to France. Her calm manner could also have been interpreted as indifference.

'Oh, Jake,' she said quickly, 'it will be, I can see that. You'll be leaving so many friends and memories here. But do you think that I could come with you?'

She waited for his look of joy, the straightening of his

shoulders, the outstretched arms, knowing he would not mis-understand or play games with her. This was far too important . . . He was staring at her in disbelief.

'I love you, you see,' she said, rushing on, trying to remove all the past pain of rejection. 'I realized when you were away. I always have, I can see that now. It's taken me too long to grow up. Oh, honey, I missed you so much.'

Jake sat down abruptly on the arm of the sofa, fists be-tween his knees. He closed his eyes for a moment and she came to kneel behind him on the cushions, her cheek against his shoulder.

'I can't believe this,' he said quietly. 'No. Wait. It's no good, Kit. It's too late.'

She kneeled up abruptly, fear in her heart. 'What d'you mean? Oh, Jake, it doesn't matter about going back to France. I don't mind. It'll be fun.'

'Wait!' he shouted. 'Shut up, Kit! It's too late. I told you. I'm engaged to be married. She is a cousin of mine. Madeleine . . .'

In the silence that followed, the name seemed to drift, echo-ing on the air. He'd said it in the French way, with the middle vowel ignored, lyrical, romantic. In Kit's mind an image rose: a young girl with a sweet, gentle face and long red-brown hair, smiling adoringly at Jake. She'd been charming to Kit, the guest in her grandmother's house, but her attention had been all for Jake.

Kit straightened up, still kneeling on the sofa, her brain too stupid, too shocked to take it in properly.

'I remember her,' she murmured – and her heart ached in her breast.

'Gran'mère always wanted us to marry. Madeleine's father

was a second cousin to my father and they were great friends. But there was always you, Kit, until last time. Not now, for the funeral, but back in the summer. You remember you didn't want to come? You were too busy with Mark and your new job.' He shrugged. 'I felt we'd come to the end somehow, that you were in love with him. You were moving on. I was pretty low and Madeleine was so sweet, so loving. Can you imagine how comforting that was? How boosting to the ego? Pathetic, isn't it?' he said savagely. 'Well, she was there and I took full advantage of her.' He put his head in his hands. 'I am very fond of her,' he muttered desperately.

'But does that mean that you have to marry her?' She tried to keep her voice level, despite her very real terror. 'I can understand everything you've said. But to marry her, Jake? Is it fair, anyway, if you don't truly love her? I don't mean to sound so prosy but—'

'She's pregnant,' he said flatly. 'Three months. She wasn't going to tell me, but after the funeral it was all too emotional for words and she wasn't very well, poor girl. I think I guessed, anyway. She was so nervous and brittle, so unlike her usual self. She admitted it in the end and, well, it didn't seem to matter too much, after all. I never guessed that you'd . . .' He raised his joined fists and drove them down on the arm of the sofa. 'For Christ's sake, Kit!' he shouted. 'Why now? Why bloody now? When it's too late. Twelve bloody years and you're three months too late.'

A quad bike swings round the bend in the lane and Kit clutches her coffee mug and calls out to Mopsa, who comes to her at once. The driver raises his hand and Kit waves back. If he's noticed that she is in her dressing gown he gives no sign of it. She turns back towards the smithy, thinking of how she might tell Mungo about Jake; about that meeting, brief and magical, after his marriage to Madeleine; about the letter telling her that Madeleine has died.

She decides that she won't tell him at the smithy where Camilla or Archie might suddenly appear. No, she will take him for a drive. Mungo likes to be driven, to be taken somewhere for coffee or tea: Totnes, perhaps? Ashburton? As they go into the kitchen she has an idea. The Dandelion Café at Haytor is just the place. They can sit on the sofa and have a long, intimate talk.

Mungo is getting breakfast ready and she studies him appreciatively. Tanned and muscular in his jeans and white shirt, his fading fair hair sun-bleached, he looks almost youthful.

He wishes her good morning and, passing behind him, she gives him a very quick kiss somewhere behind his left ear.

'I shall take you out for coffee,' she tells him. 'Perhaps lunch. The Dandelion Café. What d'you think?'

'That will be very nice,' he answers almost primly. 'And I suppose you've been out in the lane again in your dressing gown?'

'Mopsa's fault,' she says. 'Anyway, we only saw young Andy on his quad bike. He won't care. I'm going to get dressed ready for our jaunt.'

Making toast, putting the marmalade – Camilla's home-made – on the table, Mungo wonders why the café at Haytor has been chosen for their tête-à-tête. He guesses that Kit is having difficulty coming to the point and he feels almost nervous. After all, they've exchanged many secrets over the years; what can be so special about this one? He puts Mopsa's breakfast – a handful of dried food and a few biscuits – into her bowl and gives her fresh water.

'I hope I'm ready for this,' he murmurs, ruffling Mopsa's ears, but she is too busy with her breakfast to pay attention to him.

Someone else, apart from young Andy Judd on his quad bike, has seen Kit in the lane. In the little cottage further down Joe, standing at his bedroom window high up under the eaves, can just glimpse her though he cannot see what it is she is carrying. In her long gown, with the little dog running ahead, he thinks she looks like someone in a story; a princess or a witch, perhaps, but not a bad one. He notices that she walks very slowly, raising both her hands to her lips as if she is drinking. Sometimes she stands quite still. When the quad bike comes she jumps quickly to one side and the little dog comes running back to her.

After she disappears from sight Joe remains at the window. He and Mummy and Dora have been at the cottage for just six days and he is still deciding whether or not he likes it. Dora's too young to know – she's just a baby – but Mummy loves it.

'It's great, isn't it, Joe?' she says, really excited. 'There's so much to do here. You can ride your bike in the lane and we can go for walks on the moor.'

He has an odd feeling when she gets like this; as if she's playing a game, not being quite real. Sometimes he plays the game, too, because he loves her, but sometimes it frightens him, especially now that Daddy isn't around. Joe misses him; he says so.

'Daddy has to go away,' she says. 'You know he does, Joe.

He's a doctor. He has to go away to where the fighting is so that he can look after anyone who needs him.'

And of course he knows that but there's something different about her. Once she would have said, 'I know, darling. I miss him too,' but just lately she doesn't want to talk much about Daddy. Joe had listened to them arguing about moving to the cottage.

'Why don't you wait till I come back?' Daddy asked. 'Why decide to do this now?'

'Because I don't want to wait,' Mummy answered. 'It's terrific luck to get the cottage, and it's only because Mum says that Camilla is getting fed up with holiday lets and is trying it on a long let. It's an experiment. We're going to be guinea pigs.' She laughed at Joe, who was sitting on the floor with his Lego. 'Do you like the idea of being a guinea pig?'

He didn't understand what she meant but he could see that she was trying to jolly Daddy along so he laughed too because he hated seeing him upset. But suddenly Daddy looked more cheerful.

'Well, Camilla will keep an eye on you,' he said.

'What d'you mean?' Mummy wasn't laughing now. She frowned – and he shrugged.

'I just like to know you've got a friend around when I'm a long way off, that's all.'

'I've got plenty of my own friends, thanks,' she said, a bit snappy, not smiling. 'I don't need my mother's friends, too.'

And then Dora started howling and Mummy rushed out, and he and Daddy were left alone. He looked as if he were a long way off, seeing something Joe couldn't see, so he got up and perched on his knee.

'Don't you like the cottage?' he asked, taking Daddy's hand in his and bending the long strong fingers round his own.

'I haven't seen it yet,' he answered, but he looked sad so that Joe put both arms round his neck and hugged him really hard, and Daddy hugged him too.

Remembering it now, thinking of Daddy a long way away, Joe feels like he might cry but then Dora really does cry, screaming for attention, so he goes out of his room and down the steep stairs to comfort her. Mummy comes out of her room as he reaches the landing. There are only two bedrooms on this floor, which is why he is up in the little room at the top of the house. He likes it, though, being so high up. Mummy is pushing her mobile phone into the pocket of her flowered slouchy pyjamas; she's all smiley as if she's excited about something and Joe feels anxious though he doesn't know why.

'Did she wake you up?' she asks him. 'What a horror she is.'

They go into Dora's bedroom and Mummy whisks Dora up out of her cot and swings around with her high above her head. Dora begins to chuckle and he laughs too and it's fun.

'Shall we go up on the moor today?' Mummy asks, laying Dora down on her changing mat and beginning to change her nappy. 'We'll set out early before it gets too hot.'

She looks at him and her eyes are bright, as if it's a birthday or Christmas, and it's like she's thinking about something else, not him or Dora, and the little worm of worry wriggles up again.

'Where shall we go?' he asks. He picks up one of Dora's toys – a pink plush cat – and dangles it over her face. She reaches for it but he keeps it just beyond her grasp. 'Can I climb on the rocks and have an ice cream?'

'I don't see why not.' Mummy picks Dora up, cuddles her.

Dora shouts, stretching her chubby hands for the toy, and he makes it dance up Mummy's arm before he gives it to her. He trails down the stairs behind them, thinking of the lady in the lane with the little dog. As they go into the kitchen, Mummy's phone bleeps. She sits Dora in her highchair and takes the mobile from her pocket. Although she turns slightly away he can see that she's smiling secretly as she taps an answer to the text. He wants to interrupt, to distract her.

'I saw a witch this morning in the lane,' he says loudly. 'She was wearing a long dress and she had a dog with her.'

She continues to tap, and to smile, and, 'Did you, darling?' she says brightly. 'How exciting,' but he knows that she's not really listening to him.

'It's so lovely to have littlies around again,' Camilla is saying to Archie as they eat breakfast. 'Joe is such a dear little fellow and Dora is going to be a real character. Emma will have her hands full with that one.'

Archie pours another cup of tea from his big blue teapot. Kit brought him the teapot from London. It's a Whittard teapot with its own special tea-strainer inside, which can be removed so that his tea can remain in the pot without getting too strong. Archie likes two and sometimes three cups of tea at breakfast and he is touched by Kit's thoughtfulness.

Boz and Sammy lie by the open kitchen door, their eyes on Archie as he finishes his toast. After breakfast he will take them for a walk. They are too well-trained to nag but they are alert to his every movement. Noses on paws, eyes swivelling, eyebrows twitching, they watch for the moment when he'll push back his chair and say: 'Well, time to get the dogs out.'

'Rob's told me that he's a bit worried that Emma will be lonely without the other service wives around,' Camilla says. 'But I've promised to keep an eye on them all while he's away.'

Archie has been only partially listening. As usual his mind is marshalling the pressing tasks that need to be done – mowing, fencing, redecorating – rather than on their new tenant. Now he considers Emma: she is a pretty young woman, rather fun and very friendly. His two daughters-in-law are capable, busy, confident career girls, and, on occasions, they rather unnerve him. He knows that his old-fashioned tendencies to stand up when women come into the room, to open doors for them, can be misconstrued as patronizing, and this makes him slightly nervous with the younger generation, but Archie feels very much at ease with Emma.

He took the dogs with him on that first visit when he went to meet her and the children at the cottage, where Camilla was showing them around. He introduced Sammy and Boz and was pleased to see Joe's face break into smiles of delight. It was clear that he considered having the dogs as neighbours was an extra bonus. In Archie's experience, dogs always help to break the ice, cause a diversion and offer a talking point. He liked the small, solemn boy, Joe, and was amused by Dora with her passionate, greedy approach to life. When they came for a second viewing, bringing Rob this time, Archie was rather touched by the way small Joe held his father's hand, towing him from room to room, anxious that he should like the cottage, watching his reactions anxiously. Once again the dogs removed any tension. Rob asked if, as tenants, they'd be allowed to have a dog at the cottage, and Emma said it was one of the reasons she'd wanted to be in the country.

'I thought we might get those toys down from the barn loft,' Camilla is saying. 'The tractor and the little bicycle. Joe's just the right age for them. Dora's a bit young for any of them yet.'

'She's a good screamer,' he observes.

'I don't recollect Emma being like that,' Camilla remembers. 'She was a rather quiet, gentle child. She's loving it here, though, isn't she? She's such a positive girl. It can't be easy with Rob away in Afghanistan but she is so cheerful and brave.'

'Mmm.' Archie doesn't agree or disagree. He drinks his tea and thinks about Emma and how he thought she was a tad excitable when they all came up for tea the day after they'd moved into the cottage; not quite like a girl who's just said goodbye to her husband for three months. He wonders if it might simply be her way of coping with Rob's absence. After all, it must be very difficult to deal with the separation, knowing Rob might be in danger, having to cope with two small children. Emma is probably just trying to keep her spirits up for the sake of her little boy as well as for herself.

Archie remembers how Joe greeted the dogs as if they were old friends. He sat himself down between them and suffered their enthusiastic face-washing whilst Dora shrieked and flolloped about in Emma's arms, and Emma shouted above Dora's noise that she and Joe loved the cottage and that everything was utterly amazing. He watched Joe with his arms round the dogs' necks and wondered at his expression of long-suffering, of patience, as he looked up at his mother and sister. It was a surprisingly adult expression and Archie's heart was slightly wrung by it. He wondered how much Joe missed his father and if he was as happy in his new home as Emma was implying.

'Come on, old chap,' he said. 'Let's take the dogs out for a walk while tea's being made, shall we?'

And Joe scrambled up gratefully as if glad to be away from the noisy busy scene.

'Joe's a nice little fellow,' Archie says, finishing his tea. 'I'll get the toys down after I've taken the dogs for their walk. I want to get them out before it gets too hot.'

'I was wondering whether to invite Emma to supper with Kit,' says Camilla, gathering plates, putting the lid on the marmalade. 'The children could go into the bunk beds in the old nursery.'

'No, I don't think we should,' Archie says rather too quickly. He's looking forward to an uncomplicated evening. 'Not quite fair on Kit, is it? She and Emma don't know each other, after all, and the children might not settle.'

'Perhaps not,' agrees Camilla, though reluctantly. She loves a bit of a party. 'You could be right. Perhaps another time when they've got to know each other. I must introduce Emma to Mungo and then have a lunch or supper for all of them together.'

'That's it,' he says, relieved. 'Good idea.'

'I wish I could persuade James to come along. He works so hard I'm sure one little supper wouldn't be too distracting.'

'Leave him alone, he's working,' says Archie, who finds James just the least bit self-centred and boring, always banging on about his book. He pushes back his chair. 'Time to get the dogs out.'

Bozzy and Sam are already up and out of the door, feathery tails waving, eyes bright with expectation. Archie walks across the yard, up through the steep mossy garden, to the moor's edge. The dogs squeeze beneath the stile and race out on to the open moor. Archie climbs the wooden steps, pausing to glance around, checking that there is no stock near at hand. Below the stony scrawl and scribble of the high tor a dark crimson tide of bell heather spills across the steep slopes, washing around rough chunks of granite, pouring down towards the stream. As he follows the ancient ridges, those centuries-old sheep paths that wind around the side of the hill, he breathes in the honey-scented air. The sun is hot on his bare head and he raises his arms to shield his eyes as he turns to look far westward where the glitter and dazzle of seawater rims the edge of the world.

Below him a movement catches his eye. A small car travels along the lane, past the smithy and the cottages, heading towards the farmhouse. There have been Judds at Home Farm ever since Archie can remember. Billy and his brother, Philip, live there together; both widowed, keeping each other company with an old Welsh collie. They are a part of this small community, thinks Archie, just as he and Camilla and Mungo are – and now Emma and Joe and Dora. But for how long can he hold things together, keep on meeting the bills from such a small income? There is so much to do; so much to paint; so much dilapidation. Then there is the farm. If Philip and Billy were to decide to carry out some much-needed repairs where would he find the landlord's share of the cost?

At least, now the cottage is being let on a six-month tenancy, there is a regular rent coming in, but it's not enough to hold back the slowly rising tide of damp and rot that threatens the house. There are solutions, of course: sell up and downsize is the obvious one, but Camilla throws a wobbly each time he mentions it. And, of course, he'd hate to leave this valley, his home, this small community. He wills his mind to a more cheerful prospect: Kit is coming to supper; they'll have a day on the river. Archie turns back to the path, whistling for the dogs, and continues his walk.

CHAPTER THREE

From the kitchen window Philip Judd watches his cousin Mags climbing out of her car. He doesn't go out to meet her; she knows her way around. He stands, hands resting on the Belfast sink, waiting for her to come in. Ferret, he calls her to himself. Ferret-woman: sandy and twitchy-nosed and quick. She glances round the yard, up at the house, assessing, calculating, as if she's planning to buy it. He snorts derisively. She'd like that; she'd like to be part of the set-up here, part of the family, friend to Archie and Camilla and Sir Mungo. She always calls him that: Sir Mungo. Nobody else does.

'He's really famous,' she says, like they never see a newspaper or watch the television. Yet part of her is pleased that he and Billy call him Mungo; shows they're friends. She boasts about it to her little group of women friends. The Coven, he calls them.

'They'd love to meet him,' she says wistfully, as if Mungo's open to visitors like all those National Trust places they're always going to, but he blocks her attempts to muscle in on their friendship. All his life he and his older brother, Billy, have blocked her when they could. From a small child up she was a troublemaker. She'd tell tales, go whining to their mum or hers: 'The boys won't let me see the baby chicks . . . ride on the tractor . . .' but the adults took no notice and he and Billy didn't care. The age gap gave them seniority, power.

She's thrilled to get that ferrety snout round the door now poor old Billy's given her the chance. They had to show they had proper care before they'd let him home from hospital after his stroke, and cousin Mags was the obvious answer. She jumped on it quick as a stoat on a rabbit. He's grateful, of course. She's been cleaning and cooking and sorting Billy out a treat. She trained as a nurse, which means Billy can be at home instead of being cared for by strangers. He'll put up with Mags for a few weeks for that. Billy looked out for him when they were young. After their mother died their father lost heart with the farm. When he became a rep for an agricultural machinery company, and then had to move nearer to Bristol, it was Billy who persuaded Archie's father that he and Philip could manage the farm. Along with their little logging business and some gardening work they'd survived and kept their home. It's worth having Mags around to make sure Billy's safe and comfortable.

'Morning, Philip,' she says, putting the cold-box on the kitchen table. She unloads pies and jellies and soup, all guaranteed to tempt the invalid appetite, and stacks them into the fridge. 'Something to be going on with. How's the patient?'

'He's fine. Had a good night. He'll be having some physio this afternoon.' Philip watches her moving things about, reordering the shelves. He'll change it all back later. Given the chance she'd take over; she'd be moving in. His Joanie would have had a fit.

'Give her an inch and she takes a mile,' Joanie used to say. 'Keep her out of my kitchen.'

Well, Joanie's gone now and he must fend for himself, and for Billy.

'Tea's made,' he says. 'Want a cup?'

'I'll see to Billy first.' She picks up her bag purposefully, almost triumphantly: she is about to perform her good deed for the day. 'He was a bit mazed yesterday when he woke up from his nap. Away with the fairies. Talking about the old days and Sir Mungo and Isobel Trent and I don't know what else. He kept saying: "He's still here," and laughing fit to bust. I said, "Of course he is, dear, he lives just down the lane," but he was in a world of his own back in the past somewhere. "He walked all over her," he said. "Now we walk all over him." And then he goes quiet and won't say another word.'

'It's his medication,' he tells her. 'Nothing to worry about.'

She bustles off out of the kitchen and across the hall into the parlour, which has been turned into a bedroom for Billy. He hears their voices – and just for a moment he, too, travels back to the past: to the glamour and the excitement of those weekends at the smithy.

'Come and help us, Philip,' Mungo would say. 'I'm in a muddle and I've just remembered that Ralph is coming down on the four fifteen. Any chance you could fetch him?'

It might be Ralph, or any of Mungo's actor friends. Or it might be Izzy, and that was the best, of course. Driving back with Izzy from Newton Abbot was heaven on earth. If he closes his eyes he can see her: that expression, half anxious, half delighted. 'Oh, Philip,' she'd exclaim, 'how wonderful!

I thought Mungo might forget me but I know you never would.' She'd tuck her hand into his arm and reach up to kiss his cheek and he sometimes felt that he might topple over, all six foot three of him, weak with joy and love. She was so small, so delicate: a little waif with her mini-skirts and Mary Quant haircut. He'd take her case, open the car door for her and help her in as if she were a princess.

'Tell me all the news,' she'd say. 'How are Camilla and Archie and the babies? What's been happening at the farm? Has Smudgy had her kittens?'

Izzy made him feel strong and reliable and important. At the smithy nobody cared that he was the son of Archie's tenant farmer; Mungo made sure that he was part of the scene. Only Ralph liked to put him in his place with subtle hints and jokes about his size and his West Country accent. Oh, he knew that he wasn't really one of them; he was bright enough to realize that he was very useful to them, and he was careful to keep a little distance and slip away at the right moment. He always knew when to make himself scarce. Yet he valued his position. He was fascinated by them all: the way they talked to each other, quoting chunks from plays, singing, even dancing. Izzy especially loved to dance and sing, and the others would make a chorus around her. Oh, it was a wonderful thing to see, just like being at the theatre. Sometimes, afterwards, she'd slip round to where he'd been standing, just out of the circle, and take his hand as if she were a child.

'Do you think we're all crazy?' she'd ask him wistfully. 'You don't know how lucky you are, Philip, being rooted. Belonging.'

He never knew quite how to answer her. His love for her,

and his tenderness, seemed to flood up from his heart, choking the words in his throat and making him speechless. He'd hold her hand tightly and then Ralph would come sliding round, smiling that knowing, cruel smile.

'Come on, Bathsheba,' he'd say. 'Stop tormenting Gabriel Oak and give us another song.'

Oh, how he hated Ralph, then, but Izzy would squeeze his hand and smile up at him with a little shake of the head as if to say, 'Don't mind Ralph.' She'd slip away, going with Ralph back to the group and he'd be left alone.

Standing here, if he concentrates hard, he can just catch the faintest whiff of the flowery smell of her. Izzy: reaching up to kiss him, leaning sideways in the car to laugh with him, singing in Mungo's kitchen.

'You OK?' Mags is in the doorway staring at him, brows creased, summing him up.

'Yeah.' He stares back at her, not giving her an inch. 'Why not?'

She shrugs. 'You looked a bit funny standing there with your eyes closed.'

He thinks about Billy rambling in his mind, talking about the past, about things that need to be kept secret. Mags likes to know a secret; she's good at ferreting out private thoughts and hidden deeds and then dropping her knowledge into conversation like tiny bombshells. He must be watchful.

'So how is he, then? Not away with the fairies this morning?'

Mags shakes her head. 'He's very quiet. Just staring out the window. What did you do with that bib I made him? He's still dribbling quite a bit.'

'Chucked it out. He's not a baby.' He'd been seized with rage when he saw Billy sitting there with a bib tied round his neck looking like an oversized child. 'He knows how to wipe his mouth. No need to humiliate him in front of his friends.'

He hates to see his handsome older brother with his twisted face; the eye and mouth drawn helplessly downwards, like a statue that's had a careless hand dragged across its face before the clay has hardened. He's given him an old, soft flannel so that Billy can take a swipe at his chin from time to time.

Mags bridles, chin drawn in, shoulders shrugging. 'Sorry, I'm sure. I had no idea that he'd be receiving visitors just yet.'

'Not visitors. Friends. Archie comes down to see us. And Camilla and Mungo.'

He watches her expression change; the indignation falls away and her expression becomes speculative. She glances out of the window as if, even now, Archie might be striding into the yard, or Camilla.

'I'll give the kitchen a clean out,' she says thoughtfully. 'And the parlour.'

He watches her sardonically. He can read her like a book. One: if she stays long enough she might see Archie, or Camilla or Mungo. Sir Mungo. Two: if any of them should come she'd want the kitchen and the parlour to be clean, everything spick and span.

'Suit yourself,' he says easily. 'If you've got the time. I shall be cutting the grass in the orchard.'

'You're always in that old orchard,' she says.

'That's right. Good place to be in this hot weather. Do you want that tea or not?'

'It'll be stewed by now,' she grumbles. 'I'll make fresh and take some in to Billy.'

'I'll take it,' he says firmly. Billy has to have a special cup now and he hates to see Mags holding the spout to the misshapen mouth, brightly urging Billy on as if he's a two-year-old.

The sunny parlour has been made into a bed-sitting-room so that Billy can look out into the orchard when he's resting. He can walk a short distance with a stick, and there's a wheel-chair to help him get further afield, but mostly he likes to sit at the window with old Star, the grey and white Welsh sheep-dog, curled beside him. Star looks up at Philip with those strange blue eyes when he comes in with the tea. Her tail gives a little welcoming thump before she settles again, her head against Billy's legs. He wonders if Billy can feel the warmth of her head penetrating that dead, dragging leg and he is moved with sorrow and frustration. Wasn't it only yesterday they were young and strong and fearless: courting pretty girls, working the land, bringing up sons? Now those girls are dead and gone and their sons are farming their own land further up the valley with boys of their own.

Billy is smiling at him, eyes crinkled up even though his mouth isn't obeying him. He takes the plastic mug very care-fully in his left hand and raises the spout shakily to his lips.

'She's giving the place a right going-over in case Sir Mungo comes to visit you,' he tells Billy. 'How about a little walk?'

Billy nods, indicates the wheelchair, and presently they go out into the yard with Star following close behind them.

*

'I see Mags is here,' says Mungo, as he and Kit drive along the lane a little later. 'Poor Philip must be hating it but at least she's making it possible to have Billy home again. It's a pity she's such a tiresome woman. Not surprising, really. She was one of those whingeing, whining children that was always trying to get us into trouble. She'd sneak and tell tales. Billy and Philip used to avoid her like the plague and I used to tell her stories about hobgoblins and witches to try to scare her away from our hide-outs. She'd always find us, though. Ah, and there's James. Give him a wave. Oh dear, the shorts are a mistake with those legs. Not a pretty sight. I suppose I ought to see if he'd like to come in for a drink some time. Mustn't disturb the muse, though. Have you read his book? Camilla lent it to me when she knew he was coming. She'd bought it specially. Very loyal of her.'

'I don't know. What did you say his name is? Is it good?' Kit waves obediently at a small, thin, whippy man, probably early forties, who raises a hand in greeting as he comes out of the cottage door.

'Absolutely dire, sweetie, but don't say I said so. Plot not too bad, a bit derivative, but one-dimensional characters, all very stereotypical, straight out of central casting. Don't slow down.' He lowers the window and shouts a greeting, then mutters: 'That's right. On we go. Don't need him just at the moment when we're off on a jaunt.'

Kit accelerates away, laughing at Mungo's waspishness, aware of the twinkle in his eye. She is still mentally trying opening conversational gambits in order to bring Jake into the conversation. It's much more difficult than she imagined and she wonders if she's crazy even to attempt it. Jake's letter coming out of the blue has thrown her into complete confusion.

'Shall we stay in touch?' she asked Jake tremblingly, all those years ago. 'Just . . . just letters now and then?'

He held her hands tightly, reaching across the little table in the coffee bar where they'd arranged to meet. She was unaware of her surroundings, unable to take in the terrible truth that she might never see him again. The door swung open from the kitchen and the music from the radio became clearer. It was Roberta Flack singing 'Killing Me Softly with his Song'. At the sound of it scalding tears slipped from her eyes and he lifted her hands, holding them against his mouth.

'Oh, Kit,' he said sadly. 'How can we? You know how dangerous it would be.'

'I can't bear it,' she gasped. 'I'd no idea how much I needed you, Jake. How can you leave me now?'

'Please,' he whispered fiercely. 'For God's sake, Kit.'

The waitress put the coffee down, forcing them to draw apart, and Kit stared round her in the gloom, wiping her eyes.

'Why did we have to meet here?' she asked, trying to sound normal. 'It's a dump. I could have come to your flat.'

'Coming to my flat doesn't work any more,' he answered grimly. 'We always end up in the same place and it leads on to one more meeting. I'm flying over to Paris tomorrow, Kit.'

She stared at him, watching his long-fingered hand holding the spoon, stirring the black liquid round and round and round.

She thought: I know now why people talk of dying of a broken heart. Whatever is the point of life without him?

'I've got to try,' he was saying. 'You must see that. I made this muddle. It's not Madeleine's fault. She's the victim of our muddle. I owe it to her to give it everything I've got. It would be wrong to try to hold on to you, too. We had our chance and we blew it.'

She shut her eyes. It was as though he had struck her, brutally emphasizing all that she'd had within her grasp – and lost. She picked up her cup and gulped at the hot bitter coffee, burning her mouth.

He watched her, seeing her anguish, making up his mind. 'I have something for you,' he said at last, reaching into his jacket.

'You said "no presents".' Her mind was already leaping to and fro, trying to think what she might give him, wishing she'd brought him some keepsake.

'I can't take anything from you now,' he said. 'I want nothing I might have to hide or explain away. Women can be very perceptive about such things.'

'But you have a whole past behind you.' She couldn't hide her pain. 'Are you going to throw away all the presents you've ever had?'

'No,' he said impatiently. 'Naturally not. But I have no guilt about anything in my past. It is only from now forwards things must change. Anything you gave me now would be charged with emotion and memories. I couldn't bear it. I know I'm cheating with this, but you're not going to be married. Not yet anyway, and then this will belong to your past. It belonged to my mother. She gave it to me on my twenty-first birthday and told me that I should give it to the woman to whom I gave my heart.' He held out a heavily chased silver locket. 'I remember that she said that this might not be the woman I married and

I thought that it was quite a sophisticated viewpoint – for an old-fashioned Englishwoman.' He smiled bleakly. 'I always hoped that it would be my morning gift to you but now I see that she was right . . .'

'You might just as well come right out with it,' Mungo says. 'It can't be that terrible. Come on, Kit.'

'I'm just afraid you'll think I'm a fool,' she says. 'It sounds so silly when you say it out loud. I've had a letter from a man I was in love with for years; from Jake. I've told you about him. We were lovers but he married someone else because I kept playing the field and now she's died.'

'Is he asking you to meet him?'

'He's suggesting it.'

'And you feel nervous about seeing him again?'

'Yes,' she says. 'Yes, I do.'

'Have you seen him since you broke up?'

She nods. 'Just once. About twenty years ago. I met him quite by chance.'

They are up on the moor now and suddenly she is able to talk, to tell him about Jake and Madeleine. She drives slowly through the immense landscape, its sense of infinity setting her free to speak without reserve. Mungo listens, as he always does, in silence: no interruptions, no questions, no reaction except an attentive silence. She slows the car, dawdling on an old stone bridge to watch the clear water slipping between smooth round boulders, and reaching into her bag she takes out the locket to show him.

'I wore it for years,' she says. 'And then we met again.'

She is silent for a moment and then she tells him about the meeting: taking her time over it, reliving it.

She bumped into Jake in Dover Street. He was coming from the Royal Academy and she'd been lunching with a client at the Arts Club. The shock galvanized them into a moment of silent stillness. At last she stretched out her hand and grasped his sleeve.

'It *is* you?' It was partly question, partly disbelief, and he smiled with complete understanding, covering her hand with his own.

'If it's you, then it's me,' he said – and, at such a silly, Jake-like answer, they both dissolved into laughter.

It exploded out of them, a bubbling issue of joy, buried for sixteen years and now bursting up from somewhere deep inside to greet the autumn sunshine. They clung to each other – though at arm's length – bound by convention, yet subtly acknowledging the danger of this unexpected meeting. She guessed that each would wait for the other to make the first move.

'Oh, Jake,' she said, 'you've hardly changed. How dare you look so good? You must be fifty. Oh, I can't believe this . . .'

'But you *have* changed,' he answered teasingly. 'There's rather more Kit than I remember . . .'

'Don't!' she cried. 'Don't look at me. I'm old and haggy.' But inside she was singing a tiny prayer of thanksgiving that it should be today, when she was all dressed up for lunch, that they should meet.

His glance travelled over her in the old Jake the Rake manner and she felt the long-missed gut-melting excitement weakening her as she took his arm, unable now to meet his eyes. They walked along together towards Piccadilly and he pressed her arm close to his side.

'It suits you,' he murmured.

'What does?' She sounded almost aggressive, suddenly sullen, frightened by the strength of her emotions.

'Middle age.'

She felt him laughing silently, hugging her hand close, and she laughed too, the tension running out of her.

'Pig!' she said, without rancour. 'OK, so I've put on weight.'

'But I mean it.' He took her hand from his arm and touched it briefly with his lips. 'You're beautiful. How thoughtless of you, Kit, still to be so attractive.'

'Oh, Jake,' she said sadly. 'I've missed you so much . . . Where are we going?'

'Who cares?' he said. 'This looks OK,' and he steered her into a coffee bar and settled her at a corner table.

They sat there for hours – or so it seemed – yet only briefly did they mention the present. He took her left hand, running the ball of his thumb along the third finger.

'No one?' he asked softly, without looking at her, and she admitted it harshly, ashamed that he'd retained his power for so long whilst she had been displaced so completely . . . How had he managed?

'And you?' she asked reluctantly, cursing herself, wishing she could be proudly indifferent. 'Madeleine . . . ?'

'Oh, yes.' He nodded, almost absently, still staring down at their joined hands. 'Madeleine and four little girls.'

The silence was full of bitter memories – she could almost taste the sharpness on her tongue – but when at last he looked at her she realized that, after all, none of it mattered. He was still Jake – and she was Kit; the two of them together as they'd always been, back in another life where Madeleine and her four little girls had no place. With that one long look the intervening sixteen years vanished into the smoky atmosphere that drifted about them. How swiftly the old intimacy was established between them. Heads together, chuckling away, they drank endless cups of coffee until Jake glanced at his watch. Kit seized his brown wrist, covering it with her hand.

'Don't say you have to go.'

'A meeting,' he said. 'At the Bank. I shall be late. Are we going to do this again?'

The tension was back. Warily they watched each other, waiting. Neither could quite bear to say goodbye; neither wished to be the one to break the rules.

'When do you go back?' She tried to make the question casual.

'Madeleine is in Florence with the girls for another fortnight.' She translated it not as an answer but as an invitation. He waited.

'Perhaps lunch tomorrow, then?' It was an effort – after all, she had her pride – but lunch still sounded respectable. Surely two old friends could have lunch together without suspicions being roused?

'Lunch?' He was laughing at her. 'Why not? Lunch would be good. Shall I pick you up?'

'No,' she answered quickly, much too quickly. 'No, I shall be with a client tomorrow morning. What about Le Caprice? At a quarter to one?'

He pulled back her chair, helping her into her jacket, barely touching her, but his proximity was disturbing, exciting. She suspected that each would be waiting for the other to give way and she feared that it would not be Jake.

This time Kit remains silent for so long that Mungo speaks at last.

'And did you?' he asks.

She shakes her head. 'It never happened. One of his little girls fell ill and he flew back to Paris before either of us could weaken.'

'And did you stay in touch after that?'

'I wanted to but he wouldn't. I would have taken anything he could have given me but he refused. Only a birthday card every year. He never forgot.'

'And now,' says Mungo shrewdly, 'with Madeleine dead he would like to come back into your life and you're feeling just a tad resentful about it.'

She looks at him and begins to laugh. 'That's exactly it. Irrational, isn't it?'

'But very human. You don't want to give the impression that you've been sitting around waiting for him all these years.' A pause. 'Have you?'

'Nobody ever measured up,' she answers sadly. 'Once or twice I thought it might be the real thing.'

'Yes,' Mungo says feelingly. 'We all remember those moments.'

She begins to laugh. 'I feel such a fool, Mungo. Why can't I be grown-up and adult like everyone else?'

'Oh, don't, sweetie. You're so much more fun than everyone else. So now I want to hear properly about Jake. Not just the storyline. I want details. You've always been such a dark horse about him. We need some coffee and a good natter.'

Kit puts the car into gear. 'I still love him but I don't want to make it too easy. And anyway, it's a huge thing. It could be a complete disaster. I don't know how to start.'

'You haven't answered his letter?'

'Not yet. I might let you read it. Just to be sure I'm not reading more into it than there is.'

'Only if you're absolutely certain. First things first. No more secrecy. I need to know all about Jake.'

CHAPTER FOUR

The café is busy with a party of walkers who are occupying several tables. They look happy and healthy in their shorts and boots; calling to one another, joking and laughing. Mungo leads the way down the steps into the bar. It is quieter here, only one family at a corner table, and he leaves Kit to settle Mopsa on her rug on the sofa while he goes to order the coffee.

He is glad to have a moment to reflect on all that Kit has told him. He is rather surprised to find that he feels quite jealous of this Jake: that he might come suddenly into their lives and change the relationship that he, Mungo, shares with Kit. He adores Kit – and he wants her to be happy, of course he does – but how could it possibly be the same with a third person? No more intimate suppers and lazy mornings planning the day ahead. No more curling up on the sofa together to watch an old film on a wet Sunday afternoon. No more jaunts in the car. The old truism: three's a crowd. He knows that he has the power to affect Kit's decision. Like Izzy before her, Kit is unsure of herself when it comes to relationships and he can see how he might direct the way forward to his own advantage. Even as he stands there waiting, in his head he is writing the dialogue that might influence Kit. Guiltily he is aware that his Machiavellian tendencies – which made him such a good director, he reminds himself – are coming to the fore just as they did with the Awful Michael and he feels the old sizzle of excitement: a gut-clenching challenge.

He turns to survey the scene and his attention is immediately gripped by a couple standing together talking. Perhaps it is because he is already hyped up that the director in him responds to them at once. They stand close, but not too close, and he can see that the man is barely able to restrain himself from touching the girl. This is good theatre and something he liked to use in love scenes to raise the tension. 'Don't touch each other,' he'd shout. 'Make us see that you want to but don't do it!' The man leans towards the girl, talking very quietly, very intensely, and she listens, arms crossed tightly across her breast, her eyes shut. Her body language shows that she is resisting him – but only just. She's a pretty girl with short, very dark hair, denim shorts and a halter top. He's attractive, too. He has a lean, taut look in his faded jeans and cotton shirt: very tanned, tough.

Mungo watches, fascinated. Not lovers, he thinks. Not yet. But they want to be. His eyes flick to the table beside them. A baby is asleep in a little carrying chair. Her rosy face is peaceful, starfish hands outstretched; a soft toy, a pink plush cat, rests on her chest. At the table a little boy is sitting, drinking a milkshake through a straw. He might be four or five years old, his face is very serious; beneath the table his legs dangle, ankles crossed, feet swinging. The man and the woman stand slightly behind him but the little boy is not aware of them: he is watching Kit.

Mungo orders coffee, two Americanos, and goes to sit beside her on the long leather sofa. She sits gazing at nothing in particular and he sees that her thoughts are all inwards; she is still thinking about Jake. He is consumed with curiosity to know more of this man about whom she has always been so cagey; this Jake, who was the love of her life but who left her. Even Izzy could never persuade Kit to talk much about Jake. It's as if he is still too important to be discussed lightly. Mungo gives her a little friendly nudge.

'Come on then,' he says. 'New readers start here. Tell me all about Jake.'

Joe drinks his milkshake slowly, savouring it, making it last. He was amazed to see the lady from the lane, who looked like a witch or a princess, come walking in with her little dog. In her jeans and long loose shirt she doesn't look like a witch or a princess but he knows it's the same lady and the same dog. The dog is a rather untidy person, with big dark round eyes, and he watches as it is lifted on to a rug on the sofa, where it turns round and round as if it is making a nest before it settles down. He wonders what the dog's name is and he looks again at the lady who seems to be in a dream, not noticing anything but sitting stroking the little dog and staring at nothing.

He glances up at Mummy, who is saying goodbye to Marcus, who is Daddy's friend. He'd been out walking on Haytor, too. Mummy put Dora in a sling on her back and they walked right up to the top where you could see for miles and miles. He was climbing the rocks when Mummy called out,

'Oh, look. There's Marcus.' She went down a little way to meet him and they stood talking together until he shouted: 'Look at me!' and they turned and waved at him standing on the rock.

'Well done,' Marcus shouted back to him, and he felt pleased and proud of himself, balancing on the high rock.

Then they all walked down to the car park together and Marcus said, 'What about a nice cold drink? I bet a milkshake would go down well after that climb.' So they'd come in to this café. Dora was asleep but Marcus bought him a milkshake and told him about the zoo at Sparkwell where there is a lion and a bear.

'Perhaps we should go?' Mummy said. She was all bright and sparkly and excited about going to the zoo. 'Dora would like to see the bear.'

'So would I,' he said at once. 'I'd like to see the bear.'

Then, when Marcus said he must be going and stood up, Mummy got up as well very quickly.

'Oh, by the way,' she said, and they moved slightly aside and began to talk, but he couldn't hear what they were saying and just then the lady and the dog came in.

Now he reaches out and tugs Mummy's top and she turns quickly and smiles at him but not as if she's really seeing him, and as she turns back to Marcus he has the old anxious feeling again. So he joggles Dora's chair and she wakes up and starts to grizzle and Mummy says goodbye to Marcus and hurries round to comfort her.

'I was just asking Marcus if he'd like to come to the zoo with us,' Mummy says. 'You'd like that, wouldn't you, Joe? It would be more fun.'

And he doesn't know quite what to say because it might be more fun. He'd be able to do more things with Marcus there, like when Daddy's home, but at the same time he feels that there's something wrong.

'I don't know.' He makes his face a bit sulky, a bit sad, because that always makes Mummy more ready to do what he wants.

But now she looks a bit sulky and a bit sad too, and she says, 'Well, we'll see,' rather crossly, so he says, 'It would be nice if Marcus comes too,' and she beams at him like she's really happy again, which makes him feel better.

He wants to stop talking about Marcus and the zoo, so he says: 'I saw that lady over there in the lane this morning with her little dog. I thought she was a witch or a princess . . .'

Mummy turns quickly to stare at the lady and she looks almost frightened.

'What's the matter?' he asks anxiously. 'She isn't really a witch, is she?'

'No, no, of course not,' Mummy says. 'I was just wondering who she is, if she really was in the lane.'

'It was her,' he insists. 'It was very early and she was drinking something.'

'Well, we'd better go home.' Mummy gets her things together and picks Dora up, but she keeps her back to the lady and doesn't look at her again.

Mungo watches them go out. Although he's fascinated by Kit's word-picture of Jake he's kept an eye on the little group. He sees the man leave and the small boy point at Kit and the woman's quick, anxious glance round at them. He files these things away whilst he listens to Kit and tries to discover what it is she really wants. Does she really want Jake back, with all the disruption that would cause, or does she simply want to talk about the possibility without having any intention of doing anything about it? It is of some interest that her first reaction on receiving the letter was to flee.

'You'd better read the letter,' Kit is saying, 'just in case I'm getting the wrong end of the stick.'

'Is that likely?' he asks. 'I'm happy to read it as long as you don't regret it afterwards. It's such a personal thing, isn't it?'

He can't help but think of Izzy. Like Kit with Jake, Izzy never really got over Ralph. She bounced from one disastrous love affair to the next, always looking for The One who might replace Ralph, who would carry her away to live happily ever after. Mungo watched over her, protected her, promoted her career so that her adoring public never knew the truth of it all. He'd never get away with it now: not with today's media. Back then he was amongst the great and the good; able to pull strings and get the right people on his side. And, anyway, everyone loved Izzy: she was one of the first 'national treasures'. It was as if there were a great web of conspiracy flung out to save her from herself: the ultimate romantic. Was he really Svengali to her Trilby? He can still remember standing in the wings listening to her singing 'Send in the Clowns' with the tears pouring down his cheeks.

'Don't ever leave me, darling,' she'd say to him. 'I can't imagine ever managing without you.'

She began to drink too much and her work suffered, and even then he tried to protect her, shoring her up in small, sustainable but very important little cameo parts, escorting her in public, making sure she had the right medical care. Ralph's abandonment was the first step on that downward slope: Ralph, and then the secret agonizing premature birth of his stillborn child. The child was to have been the means of reconciliation; the magnet to draw Ralph back.

'Someone must know where he is,' she'd say. 'He can't hide for ever,' and Mungo remained silent, still trying to protect her, wondering in the last resort if he could claim the child publicly as his own. Nobody would have been surprised – in fact, their adoring public would have been delighted – and part of him also longed for Ralph's child. Meanwhile it must be kept secret, but oh, the anguish and the tears. And then she miscarried, all alone in her London flat, one cold March morning. She had a name ready for the baby if it should be a boy: Simon. It was Ralph's second name.

Afterwards, she watched other mothers and their babies with such longing, with such intensity, that Mungo feared for her reason. He persuaded her to go abroad, to Venice for a short holiday with another actor friend, and gradually aroused her interest in a new production of Sheridan's *The Rivals*. He believed that Izzy would do well as Lydia Languish and encouraged her to audition for the part. Slowly she recovered, grew stronger, but she didn't forget Simon. 'He'd be two . . . five . . . starting school . . .' She pondered on whether he would have looked like Ralph, still hoping that one day he would return. It required such patience to keep her focused, hold her steady, but soon it became clear that those sealed-in emotions for Ralph, her unused store of mother-love for his child, were beginning to distil into her work and touch it with genius.

With difficulty Mungo wrenches his attention back to Kit.

'I just don't want people rolling their eyes and thinking "Here she goes again," or stuff like that,' she is saying. 'I can just hear my dear brother on the subject, though he was very fond of Jake. I want time to really think about it. This is just between you and me, Mungo. I need a breathing space.'

'Fine,' he says. 'That's fine. So Jake doesn't know where you are?'

She shakes her head. 'No idea. I could be abroad on holiday, for all he knows. There's no way he could tell whether I've even had the letter yet.'

'Well, I'll read it if you want me to, sweetie.'

'Not here, though.' She picks up the cup and drinks her coffee. 'I feel really weird after talking like that about Jake. It's funny how you remember things you haven't thought about for years.'

'Yes,' Mungo says sadly, still thinking about Izzy. She slipped away from him suddenly, light as a breath, now here, now gone. First Ralph, then the child, and then Izzy. He's lost them all.

'Shall we give Mopsa a little walk?' asks Kit. 'Do you think she'd make it up to the tor?'

'*She* might, sweetie, but I'm not sure I would. It's very hot out there.'

Kit laughs. 'Let's give it a go. Then we'll come back and I'll buy you lunch.'

His spirits rise a little; Kit can always cheer him up. Outside he glances around but there is no sign of the little family. Odd that they've captured his imagination: the intense young man, the small boy pointing at Kit, and the girl's last hasty, worried glance. He longs to know their story, to create one around them, but Mopsa is tugging on her lead, anxious for the freedom of the moor, Kit seizes his arm and they all set out together in the bright sunshine.

CHAPTER FIVE

A warm, still evening; the scent of the cut grass drifts and mixes with honeysuckle and meadowsweet and the moon is just visible in the pale sky. Swallows swoop and wheel in and out of the barn where their babies wait eagerly for those nourishing beakfuls of food, stoking up for the long journey ahead.

Camilla, setting the table on the veranda outside the kitchen door, pauses to watch them. She'll miss them when they go, despite the mess they make on her washing. She likes the way that the young from earlier broods are all helping to feed these last nestlings; a family at work together. Her sons and their families have been here during the summer; separately, overlapping, singly, in groups; the summer has been full of visitors – and she loves it. She loves to cook and nurture and entertain. Now she misses them just as she will miss the swallows. As the grandchildren grow older, and their lives grow busier with their own friends, visits to the valley aren't the great treat they once were. They are outgrowing the toys and demanding more sophisticated entertainment, but at least the two eldest cousins, Ollie and Luke, love sailing, Annabel adores cooking, and Lucy can practise her flute without neighbours complaining.

Camilla lights the candles in their prettily painted glass bowls. This veranda, with its slate floor, fluted stone pillars and glass roof, is perfect for summer evening entertaining. It looks out across the sloping lawn to the Horse Brook, slipping its shining way through the trees, and it is Camilla's favourite summer place. Even in the rain she will sit here planning: menus, spring bulbs, a present for a grandchild.

The candles flicker and gleam as the daylight begins to fade; the moon grows brighter in the east. Camilla's thoughts dwell briefly on her supper: roasted tomato, basil and parmesan quiche, beetroot salad with rocket for colour, a honey-roast ham. A jug of Pimm's is in the fridge with several bottles of rosé and bowls of raspberries and meringues.

She can hear voices. Mungo and Kit are with Archie in the hall and she hurries in to meet them. Tall, thin, elegant Archie is stooped in an embrace with Kit, who stands on tiptoe to hug him, and Camilla smiles at the sight of them. How different Mungo and Archie are, in almost every way possible. Serious, responsible Archie, working in his father's law practice in Exeter from the moment he left university: imaginative, emotional Mungo, risking parental disapproval and security to follow his star. She loves Mungo's gay friends and his girlfriends and, because nothing seems to get too serious for too long, her relationship with him has never been strained. He beams at her, opening his arms for a hug.

'Are we on the veranda, Millie?' he asks. 'Oh, good. A perfect evening for it.'

'Come and have a drink,' she says. 'How are you, Kit?'

She senses that Kit is a tad stressed; a little bit tense.

'It's great to be here,' Kit says, kissing her. 'London is an oven.'

Camilla takes the Pimm's from the fridge. 'I hope you don't have to go dashing back?'

Kit shakes her head. 'I work very part time these days and anyway everything's gone dead. People rushing away, hoping the hot weather will last. This late heat wave has taken everyone by surprise. So what's new? How's the family?'

Camilla pours her a glass of Pimm's. 'They've all come down during the holidays and it's been wonderful. I'm just rather sad to see all the children growing so fast. I do so love them when they're small. Actually, we've let the cottage on a short-hold tenancy to a nice little family, did Mungo tell you? Not that he's met them yet. Emma is the daughter of a friend of mine and her husband is an MO in the Royal Marines. He's just gone back to Afghanistan for three months. She's got two little ones, which is such fun. I thought of inviting her to supper but Archie wasn't too keen. I think he wanted you all to himself.'

Kit looks affectionately at Archie. 'The dear of him,' she says, and then crouches to embrace the dogs, who come wagging enthusiastically to meet her. Kit is a great favourite. They lick her ears whilst she laughs helplessly, an arm around each of their necks. Camilla watches her, amused, understanding why Mungo is so fond of her: there is something so wonderfully uncomplicated about Kit – unlike Izzy. Poor mercurial, insecure Izzy.

She helps Kit up, pushing the dogs away, handing her the

glass. 'Let's have our drinks,' she says, and leads the way out on to the veranda.

Kit pauses to sip appreciatively. She's falling under the familiar spell of being cherished. She's spent her working life advising wealthy couples on the designs for their empty new penthouse flats, choosing a pretty lamp or a dining table, sourcing materials, selecting kitchens, and it is such heaven to allow other people to take charge occasionally. This was at the root of the temptation with Michael, of course. He was so responsible; so adult. She was able to imagine a future where anxieties and problems were shared, even taken on to his broad shoulders, so that she could be free of the responsibility. His size and rather shaggy head gave the impression of a large animal: a bear, perhaps, or a huge dog. She was always able to identify with Beauty's attraction to the Beast and for some while she was blinded to Michael's blinkered views and his absolute need to conform. After years of friendship with unconventional people Michael was a novelty. She thought he was reliable when he was merely intractable; wise when he was simply stubborn. Even Hal had remarked rather anxiously on Michael's stolidity and self-regard, though the fact that he was an old naval oppo was a mark in his favour.

'I thought you'd all approve,' she said later to Mungo. 'I could see my playing Camilla to his Archie.'

'Michael isn't a bit like Archie,' Mungo answered at once. 'Michael is a bigoted control freak who just happens to look like a rather attractive dog. And you aren't Camilla. For God's sake, sweetie, open your eyes!'

How odd love is, thinks Kit. Like a virus attacking us when

we're low. Perhaps I thought it was my last chance for a relationship. Imagine being married to Michael now and getting
Jake's letter.

This idea gives her a little jolt. How quickly all Michael's
apparent virtues would have crumbled to dust in the light of
Jake's personality. Kit tries to imagine them together and fails
utterly.

She considers telling Camilla about her dilemma, about
Jake. Camilla will be fascinated, even charmed, by the romantic possibility but she will quickly become practical; cautious
about any commitment. Just at the moment Kit doesn't want
it to be up for discussion in this way. Camilla would expect
some kind of rational conversation, extracting facts, leading
to a decision. She would ask about the letter, and exactly what
it is that Jake is proposing, and it would be difficult to explain
it without the context of the past. The letter, short but clear,
unfolds in Kit's mind.

Kit, my dear, this is an almost impossible letter to write.
I've thought about it for several months and I know
now that any attempt at explanation or justification
must mean that I am either disloyal to Madeleine or
to you. We both know what happened and why. Let's
leave it at that.

Madeleine died earlier this year from cancer. She
had been ill for some time. Her death has made me
value life even more deeply and now, as I begin to
look forward again, I'm hoping that the future might
include you. I've gathered from our yearly exchange
of birthday cards that you are not married but there

might be other complications about which I have no knowledge. Would it be possible to meet? To say that nothing has changed would be trite, cheap even. But at some very deep level the love we shared *does* seem unchanged. Is this possible? Help me out, Kit. I'm a banker not a poet, and if I go on I shall make a fool of myself. I need to see you; to see your expression when I say these things. I can't begin to write how much this would mean to me.

    With my love,

    Jake

Kit is filled with nostalgia for their shared past; she longs for him. She picks up her glass and has another sip to steady herself just as Archie appears beside her.

'Come and see the moon,' he says.

It's a magic world on the veranda: candlelight, moonlight, starlight. Black bats flit and dart amongst the eaves, pale moths drift and flutter round the guttering flames, an owl screeches down in the woods. Kit is suddenly filled with envy of Camilla, who has lived her life here amongst this tranquillity with Archie and her children and her garden; giving life and nurturing it. Beside this abundance her own life seems suddenly shallow. She thinks of Jake and Madeleine, and their four little girls, and wonders what her life with him might have been like if she hadn't been so dilatory.

'I want to be Camilla,' Izzy said to her once. 'She's so . . . uncomplicated and she does so much. She's so practical and confident. She wouldn't have a panic attack about what to wear to a party or because she couldn't decide what to buy for supper. I don't think she really likes me much but she'd never show it.'

Kit didn't protest that of *course* Camilla liked her; she knew Izzy too well to make empty, automatic responses to these tiny cries of pain. Izzy hid the fear and despair so well that even those close to her would never have guessed at the depths to which she plunged.

'And darling old Archie is such a poppet,' Izzy added wistfully. 'Imagine having an Archie.'

'We'd both drive him mad in twenty-four hours,' Kit answered. 'He's so sane and normal and responsible. We must just be grateful for Mungo.'

'Oh, I am, I promise you,' said Izzy fervently. 'He saves my life over and over again. Well, I suppose it's my life. Perhaps it's someone else's life. The trouble is I've played so many parts that I don't know who I am any more. I'm not sure I ever did. I listen to myself talking and wonder if other people can tell that there's nobody there really.'

'Would you really swap your fame and success to live in a tiny hamlet, bringing up children . . .?'

'No,' Izzy said sadly. 'Not as me. Not as Izzy. The responsibility would freak me out and I'd mess it all up. That's why I want to be Camilla. Actually *be* her. That innate sense of her own worth. Those darling babies, and Archie like a rock at her side.'

'And the dogs,' said Kit, keeping it light. 'Never mind the babies. I'll have the dogs.'

Archie is smiling at her, topping up her glass.

'I'm hoping you might come out sailing with me tomorrow,' he says. 'No good asking these two but I thought that you and I could have a potter down the river. Take a picnic.'

'I'd love it,' Kit says quickly. 'Yes, please. If that's OK?'

She glances at Camilla, at Mungo.

Camilla shakes her head. 'Too hot for me. Can't cope with the dazzle on the water. And it's no good looking at Mungo. You know he gets sick in the bath. It'll be lovely for Archie to have some company.'

'I'll cook supper for us all,' says Mungo. 'And what were you saying about a new tenant at the cottage? I must go and introduce myself. And how's James's novel coming along? Do you see much of him? He seems a bit self-conscious. As if he thinks we're all talking about him.'

'But we *are* talking about him,' points out Archie.

'You know what I mean, though.'

'I know exactly what you mean,' agrees Camilla. 'When I talk to him it's as if he's waiting to get back to the fact that he's a writer. It's odd how he can turn almost any subject back to it.'

'Poor James,' says Mungo. 'I suppose writers are just as bad as we actors are. Insecure. Needing love and approval. It's the creative spirit. Or perhaps we weren't loved enough as children.'

'Oh, for God's sake, don't start all that,' cries Archie. 'You were loved just as much as I was, and I don't feel the need to make everyone love me.'

'Ah, but you have wonderful Millie and your children . . .'

'Just stop it,' Camilla says, amused by this familiar interchange. 'Anyway, the question is whether we should give a little party and invite Emma and James. Would it work? I don't see why not . . .'

Kit sits down at the table, takes an olive, listening to them talk. She thinks about Jake, trying to imagine him here amongst these special friends and a mix of excitement and terror churns her gut. Camilla goes inside, murmuring about supper, and the brothers stand together talking. Kit watches them: tall, lean Archie and short, muscular Mungo. The sense of panic recedes and she breathes deeply. Bozzy and Sam edge closer, jostling for her hand on their smooth heads, nudging her knee. She leans forward so as to embrace them both, happy as she has always been in their undemanding company and uncritical affection.

She thinks: if Jake had been a dog I'd have been fine – and gives a little spurt of laughter, buried hastily in Sammy's warm neck.

The tranquillity and the moonlight enfold her; for this space of time she can be peaceful.

CHAPTER SIX

Joe is still awake. He lies in his narrow bed gazing at the moon swimming into sight at the corner of his dormer window. Daddy phoned earlier from Af, when Mummy was getting tea, and Joe told him all about the walk at Haytor and how he climbed on the rocks and then went and had a milkshake with Marcus.

'Marcus?' Daddy said, quite sharply. 'What was he doing there?' and Joe explained about how Marcus had been out for a walk, too, and how they were all going to the zoo together. And all the time Mummy was looking anxious, frowning and biting her lips as if she didn't want him to tell Daddy about it. Then he'd given the telephone back to her and went into the sitting-room to turn the television on, though he could still hear Mummy explaining about Marcus. She talked very quickly and laughed a lot.

'. . . I've no idea. I thought he was away, too. He said that he's training on a Mountain Leader course at Lympstone to go out to California . . . Amazing, wasn't it, that he should be up there on his day off . . . No, he said he'd just climbed up to the tor . . . Yes, just into the Dandelion Café for a coffee . . . Well, he mentioned the zoo and Joe got very excited about it and thought it would be nice if Marcus came too . . . Oh, don't be silly, darling . . .'

At this point she'd closed the kitchen door so that Joe couldn't hear any more but when she gave him and Dora their tea she was very quiet, almost cross.

'Doesn't Daddy want us to go to the zoo with Marcus?' he asked anxiously. 'Anyway, it was you who asked him to come with us, not me.'

'Of course Daddy doesn't mind,' she answered impatiently. 'Why should he? He was just surprised, that's all. He thought Marcus was in Norway.'

'You said he was silly. Why was he silly?'

She stared at him, frowning. 'I said who was silly? Oh, I see what you mean. No, that was just a joke because Daddy was saying he wanted to come to the zoo, too, all the way from Af . . .'

She went on talking, explaining, but he wasn't listening. He was thinking of Daddy, far away, wanting to come to the zoo and it made him feel very sad.

As he lies watching the moon climbing higher across his window, Joe still feels sad. Shadowy, black bars lie across the carpet and on his Thomas, the Tank Engine duvet cover. He wonders if Daddy is looking at the moon in Af, and he thinks he might cry. He slides out of bed, pulls the door wider open and goes out to stand on the tiny upper landing. He can hear the quacking noise of television voices but then he can hear Mummy's voice, too. She is down in the hall and he can just see her moving in and out of sight, her hand is to her ear and her head is bent; she is speaking on her mobile phone. He can't quite hear all her words as she paces to and fro though she seems to be protesting. 'No,' she says, 'no, you mustn't. It's much too late,' but her voice is gentle, rather like the special voice she uses when she talks to Daddy. He knows that everything is all right after all and his heart is soothed.

Joe goes back into his bedroom and pushes the door nearly closed but so that he can still see the glow from the lamp on the lower landing. Anyway, the room is brimming with moonlight. He closes his book – *Room on the Broom* – scrambles into bed and reaches for the various soft toys that share his slumbers. The moon slips away out of sight but the dark blue square of sky is full of stars. Happier now, comforted, he watches their flickering, glimmering dance until he falls asleep.

Kit climbs between the cool cotton sheets, sits for a moment debating whether to read her new William Boyd, and then slides down the bed with a sigh. Mopsa watches her, head cocked, waiting for her moment. As soon as Kit is settled she jumps up and curls beside Kit's knees on the mound of duvet that has been pushed aside. It's much too hot for the quilt. In fact it's too hot to have Mopsa on the bed but Kit strokes her, murmuring loving words, and then switches out the bedside light.

She lies on her side facing the open window. The pale, pretty curtains are drawn together to discourage moths but the moon's brilliance floods around the edges. Kit's thoughts are jumbled with different images: the candlelit table on the veranda covered with plates and glasses; half-empty bowls of food, tall bottles, half-full of wine; Bozzy, Sam and Mopsa sharing an unexpected mid-supper treat, ears flopping forward as they eagerly inspect their bowls; Archie and Mungo locked in animated discussion whilst Camilla gazes out across the garden, thinking about the pudding. Memories of Jake jostle with these images.

'You have the locket,' he is saying. 'You were my first real love, Kit. Nothing's changed that . . . I must go . . .'

Is it possible that she can reabsorb him into her life? How would it work? Six months in London and six months in Paris? What would his daughters and their children think? Family is so important; they can make or break. And now Izzy has appeared among the images. They are sitting together at a table on a pavement outside a café in Totnes.

'The thing is,' Izzy is saying, 'if you're really lucky you get born into this little family unit. This is your place, where you belong; where you are safe. And then there's the rest of the world, strange and unknown, but that doesn't matter as long as you've got these people. Your people. If you lose them, you lose your bearings, your sense of being known. It's unbelievably frightening and unbearably lonely. It's odd, isn't it, how we are defined by other people knowing us? It's as if we don't exist unless we are recognized by other people. When you lose your own special unit you are in real danger of losing yourself. Gradually, as you grow older, you make other connections, of course, but it's never the same . . .'

Kit remembers how hot the sun was on her arms and hands as she lifted her cup and watched Izzy's face: so expressive, so beautiful, so sad. She remembers the smells of spices and coffee, the background buzz and bustle of the market across the road, the heart-jerking sound of the busker's clarinet playing 'I'll Remember April' . . .

Now, Jake reappears. 'Our love has to be put where it belongs . . . A memory . . . we have to live in the real world, Kit . . .'

Kit turns over; away from the window, away from the moonlight. She reaches out to touch Mopsa's rough coat. Deliberately she does what she always does when she can no longer bear to think: she recites poetry silently to herself. 'Augustus was a chubby lad; Fat ruddy cheeks Augustus had . . .'

Mungo lies, propped about with pillows, reading the Duchess of Devonshire's memoirs. He thinks of her as Debo. He has been asked to write his own memoirs – his agent tells him that he could get him a splendid deal with a top publisher – and so he broods about it from time to time. There are many names to conjure with – and many memories. He could cause a few scandals, there would be some very red faces – his own amongst them – but an expurgated watered-down version of his career doesn't really appeal. Izzy, for instance: he would have to write about Izzy. Mungo shakes his head. How would it be possible to do that without betraying her? She is still well-loved, remembered with such pleasure. Towards the end of her career, her life, she decided to experiment in cabaret.

'After all, darling,' she said to him. 'I started as a song-and-dance man. Why shouldn't I have a go?'

She'd been a huge success. The public flocked to see her, admiring her warm, flexible voice, applauding her natural humour, which informed the comedy numbers, appreciating her faultless timing and genuine emotion. She went on tour; she recorded some favourites on an album that went immediately to the top of the popular music charts: Joni Mitchell's 'Both Sides Now', 'Send in the Clowns', 'Yesterday'. The public adored her; she had the knack of making them believe that they knew her, that she was one of them, whilst retaining a classy glamour that kept her just tantalizingly out of reach.

'Tragic, isn't it?' she'd say sadly, reading fan mail, opening little presents. 'What would they say if they knew the real me, Mungo? Anyway, who *is* the real me? I'm such a fraud.'

'No,' he'd say, putting an arm around her. 'No, you're not. It's just that besides being complicated like the rest of us, you have this genius as well. Don't beat yourself up all the time.'

By now she was taking uppers and downers, sleeping tablets – and she was drinking heavily – but there were still flashes of the old Izzy: singing and dancing in the kitchen, laughing and gossiping across the table during a candlelit supper, appearing apologetically at his bedroom door. 'I can't sleep, Mungo. Such terrible nightmares, darling. May I come in with you? Just for the cuddle.'

Mungo closes his book and puts it on the bedside table; takes off his reading specs, switches off the light. He misses Mopsa's weight at his feet and suddenly imagines himself going into Kit's room and climbing in with her and Mopsa. 'Just for the cuddle.'

She probably wouldn't mind, she'd probably be totally cool with it. Unexpectedly he thinks of Ralph and a title for his memoirs occurs to him: *Entre deux lits*. He gives a little snort at the thought. Still smiling, he falls asleep quite quickly, one arm across his eyes to shut out the moonlight.

*

Archie is in bed first. Once he's filled the dishwasher Camilla likes the kitchen to herself to do the last of the clearing up. He takes the dogs out for a last stroll, locks up and goes upstairs. He is pleased with the success of the evening and the prospect of a day on the river with Kit. He makes a little murmuring, humming noise, like a contented bee, as he prepares for bed and by the time Camilla comes upstairs he is already deeply asleep, lying half on his side with his book, Patrick O'Brian's *Master and Commander*, on the floor.

She puts a glass of water on the chest beside Nigella's *Forever Summer* recipes, turns off the light and slides in carefully beside him though she knows that he won't wake. He's always had this gift of sleep; dropping off suddenly, relaxed and peaceful, nothing to trouble his conscience or his dreams. It is in the early hours that Archie's demons gather to torment him. Then he will lie awake, his worries refusing to allow him to sleep, and often he will slip out of bed and go downstairs to read, leaving her to lie awake in his absence, prey to her own anxieties.

Now she curves herself against him, so that she can feel his comfortingly familiar bony warmth, and she thinks about the evening with a sense of satisfaction. There is simply nothing she enjoys more than friends or family – or both – gathered around a table laden with delicious food and good wine. Just two extra people can make the act of eating and drinking a celebration; even if it's only dear old Mungo and Kit. And Kit was in good form, making them laugh about some of her clients' requirements and a trip to a reclamation yard in Gloucestershire to find some particular kind of tiles. There had been a rather sombre note when Mungo suggested that they should raise a glass to Izzy 'for her birthday yesterday', but the moment passed.

Camilla shifts a fraction closer to Archie, disturbed as always by the memory of Izzy's death: the sudden collapse brought on by an overdose of some medication she was taking. Nobody knew if it was by accident or design, but the public version was that she'd been struggling with a debilitating illness: 'Dame Isobel Trent died yesterday. She had been in poor health for some time . . .' Something like that.

Poor Mungo was devastated but, in another way, relieved. He'd been so afraid that she'd give herself away. Camilla could hardly believe it when he told her some of Izzy's problems.

'But she was always such fun,' she protested. 'The life and soul of the party. I know she loved attention and craved approval but she was the one who cheered us all up. She should have put all that business with Ralph behind her and married some nice fellow . . .'

Now, lying against Archie's back, she remembers Mungo saying earlier: 'I regret Ralph.'

Camilla gives her head a tiny shake. It's all too complicated to worry about now. Instead she begins to think about the picnic she will make for Archie and Kit to take on the river tomorrow. Smoked salmon sandwiches, perhaps. And egg mayonnaise; Archie loves egg mayonnaise sandwiches. A little salad with tiny yellow tomatoes, and some of her cherry cake. Camilla drowses; Archie shifts a little and begins to snore.

Billy Judd cries out in his sleep. His bed is washed in moon-light, adrift on a white flood of light that drips from his pillow and pours across the blackened oak boards of the floor.

'Put 'un in deep, boy,' he says. 'Foxes'll get 'un else.'

He turns restlessly, muttering.

Philip watches him from the doorway. He wonders what Billy might say to the ferret woman, or what she might hear when he dozes in his chair.

'Got something on his mind,' Mags said, jerking her head back at Billy, sitting staring out into the orchard. 'Saying all sorts, he is.'

'It's all that television,' Philip said. 'Those *Midsomer Murders* and God knows what. Gives him strange ideas.'

She raised her eyebrows at him, pursed her lips, and he wanted to pinch her, like when they were children; give her a slap.

He moves closer to Billy, picks up the book he's been reading to him. Agatha Christie – *Death on the Nile*. Way back it was Billy who'd be reading to him.

'Come on,' he'd say, when their mother had gone downstairs, leaving them in the dark, calling back threats should they stir from their beds. 'Where'd we get to?' and he'd fish under the pillow for his torch and make a tent of the sheets with his knees for the book. Even now it seems that Philip can hear his big brother's husky twelve-year-old voice reading to him by torchlight – *The Secret Seven, Biggles, Jennings*. He outpaced Billy in the end, passing the eleven-plus, going to grammar school, but Billy didn't care. How proud he'd been of his small brother in his smart school uniform, how ready to defend him from teasing, and how quick to get him out of any kind of trouble. It would be a pity if Billy were to be the one to drop them all in it at this late date: himself, Billy, Archie and Camilla, Sir Mungo.

As he stands looking down at Billy, watching the fluttering eye movement behind the closed lids, the clenching and un-clenching of his large hands, Philip wonders how he can now protect them all.

He remembers another moonlight night – but cold, cold. The cobbles were like glass beneath his boots, light stream-ing from the kitchen window where Mungo and Ralph were framed with Izzy between them. He sees again her hands fly to her face and her rush from the room, the sudden stretch of Mungo's arm and the connection of his fist to Ralph's face and his stagger backwards . . .

Billy cries out, startling him, and struggles to sit up, and Philip kneels on the edge of the bed, taking him in his arms as though he were still a child.

'There now. There now. It's me, Billy. It's Philip. Hush, boy. Hush.'

He holds the big, helpless, trembling frame and his eyes fill with tears. Billy rests against him.

'I didn't say nort,' Billy says at last.

''Course you didn't. Not to old ferret woman.'

Billy starts to chuckle. He wheezes and gasps for air. 'Used to walk all over her,' he says. 'Remember? And then she walked all over him.'

Philip laughs too. Suddenly, they're both young again: in-vincible.

'How about a cuppa?' he suggests. 'And another chapter? Like that, would you?'

And Billy nods and settles himself contentedly to wait.

*

James is also awake. His head seethes with ideas, scenes, fragments of conversation, plots and counterplots. He was right to come to this valley where nothing has happened for a thousand years; where people live in simple contentment. It is the perfect place to enact his own drama, to allow his thoughts to spill out and take form. There is no noise, nothing to interrupt the process. He can't decide what kind of woman his main female character should be; he can't quite pin her down. He watches women, trying to fit them into his book, making up a history for them, but he can't always hear their conversations in his head when it comes to writing about them. Women are so difficult to portray. Yes, he's got a mother – but no sister – and had girlfriends, and he lives with Sally and knows how she thinks (up to a point) but even so, it's almost impossible to imagine what's really going on in women's minds. To be on the safe side he makes sure that Sally reads everything he writes.

'You can't have that,' she'll say sometimes. 'No woman would ever think like that. No way.'

Often this irritates him – how does she know how every woman thinks? – but mostly he's too unconfident to ignore her. He tries to read women's fiction, chick-lit and stuff like that, but it does his head in; he simply can't hack it.

'You're not in touch with your feminine side,' Sal tells him – and she's probably right though he always remembers Valentine's Day and her birthday so she can't complain. Anyway, characterization isn't so important. It's the plot that's crucial. It's good to have the love interest as well as the suspense, though, but by writing this book in the first person it's letting him off the hook of having to record the thoughts of the female character in any great detail.

James turns on to his back wondering if he should get up and make himself some coffee or a mug of tea, but he knows it will merely keep him awake longer, so he resists the temptation. Nevertheless, he slides off the bed, goes down to the big living-room-kitchen and switches on his laptop.

A quiet night in the valley, Sal. Everyone asleep but me. None of the locals will be troubled by tiresome characters and difficult plots. I can imagine them sleeping peacefully. Camilla and Archie, those two old boys next door at the farm, and Sir Mungo. Sir Mungo has a visitor who drives a yellow drop-head Beetle. A fellow thespian, I suspect. They waved to me as they drove by and I waved back but I didn't want to encourage them to stop. Too much tied up in my head. Hope I didn't offend them. And I've had another glimpse of the family in the cottage next door. Friendly woman, early thirties, I'd say, but very much occupied with her kids. The baby's a bit noisy from time to time but the boy is quite a quiet little fellow. I don't want to encourage them either, to be honest. I don't need a small kid poking about in here and fiddling with my laptop. She's an army wife, I think Camilla said, so I expect she's very competent and tough. You'd need to be, wouldn't you? Not much copy here but I don't need copy. I'm getting to know the area really well and everything's falling into place.

I was looking for a village for a bit of the action for the subplot this morning. Somewhere for a liaison between the lovers, out of Totnes, just for a change, where the main action will take place. Difficult to know where they might meet. I suppose you might say the bigger the better – Exeter, perhaps – but then I decided that an element of risk ought to come in here. I mean it would be a bit edgy, wouldn't it, to be meeting under your husband's nose? Or wife's, for that matter. Remember we talked about it and we agreed that the woman would be divorced but the man has a wife and kids? The woman's got nothing to lose so maybe she's hoping they get caught out so as to speed a separation? Anyway I decided that I needed somewhere not as big as Ashburton or Totnes, but not as small as say, Dartington. I drove about a bit and found myself in South Brent. I parked in the old station yard and wandered round the village and I think it might come in very useful. Went into the deli and had a coffee, chatted to the locals as they came in and out – a very friendly bunch of people – and then on the way back to the car stopped off at the pub for a pint and a snack. Walked down by the church and out to the river and I think it will do very well as the place where my two lovers meet clandestinely. In the car park, perhaps, huddled in one car? In the pub more openly? Where would you meet your lover if you had one? Don't answer that! Wouldn't it be wonderful if this book made the big time and we could buy a little weekend cottage like this and live the good life? I've got really good vibes about this book, Sal. Perhaps Sir Mungo and I should get together. I suppose it would be crazy not to take advantage of such a connection, wouldn't it, even if he is a bit past it? He seems very friendly. You'll have to chat him up when you come down.

Better try to get some sleep. Goodnight, my love. J xx

He closes down, goes back upstairs and gets into bed. He makes himself comfortable and picks up his book: Dave Eggers' *A Heartbreaking Work of Staggering Genius*.

CHAPTER SEVEN

'It's crazy,' says Emma, keeping her voice down, glancing at the group at the next table, 'but he makes me feel alive, if you see what I mean. I'm beginning to realize now just how really dull and empty my marriage has become.'

She's driven into Totnes with Dora, leaving Joe with Camilla, and is now in Rumour meeting a very old friend. Emma stirs her coffee, looks at Naomi – dear, gentle, rather plain Naomi – and experiences this odd desire to burst out laughing, to dance and sing and jump up and down. Deliberately she schools her face into a more serious expression. How could earnest, sensible Naomi begin to understand these wild, mad emotions? This sudden flowering of love?

'Are you sure,' Naomi asks quietly, 'that you're not just talking about sex?'

Emma puts down her spoon and stares at her.

'You know?' says Naomi gently, as if Emma is about ten and has yet to understand anything about sexual urges. 'It can be such a powerful feeling, can't it? But it would be disastrous to confuse it with the real thing.'

'Meaning?' asks Emma. Her excitement has diminished a little in the face of Naomi's pragmatism. She thought Naomi might be rather envious, might want to know a few details of this rather thrilling love affair that seems to be burgeoning between her and Marcus, but Naomi seems remarkably unimpressed.

'Meaning that your marriage is under strain with Rob being out in Afghanistan. He's operating on his friends who have been blown up and he's watching others being flown home in body bags. Not easy for him. Not easy for you. It's no wonder if your marriage is a bit stressed.'

Emma is silent. This isn't what she expected from Naomi, whose husband is a junior doctor at Derriford Hospital, and she's rather wishing now that she hadn't told her. It's just so difficult keeping these exciting emotions to herself and she certainly can't tell her other close friends, who are not only military wives themselves but very fond of Rob. She'd rather counted on Naomi being a bit sympathetic, a bit impressed.

'Well,' she says lightly, leaning over to check on Dora, 'it's just rather nice to be seen as a woman again, I suppose. Actually noticed and appreciated.'

She knows that Naomi will make some banal remark assuring her that Rob does all those things but that just now life is a bit tough for him. Naomi does exactly that.

'You know,' she says, when she's finished reassuring Emma about Rob's love for her, 'my old mum used to say that all marriages have a funny five minutes at some point. After all, you have to think about Dora and Joe, too, don't you? Does Marcus have children? I know you said he's separated from his wife. Where does she live?'

'In Sidbury,' says Emma. She feels a bit sulky now. She doesn't want to discuss Tasha or her two sons. They aren't really part of this. 'He goes to see them regularly.'

'Hmm,' says Naomi. 'Well, just don't do anything crazy, Ems. There are a lot of lives involved. Not just yours. Look, I've got to get going. See you soon.'

She gets up, gathers bags together, gives Emma a kiss, touches Dora's head with a light caress. Emma waves as Naomi goes out, drinks the last of her coffee. Her high spirits have evaporated and she feels flat and rather irritable. It was foolish to imagine that Naomi could possibly understand and she wishes now that she hadn't told her. At the same time, she's got a point: there *are* a lot of lives involved. She looks down at Dora, who has fallen asleep; how vulnerable she looks. And suddenly Emma thinks about Rob, so quiet and withdrawn during that last leave, and she wishes that she'd been more perceptive, kinder. Those odd meetings with Marcus, so charged with excitement, made Rob seem very dull in comparison. Guilt and anxiety threaten these more recent feelings of euphoria and she slumps in her chair, thinking about what Naomi said.

A figure appears from behind her and slides into the chair opposite. Emma gasps with surprise and then beams with delight.

'Marcus! I didn't see you there.'

'You were occupied with that rather severe-looking woman so I thought I'd take a back seat. How are you?'

'But what are you *doing* here? I can't believe it.'

'When you texted you said you'd be coming into Totnes to meet a friend so I thought it might be worth the trip to get a glimpse of you.'

His smile makes her gut churn so that she feels embarrassed and excited and happy all at once. He leans across and strokes the back of her hand with one finger. As usual she feels a kind of shock when he touches her, but instinct makes her snatch her hand away and she glances round quickly and looks down at Dora as if to reassure her. She notes that he regrets his gesture – he sees that it was mistimed and she isn't ready for any kind of public display – but he has no intention of giving way.

'Have you thought any more of my plan to have some time on our own?' he asks. His gaze is so keen, so alive, that she feels her willpower beginning to dissolve in its laser-like beam.

'I can't get my head round it,' she says. 'Not yet. It's a bit difficult with the children.'

'Where's Joe?'

'With Camilla. She came down this morning and asked if he'd like to go up and play. She's got loads of toys up there and, of course, he loves the dogs.'

'Would she have Dora, too?'

'I'm sure she would.' Emma hesitates; she feels the least bit as if she's being stampeded. At the same time it's very flatter-ing and exciting. Marcus is so vital; so charged with power that you feel he might explode with it. He's smiling at her again and she finds that she's responding, weakening.

'It's not that I don't want to,' she says. 'It's just . . . I have to be careful. I have to think about Joe and Dora . . .'

'I know,' he says. 'Of course I do. I understand. But I'm not going to give up either, Emma. I think we would be so good together.'

'It's just that there are so many lives involved.'

He laughs and she feels a fool. It's as if he knows that she's been influenced by Naomi.

'Is that what that boot-faced female said?' he asks. 'Come on, Emma. It's your life.'

'I know it is,' she says quickly. 'I know that. But it's not *just* my life. I have to think about Dora and Joe. And Rob. This will change everything.'

As soon as she says it she knows it to be true and panic flutters just beneath her ribcage. Marcus continues to watch her with that cool grey stare, as if he is assessing the level of her feelings for him: his power over her. He has picked up the spoon – one of Joe's with a pirate on its blue plastic handle – that she used earlier to give Dora a little snack and he is turning it and turning it in his hand with a little tap on the table between each turn. There is an oddly controlled rhythm to his action and, just for a brief second, she almost feels frightened of him. Then he leans closer, though he doesn't touch her, and speaks gently.

'Sorry,' he says. 'It's just I can't bear the thought of losing you, that's all. I don't think you have any idea of how I feel about you.'

His expression is tender now, almost humble, and she feels her own power over him, which is rather gratifying and exciting.

'I will try,' she says. 'I'll talk to Camilla and see if we can have some time on our own together. It's just that it's all happened so quickly.'

'Of course,' he says, sitting back. He stares around, calmly, easily. 'Time for another coffee?'

Emma glances at her watch. 'A very quick one. Then I must go home to feed Dora, and Camilla has invited us to lunch.'

Emma can't quite decide why the thought of Camilla, looking after Joe and making lunch for them, is such a comforting one. She watches Marcus go to order the coffee; takes another look to make sure there's nobody she knows, though that's very unlikely here in Totnes. And anyway, Rob and Marcus are friends. It's not that amazing that she and Marcus might be having coffee together – and Dora is an excellent chaperone. She tries to capture that earlier warm glow of light-hearted excitement but Naomi's cool common sense has made it seem rather silly; cheap even. Marcus comes back towards her. He is lean and tough and sexy, and her gut still behaves oddly at the sight of him.

He sits down, smiling and friendly; no stress. He begins to tell her about some incident in Norway, which makes her laugh, things are easy between them again, and she relaxes and it's good.

It is not until Emma begins to collect her things together that she sees Joe's spoon. It is crushed and twisted almost in half. Somehow the sight of it is shocking; frightening. She glances quickly at Marcus, but he is occupied shrugging himself into his jacket, and she takes the spoon and drops it into her bag.

Marcus walks back to the car park with Emma, waves her off. He must be careful; very careful. He likes being with her; likes the way that she's attracted to him but playing it cool. He respects that. But he needs something to happen; to move things along. All the time she was with the girlfriend he was watching her. He saw her face change from excitement – that need to tell someone, to be girly and gossipy – to wariness. He could tell at once that the boot-faced friend was putting the mockers on it; damping things down. The way Emma put her head on one side, her more serious expression, showed that doubt was creeping in. How glad he was then that he'd decided to take the chance to trail her. He's done it before – checked out where the cottage is – but he needs to be careful. There's that guy next door, for a start. Emma says she thinks he's a writer. He comes and goes; he's a bit of a loner.

Marcus unlocks the door and gets into his car. He can't help smiling. If people only knew how easy it is to follow them, watch them, they'd never know a minute's peace. And after all, it was fair enough. She'd sent the text telling him that she was meeting a friend for coffee in the bistro Rumour, more or less suggesting that he should be there, too. It was easy to slip in early and sit at a table at the back, behind a small partition from which point he could watch the two girls together. He needs to see her; to be reassured that she's attracted to him. He longs for that warmth, that female companionship that he misses so much since Tasha told him that she'd decided she wanted a trial separation; that he was becoming impossible to live with. It's been less than a year – and he's been away for most of that – but he misses her, the bitch. God, he misses her and the boys. Not all the time, of course. Not when he's with the lads out in Norway or in Af. That kind of companionship surpasses everything; nothing like it. But when he's back he doesn't want to live in the Mess. He wants to be with his wife and with his boys. He and Tasha keep up the pretence that

Daddy's away working most of the time – he still has most of his stuff at the little cottage in Sidbury – but he needs the stability that Tasha always gave him.

He's got only these few days of leave and then at the weekend he's going to see his boys. Thinking about them upsets him. They're used to his being away, of course, but soon they'll begin to know something's wrong. They're only two and four years old; they don't really remember anything different, to be honest. Even so, he's not going to lose them. And, to be fair, Tasha makes sure he sees them when he can. She thinks it's important. Sometimes he wonders if she's just trying to teach him a lesson, to shock him into showing more respect and being more responsible when he's home. Well, it works both ways. She threw him out so she can't complain if he finds someone else. He's always fancied Emma but now she's become a challenge. He can't get her out of his head and he's determined to have her. But he hasn't got much time; he must keep up the pressure on her if he wants to succeed. That night he'd been watching her cottage he'd have knocked on the door, taken her by surprise, if her nosy neighbour hadn't appeared, peering out in the dark.

Marcus clenches his fists, remembering his frustration. He was waiting under the trees, watching the lights go off upstairs to be certain that Joe was asleep; hoping to catch Emma off guard for a moment. Last night he phoned her, asked straight out if he could come round, but she blocked him. Joe was still awake, she said, fobbing him off. She wants him, he knows that, but just at the moment it's a game to her. Thrill of the chase and all that. For him it's a need to prove to himself that he can make another woman love him; take chances for him. If he can just get her alone he knows he can convince her. He hoped that she was going to be on her own this morning, without her children, so he could persuade her to stay and have lunch with him, but no such luck.

A car pulls into the space beside him and a small, thin, nerdy-looking guy in shorts gets out. Marcus lowers his window.

'Want my ticket?' he offers. 'I put way too much on it. Couple of hours enough for you?'

The nerdy guy hesitates, then shakes his head.

'That's very kind but I never quite know how long I'm going to be when I'm researching.'

He looks as if he might be going to explain what he's re-searching but Marcus isn't interested. He starts the engine, backs out and drives away.

CHAPTER EIGHT

'Such energy,' says Mungo, watching Joe pedalling at high speed round and round Camilla's yard on a brightly coloured plastic tractor. 'Can you remember being like that?'

He feels he has seen Joe somewhere before but can't think where.

Camilla frowns. 'I don't remember much before I was about seven and had my first pony. Anyway, it's difficult to know what it is you actually remember and what is received wisdom, isn't it? I think I was rather a bossy little girl. Archie says you were always making up games and bullying your friends into taking part. Either that or playing with pretend friends. He says you preferred pretend ones because they always did exactly as you told them.'

They both laugh.

'Not much change there then,' says Mungo. 'It was clearly an excellent apprenticeship for my career.'

'Did you read that review in the *Telegraph* of whatshis-name's autobiography? He says you were an absolute martinet.

Terrified him into submission when you were directing him in some play or other.'

'Nonsense,' says Mungo indignantly. 'I was like a father to him. Taught him everything he knows. Millie, that child will get heatstroke if he goes on like that. I left Mopsa in the kitchen because the midday heat is too much for her.'

'Emma's due back any time now.' Camilla glances at her wristwatch. 'Are you sure you won't stay to lunch? I wish you would.'

'I'll wait and see if I like her,' says Mungo candidly. 'We'll have a code so that there's no embarrassment. Now what shall it be?'

'Too late,' says Camilla. 'I hear a car coming up the drive.' She calls to Joe, who is still circling on the tractor, 'I think Mummy's back,' and then walks round the side of the house where a small car has come to a stop. 'Yes, it's Emma.'

Mungo follows her, waiting at the entrance by the barn whilst Camilla goes forward to greet her. He stares in astonishment. It is the girl from the Dandelion Café; the girl who was in conversation with the tough young man. And, of course, that's where he saw Joe: the little boy drinking the milkshake. He is seized by curiosity. Camilla has told him that this Emma's husband is out in Afghanistan, so who was the man with her in the café?

Camilla is bringing her forward, introducing her, and Mungo takes her hand, delighted by this new development.

'Hello, Emma,' he says warmly. 'Camilla says that you're settling in very happily at the cottage. I'm just up the lane if you need any help. You must come and see me.'

'Thank you,' she says.

'I've been invited to lunch too,' he says, beaming at Camilla. 'I hope you don't mind.'

'Of course not,' Emma says. She glances behind her at the car. 'I think I need to get Dora out. It's so hot, she'll be boiling.'

'Well,' murmurs Camilla, as they watch Emma leaning in, unstrapping Dora from her seat, 'it didn't take you long to make up your mind.'

'You didn't tell me that she was so pretty,' he says, 'but remember that I'm no good with babies. You must deal.'

Joe appears beside them. 'I've been riding on the tractor, Mummy,' he shouts. 'Come and watch me.'

Camilla takes Dora from Emma. 'Come on, sweetheart,' she says tenderly to Dora. 'Just a few minutes,' she says firmly to Joe, 'and then you must come in and wash your hands. Lunch will be ready by then.'

Talking to Dora, she carries her off into the house. Mungo glances at Emma to see if she minds Camilla's appropriation of her role, but Emma looks quite content with this relief from her responsibilities.

'She's amazing with them,' she says, as if answering his unspoken question. 'It's wonderful when somebody else takes charge for a moment.'

'Yes,' says Mungo. 'It must get tiring coping all on your own.'

'Bath-time is the worst,' she tells him. 'But you get used to it. Still, it's great to get out and have a break and meet up with friends . . .'

She falls silent and they stand for a moment, watching Joe,

who is showing off and pedalling as fast as he can. Mungo is aware of a certain tension emanating from her. From the corner of his eye he sees her fingers clench and unclench on the long strap of the bag that hangs over her shoulder.

'You must meet Kit,' he says lightly. 'She's a very old friend who is staying with me at the moment. You might have seen her already in the lane with my dog, Mopsa.'

Emma looks at him quickly, and then away again. 'I don't think I have,' she says uncertainly. 'Though Joe mentioned someone out in the lane with a little dog. He said she looked like a princess or a witch, but a nice one. He couldn't make up his mind.'

She smiles but he can feel the weight of her anxiety, per-haps even guilt, and he feels immensely sorry for her.

'A witch or a princess. That sounds like Kit,' he says cheer-fully. 'I can never make up my mind about her, either.'

Camilla appears.

'I've found the highchair for Dora,' she says. 'She's all settled. Come along,' she calls to Joe. 'Time to wash your hands. Quickly now.'

Obediently Joe climbs off the tractor and runs towards her. 'What shall we do after lunch?' he asks, seizing her hand and going inside with her. 'Shall we take the dogs up on the moor?'

Emma watches them disappear, raises her eyebrows, and gives a little shrug. 'I wonder how she does that? It would have taken me at least twenty minutes to get him off that tractor and indoors. What's her secret?'

Mungo smiles at her; gives her a tiny wink. 'She was saying earlier that she was always bossy, you know. Even as a child. Old habits die hard.'

She laughs at his little joke and just for a moment she looks relaxed and at peace. Mungo thinks of that tough-looking young man and can quite understand how he might wreck one's peace of mind. He remembers Ralph and how terrible old love nearly destroyed them all, and he realizes that Emma reminds him of Izzy; not just her gamine, waif-like Audrey Hepburn look but that same vulnerability.

'We'd better go and wash our hands,' he tells her, 'or Camilla will be after us. We shan't be exempt simply because we're grown up. Or pretend to be.'

Emma looks at him intently. 'I don't always feel grown up,' she admits. 'Sometimes I think it's quite scary that I'm responsible for two small children.'

'Terrifying,' he agrees sympathetically. 'We're all the same underneath, you know. Putting up smokescreens so other people don't know how totally helpless we really feel. Well, perhaps not all of us. Not Camilla. Camilla is very grown up. But I keep forgetting that she and your mother are old friends.'

'They were at school together and they stayed in touch afterwards. She was really good when Mum and Dad got divorced. Mum's a bit of a scatterbrain so I think she really appreciated Camilla's practical approach. I think she was quite grateful to have someone to tell her what to do.'

'Ah, well now, Camilla's just the right person for that,' says Mungo.

Camilla reappears. 'Are you two ever coming? Joe and Dora are waiting for their lunch.'

Mungo and Emma follow her meekly into the house.

'Told you so,' he whispers to her, and Emma laughs. Mungo

is pleased: he feels that he has broken down some of her defences and that a kind of rapport has been established. His curiosity is aroused and he longs to know more about Emma and the man in the café. He remembers their body language, their intensity, and he has the odd sense that she might be in some kind of danger.

Don't be such an old drama queen, he tells himself. But the feeling remains.

Kit and Archie are enjoying Camilla's picnic, anchored up in Old Mill Creek in the shade of the woods: the water soft and still as stretched silk, boats resting on their mirror images, trees leaning to embrace their reflections. A flotilla of ducks sets out from the shadowy shore, fracturing those images, splintering the smooth surface into a thousand shining ripples. Quacking encouragingly, they paddle hopefully around *The Wave*, waiting for some morsel to be thrown to them.

'Poor things,' says Kit sadly. 'The trouble is that these sand-wiches are so delicious I can't spare a single crumb. Camilla is so clever. You are a very lucky man, Archie.'

'I know,' says Archie, rather smugly, as one who has been able to pick and choose, and has chosen the best. 'And she'll be having a wonderful time with young Joe. Funny little chap. Very serious. Probably because of his father being away so much.'

'Have they got a dog?' she asks, putting a tiny yellow tomato into her mouth, crunching on its sweetness. 'We never had one at home because we lived in a very small house in Bristol but they were always there at The Keep for the holidays. Dogs are so good for children.'

'Joe certainly loves ours, and Emma talked about getting one but she might think she has enough on her hands just at the moment with Rob away.'

They sit companionably in the cockpit, the picnic spread before them. Seagulls wheel above them, heads cocked, yellow eyes fixed on the possibility of food. Kit draws up her legs and wraps her arms around her knees.

'If you had to do it all over again,' she says, 'what would you change?'

Archie breathes deeply, smiles contentedly. 'Can't think of anything. Wouldn't have minded a nice ocean-going yacht, but no point really. Camilla's not much of a sailor.'

Kit watches him as he cuts a slice of cherry cake, sprinkles a few crumbs over the side for the ducks, who come at once, quacking and splashing. How wonderful it must be to have no regrets, no feelings of remorse for those foolish mistakes of one's youth. It is so peaceful to be with Archie, so soothing and so safe. Yet she knows she will not be able to tell him of her dilemma with Jake. Like Camilla, he would take the rational, pragmatic view of one who has never been at the mercy of a mercurial nature. He would try to sympathize, to understand, but there would be none of that genuine empathy that she finds with Mungo or, in the past, with Izzy.

'What about you?' he is asking idly, finishing his cake, dropping a few more crumbs to the squabbling ducks.

'Not having my own dog,' she answers quickly. 'I always thought it wouldn't really have worked in London but some-times I wonder if I could have managed it after all. Thousands of people do.'

'Well, you still could,' he says, 'though I always feel sorry for dogs cooped up in the city and only being able to walk in parks. Doesn't seem quite right somehow.'

Kit smiles to herself: this is the countryman's view. Would Jake want a dog? She thinks about him, about how and where they might live together, and is seized with the now-familiar panic. Part of her longs to see him and part of her is in complete denial. She reaches for some cake and finishes her glass of white wine. Camilla has deemed it safe to allow them a half-bottle: no more, lest Archie should become careless. Archie is stretched out, knees drawn up, eyes closed, head pillowed on his rolled-up sailing smock, and Kit wishes she could stay here for ever in this quiet backwater, eating Camilla's cherry cake. Jake is no threat here . . .

When Mungo read Jake's letter he was silent for a moment and then raised his eyebrows and let a little whistle escape his lips.

'Whew!' he said. 'This boy's keen, sweetie. Rather touching after all these years. I'd like to meet him. He's so direct and honest, yet there's a tenderness too. It makes me feel quite emotional.'

She took the letter from him, folding it. 'I know,' she said. 'It makes me feel the same but it's such a huge step, Mungo. I remember the old Jake and he'll be remembering me in the same way. It's twenty years since we saw each other. Supposing we arrange to meet and we don't even recognize each other? I couldn't bear to see the disillusionment in his eyes. Imagine the horror!'

Mungo thought about it; she saw him entering into the whole spirit of it, preparing – as it were – to direct the scene.

He'd be mentally casting the characters, setting the stage, writing the dialogue.

'You were in love,' he said. 'And, even more importantly, you really liked each other. You were separated, never mind why and how, but the moment that he is free he thinks of you and asks to see you. You tell me that nobody has measured up to him. The trouble is that you feel resentful because he was the one who left and now he is the one who has decided to return. He's calling the shots.'

'Yes,' she said at last, reluctantly. 'That's exactly it. I feel humiliated. He put me aside for Madeleine and now that she's died he's decided to pick me up again.'

'But it wasn't like that, was it? You said he became involved with her because you refused to commit to him, that he asked you to marry him but you didn't want to be tied down. He was miserable and took comfort with this girl who adored him. Who shall blame him for that? Perhaps she got pregnant on purpose and poor Jake felt he must do the right thing.'

'Oh, shut up, Mungo,' she said irritably. 'Whose side are you on?'

'Not mine,' he answered surprisingly. 'I'll admit that I had every intention of persuading you against this. I don't want to share you, sweetie. But this letter has made me feel differently. I think I'd rather like your Jake.'

'Yes, I expect you would,' she said drily. 'He's definitely your type! But that's the point, isn't it? It would change so much, including us.'

'But there might be advantages, too. Try to be positive.'

'I seem to have lost my nerve,' she said. 'It's come as a shock and I'm afraid of upsetting the status quo, I suppose.'

'Oh, don't start telling me you're too old and rubbish like that,' he said impatiently. 'How many people would love to have a second chance at life?'

Now, Kit rests her chin on her knees and gazes across the creek. A cormorant stands on a buoy, its wings extended, immobile in the sun; on the shingly beach waders wait for the tide to fall.

Archie regards her through half-open eyes. With her knees drawn up like that, staring over the water, she reminds him of many past days with her on the river. He wonders what she really regrets: he doesn't quite believe that it's simply a dog. Surely it can't be the Awful Michael. He hadn't cared much for the fellow but nor did he approve of Mungo's brutal decision to put the boot in.

He said as much when Camilla told him that Mungo was planning to confront Kit.

'But you can't stand him,' she cried. 'She won't be happy with him.'

'I suppose we can't know that,' he answered uncomfortably. 'It's such a private thing, isn't it? Just because we don't like him . . .'

'Oh, for goodness' sake,' she said. 'You know Kit far too well to believe that she'd be happy with a prosy, pompous old bore.'

'I can be a prosy, pompous old bore,' he muttered, hoping that she might contradict him.

'Of course you can,' came her devastating answer, 'but you're not like it all the time. Michael is. Kit's much too good for him.'

He quite agreed with that. The prospect of losing Kit's

company on walks with the dogs or days out on the river was a big price to pay for the company of the Awful Michael. During the eighteen months of her relationship with him Archie really missed his times with Kit, though even now he can't quite define the nature of his friendship with her. Perhaps, because she was first and foremost Mungo's friend, it was as if he'd acquired a younger sister. Her social ease and naturalness made him feel as if he'd known her for ever. She fitted in.

'Perhaps,' Camilla said, 'it's because she's a member of a large family. She just gets along with everybody. Or perhaps it's because she has learned how to deal with her clients and instinctively responds to different people in the ways that are right for them. Whatever it is, she's a great asset.'

He is pleased that Kit has Camilla's seal of approval. These days out are precious to him. He is able to be silent – as they are at the moment – to let his thoughts wander, to enjoy the beauty of the river and the day; or to have an exchange of ideas that are always slightly unusual, and there is no stress. He doesn't feel responsible for Kit, yet there is the pleasure of her company, of simply knowing she is there.

A motor boat putters by, *The Wave* bobs and rocks in its wash, and the spell is broken. Archie opens his eyes and sits up.

'Tide's on the turn,' he says. 'Just time for coffee and then we'll have to head for home.'

CHAPTER NINE

M ags clears the plates and begins to load the dishwasher. 'Leave it,' Philip says. 'I'll do it in a minute.'

He'll rearrange it anyway; she can't get in half the amount that he can. She turns, frowning, and he watches her: little pebble eyes, mouth like a bar code. What's Billy been saying now? What maggot has she got into her tiny head?

'Want a cup of tea?' he asks. 'Before you go off? Don't want to be late for your group.'

He can see that she's torn. She's settling in now, getting her feet right under the table – but she mustn't be late for the Coven. She hesitates, fiddling about by the sink, and he gets up ready to make some tea and then chivvy her out of the kitchen, out of the house.

'He gets these turns,' she says, watching him fill the kettle. 'Repeats himself.'

'Understandable,' says Philip easily. 'We all do that.'

'But it doesn't make sense.'

'Nor do you, sometimes. Nor do I.'

He dunks a tea bag into a mug, can't be bothered to make

a proper brew, and then stares out of the window in dismay. Mungo is coming into the yard, striding up to the back door, which is standing wide open. He hammers on the door and shouts at the same time.

'I'll go.' Mags is already halfway out into the scullery and Philip can hear her expressions of delight. He curses just below his breath, makes her tea.

'Look who's here,' says Mags, beaming in the doorway. 'Isn't this nice? Sir Mungo come to see how Billy's doing.'

Mungo winks at Philip behind Mags' head and he can't help but grin back at him.

'How are you, Philip?' he asks. 'Mags says Billy's doing well.'

'Well enough,' he answers.

He feels hampered by Mags' mopping and mowing beside him; anxious about what she might say. He puts her mug on the table and nudges her towards it.

'Would you like some tea, Sir Mungo?' she asks. 'The kettle's just boiled.'

Philip can see that if she has to choose between Sir Mungo and the Coven there will be no contest. Mungo looks at him and raises his eyebrows. It's clear that he can sense Philip's irritation and has a pretty good idea of what is causing it.

'No, no,' Mungo says. 'Thanks but I've just had lunch with Camilla. And with Emma, our new neighbour. Have you met her?'

'Not to speak to yet,' says Philip, whilst Mags sips her tea and smiles ingratiatingly. 'Just to wave to, passing in the car.'

It's funny but with Mags there he can't be natural like he usually is with Mungo. It's crazy; Mungo has known Mags all his life, knows what she's like, but Philip feels awkward, uncomfortable, and he's relieved when Mungo pulls out a chair and sits down just like he always does.

'Shall I pop in and see Billy?' he asks. 'I think he rather enjoyed our little chat last time. Is he up to it?'

Mags is on her feet in a flash. 'I'll go and check him,' she says.

She wants to see if he's dribbling or if he's fallen asleep with his mouth open, snoring. Mustn't let Sir Mungo see him like that. Philip watches her go out and then looks at Mungo and shrugs.

'Driving us round the bend,' he says, 'but what can we do?'

'You never got on,' says Mungo sympathetically. 'Even as children. She was always a pain in the neck, wasn't she, but I suppose she's allowing you to have Billy at home? That makes it worth it, doesn't it? Be grateful she lives in Newton Abbot and not in the village any more.'

'She's a troublemaker. Always was. Likes to sniff out secrets.'

'Secrets?'

'Private things. Things she's not supposed to see or hear. Always been the same. Well, you know that. Remember when we were kids? She liked to poke and pry and then drop you in it accidentally on purpose.'

Mungo stares at him. 'And even if she were to . . . imagine she knew a secret, what then?'

'Who knows?' asks Philip softly, listening for the opening of the door, watching Mungo's face.

'There now,' says Mags, bustling in. 'He's all ready for visitors.'

Mungo gets up and Mags holds the door open. Philip steps in front of her as she makes to follow him.

'Best drink up your tea and then get on your way,' he says pleasantly, 'or the girls'll be wondering where you've got to.'

Her face is blank with frustration and disappointment but he waits, unmoving. They can hear Mungo's voice as he talks to Billy, and Billy's wheezing laugh. Mags turns away, swallows her tea standing at the table and then picks up her bag. He follows her to the door, herding her like a sheepdog lest she strays back towards the parlour. She goes out into the yard, climbs into her car and drives out of the gate and away down the lane.

He continues to stand leaning against the door jamb, gazing out across the yard towards the orchard. No Joanie hanging out the washing, no children playing in the old barn. The stables are empty; no stock to worry about now that the grass keep is let to his son; just a few chickens pecking in the yard and one of Smudgy's descendants washing herself in the sunshine. And now Billy is leaving him, retreating into a shadowy land where he can't follow. For the first time in his life Philip feels truly alone. His sons and their children live further down the valley but this is not the companionship he suddenly craves. Just at this moment he doesn't want to be grandfather or father, an elder of the tribe. He has an inexplicable need to be with those people who knew him as a boy, as a young man, who shared his youth. There are very few left now, but Mungo is one of them. He remembers Mungo as the imaginative child, as the spirited teenager, and later, as the actor who brought glamour and excitement into his life: Mungo brought the smell of greasepaint, the magic of theatre – and Izzy.

The sunlit yard is superimposed with images: Izzy, laughing up at him, holding his hand; singing and dancing in Mungo's kitchen. He sees Ralph's amused, contemptuous smile and hears his voice: 'Keep away from her, Gabriel Oak. She's out of your league.' He remembers the weight of Ralph's body in his arms, the jar of the spade slicing into the freezing, heavy mud, and Billy's voice in his ear: 'Put 'un in deep, boy. Foxes'll get 'un else.'

Billy and Mungo: the companions of his youth. He turns away from the images and the voices, and goes back inside to find them.

Emma reads the text message that's just pinged in, clips her mobile shut and slips it into her pocket. She feels unsettled, anxious. The excitement of the last few weeks has dissipated and Marcus' message – 'Did you ask Camilla?' – just makes her more stressed. Her morning with Naomi, followed by the lunch with Camilla and Mungo, has confused her. The disturbing sight of the fragile twisted spoon, with the faded and rubbed image of a pirate on its plastic handle, hovers on the edges of her thoughts. It is as if she and Marcus were caught up in a kind of special secret world, a delightful conspiracy, which looks rather tawdry now that it has been exposed. It's been fun, rather dangerous; a payback against the loneliness and fear she endures whilst Rob is out in Af with his band of brothers. If she's honest she gets just a tad fed up sometimes with the camaraderie bit, the sense of 'we happy few', the inability to reconnect with boring, humdrum family life on their return.

'We like fighting,' Marcus said to her, at a party back in the spring. 'It's what we do. It's what we're trained for. And it's a soldiers' playground out there, Ems, make no mistake.'

'But Rob's a doctor,' she protested. 'He's trying to save lives.'

'Ah, but he likes a bit of excitement, too, or he wouldn't have transferred from the navy, would he? He was just as proud to get his green lid as the rest of us.'

Emma tried to remember the very good reasons Rob gave for deciding to take the All Arms Combat Course – and his euphoria when he passed and was awarded the green beret – but she was too conscious of Marcus' grey gaze, the smile on his rather thin lips, to think clearly. It was like being caught in a very strong beam of light: concentrated, dazzling.

'And what's all this Rob tells me about moving into the country?' he was asking.

She shrugged. 'I just feel I'm a bit stifled by military life. A friend of my mum's is letting a cottage up on the moor behind Ashburton. I thought it would be fun.'

His smile, intense, knowing, was rather heart-bumping. She felt as though he could see into her mind and understood the complicated muddle she was in: frustration with Rob, disappointment at those leaves that promised so much and delivered so little, resentment at managing two small children and all the hassles of daily life alone for months at a time with very little gratitude or recognition of the difficulties.

'I'm going to Norway for a few weeks,' Marcus said, 'but we must get together when I return. Look, here's my card.' He slipped it to her quickly just as Rob came back with their drinks. 'Hi, mate,' he said easily. 'Just saying we should get together some time. Ems tells me you're moving.'

She put the card into her bag, and with that complicit action it was as if she entered the next stage of the game.

Now, she wonders at what point during that conversation their usual, slightly flirtatious, jokey friendship toppled over into this new dimension. Of course, everyone knew that Tasha and Marcus were having a trial separation but he'd been on his own for nearly a year. So why now? There was an email address on the card, as well as a mobile telephone number, and when she sent the round-robin email to their friends to give them the new address she added Marcus on it. The email included her mobile number: perfectly reasonable.

Marcus responded, openly and casually, and she left it for Rob to see, along with all the other emails wishing them happiness in their new home. Then she had a text from Marcus – something amusing, brief – and she'd known that this was a crossroads: that to answer the text would in some undefined way commit her to more than the easy-going friendship that existed between the three of them. She dithered. Dora was just three months old and very demanding; Rob, home on R and R, was tired, depressed, short-tempered; Joe couldn't understand why Daddy didn't want to play endless games or go for walks or kick a football. Of course she sympathized; of course she tried to give Rob the attention and love he needed. But she was tired, too; worn down with the new baby and a lively four-year-old. This amusing text was like a little sip of champagne; a reminder that there was life after babies, routines, shopping, and a grumpy husband. One afternoon, after Rob had shouted at Joe, snapped at her for trying to mediate, slammed out of the house to go for a solitary walk, she replied to the text.

As she sits on the bench in the garden behind the cottage watching Joe playing, she knows that she's taken a huge risk with Marcus. It was easy to pretend that it was just some light-hearted fun, a harmless flirtation on both sides, but since the meeting on Haytor she's realized that she's getting out of her depth and that Marcus might not keep to the rules. He's not giving her any leeway, no room for manoeuvre. When she retreats, he attacks: when she hesitates, he crowds her. He's like a pile-driver and she's beginning to feel just a little fright-ened of him. All the while Marcus was watching her, talking to her, his hand was clenching and crushing Joe's spoon. He wasn't even aware of it; he simply left it there on the table, an outward manifestation of whatever turmoil was going on inside his head. She took the spoon out of her bag when they got home and thrust it deep into the rubbish bin so that Joe wouldn't see it. Then, quite suddenly, some instinct made her retrieve it, scrabbling for it, washing it and wiping it on a tissue and then hiding it in her bag. The twisted spoon is a symbol of her fear.

This small garden, designed to withstand the ravages of holiday-makers, is peaceful. It is paved, no grass to be churned up or mowed, and dog roses and honeysuckle grow in the hedges that bound this sunny space. Camilla has planted sunflowers against the cottage wall and they stand tall and straight with sticky green leaves, their upturned faces follow-ing the sun. There is a barbecue in one corner near the French doors into the sitting-room, a heavy wooden table with an umbrella, and six green plastic chairs.

Joe has brought out his train set and is laying it down carefully, kneeling amongst his Thomas, the Tank Engines and track. He looks up and beams at her, and her heart thumps with love and fear. Being with Camilla and Archie and Mungo has somehow put her life back into perspective. Their values, their sense of place and home and family, have reminded her of what she has to lose. Naomi's reaction was the thin end of the wedge but her slightly sanctimonious approach robbed it of some of its impact. Camilla and Mungo, unconscious of her relationship with Marcus, were much more effective in their simple straightforward attitude to her, and to Joe and Dora. There was an unspoken assumption that these children would come first and that her commitment to her marriage was taken for granted. They were both very sympathetic about the difficulties of service life, they approved and admired the fact that she'd taken it on and was coping with it, and their cheerful friendliness gave her new courage and strength.

Emma watches Joe hooking his engines and trucks together, talking to himself, and she sees what she has to lose. Her own world has swung back into focus and she realizes how very precious it is to her. She mustn't risk it for this chimera of excitement and fun; for some brief sexual gratification. Yet how to extricate herself? Her mobile rings and she takes it out and looks at the caller's name: Marcus. She leaves it to ring but her gut curdles with fear. The image of Joe's little spoon, crushed out of shape, rises in her mind. She must be honest with Marcus; explain that it's gone far enough and she wants out. After all, what can he do? Her mind answers the question promptly: he can show Rob the texts. This time she feels quite sick and her thoughts double and dart, to and fro, seeking a resolution.

Joe comes to stand beside her. 'Come and play, Mummy,' he wheedles. 'You can be the Fat Controller if you like.'

She hugs him, pressing her cheek against his hair that is warm from the sun, and she wants to weep. He pulls away from her, looking at her as if trying to gauge her mood, and she smiles at him.

'Come on, then,' she says, and they kneel together amongst the tracks, playing trains in the afternoon sunshine.

CHAPTER TEN

Mungo places the drinks carefully on the round, white-painted, wrought-iron table and sits down beside Kit. Early evening shadows are gathering now in the courtyard, which is still as warm as an oven after the day's heat. A blue-glazed jug full of sweet peas stands in the middle of the table and Kit leans forward to inhale their delicate scent.

'It's fascinating,' says Mungo, tasting his gin and tonic with relish and continuing their earlier conversation. 'An absolutely lovely girl, but all this tension. And who's the man? That's what I want to know.'

'That's what you always want to know,' retorts Kit. 'I have to say I didn't notice them.'

'Well, Emma noticed you. She said that the little fellow, Joe, had seen you in the lane with Mopsa and thought you were either a witch or a princess. A nice witch, he said.'

Kit laughs. 'Right the first time. What a discerning child. I must meet him.'

'I want you to meet them both. My guess is that Emma thinks that you might have seen her in the Dandelion Café.

And since you're staying here with me, and almost part of the family as it were, she's afraid her little secret might leak out to Camilla and Archie.'

'That's a bit far-fetched, isn't it?'

'Not at all. The point is that if you're feeling guilty about something it's very difficult to behave casually. I tell you, I watched them. They weren't just two old friends meeting by chance.'

Kit sips her wine thoughtfully. Mungo enjoys a bit of drama, a good gossip, but he doesn't invent something like this just for the sake of it.

'But you like her?' she asks. 'This Emma.'

'Very much. But I kept getting that vibe that she was nervous about something.'

'You think she might be having an affair with this man?'

He sits for a minute, turning his glass thoughtfully. 'Not yet,' he says at last, 'but I think it's on the cards.'

'But it's none of your business, really, is it? She might be unhappily married. Her husband might be horrid to her. You can't just interfere like you did with me and Michael, you know.'

'I was right to interfere, though, wasn't I? You don't regret him?'

She shakes her head. 'It wouldn't have worked if I'd married him. I could see that, really. It was just that it was so nice to have one's own person, if you know what I mean. Someone always available to go to the theatre with, or a sexy weekend away. I could take it for granted that I'd have a partner for a wedding or party. There was something comforting about him, and thinking that I'd have a companion for my old age.'

'As long as you didn't die of boredom first.'

Kit makes a face at him. 'He just wasn't your type.'

'I'm the first to admit that he was very good-looking in a rugged, military, very British way. But mentally you were light years apart, and he was quite a lot older than you. It was a midsummer madness. You were bewitched, like Titania, and he was your Bottom. He rather looked the part too, with that big shaggy head.'

She sighs, acknowledging that he's right. 'Part of it was that when Sin married, the whole dynamic changed somehow. It had always been a bit like a bachelor pad – friends coming and going. Well, when she got married it altered things and then I felt that perhaps it was time to be a bit more conventional.'

'You certainly picked the right man for that, sweetie.'

'Well, I admit that you were right about me and Michael, but that doesn't mean that it's the same for Emma. Maybe she's in love with this guy.'

Mungo shakes his head. 'There's something wrong,' he says stubbornly.

Kit leans across the table towards him. 'But what can you do about it?'

'I don't know,' he says, almost crossly. 'It's just that I feel she's in some kind of trouble.'

Mopsa gets up from her sun-warmed patch on the cobbles and comes to look at him expectantly. She makes a few little jumping movements as if to will him to stand up.

'I think she's trying to tell you something,' says Kit, amused. 'Could it be dinner-time?'

He glances at his watch and gets up. 'Dead on the dot as usual. Come on then, you old nag-pot.'

They go into the kitchen together and Kit sits on alone in the quiet courtyard thinking of Emma, wondering if Mungo is right, remembering Jake and how she would willingly have had an affair with him if time had been on her side during that last meeting in London.

Way back then, she recalls, her plots and stratagems came to nothing. The trouble was that Jake was behaving as if they were two very dear friends, catching up on old times, sharing special memories, enjoying a small break from the usual routine. What was missing was the indication that it would lead on to anything else. He held her hand, kissed her cheek, laid his arm about her shoulders, but there was nothing more than deep affection in these gestures. After the theatre and their late supper – which had been such fun – he simply put her in a taxi and sent her home. Her pride did not allow her to do anything but behave as if that were exactly what she was expecting. Back in her flat in Hampstead, however, she paced around, seething and frustrated, telling herself that it was perfectly reasonable that, despite his Jake-like glances, he no longer fancied her. Nevertheless, she was deeply hurt and utterly miserable.

The next morning she was unable to work. Searching through her catalogues for a particular kind of rocking chair required by the owner of a small craft centre, she found that she'd looked up the same thing twice already and she pushed the book aside with an impatient sigh. She simply couldn't concentrate. Her small study was untidy: the sturdy pine work-table covered with samples of material, catalogues, price sheets; a length of striped ticking falling from its roll balanced on the only comfortable chair; her desk groaning beneath the weight of reference books. The carpet had almost disappeared beneath a selection of small Indian rugs, laid out fanwise, ready for inspection by the client from the craft centre. Usually Kit enjoyed the busy atmosphere of her study but that morning it irritated her. She stared out of the window, across to the pond and the Heath beyond, and thought about Jake. Leaning her elbows on her cluttered desk, watching the ducks on the pond, she wondered if she should have made her feelings clearer.

Studying him covertly when he was not aware of her – ordering drinks at the bar, paying a bill, talking to a waiter – she knew that he would have lost none of his talents. She saw, too, that other women watched him. Brown-skinned, casually elegant, his horn-rimmed spectacles lending him an academic air, he was very attractive. He had been hers and she had lost him. In chasing after the romantic shadow, she had lost the real live substance.

Kit stabbed her pencil into the blotter, breaking its point. How many times she'd imagined this very situation: Jake appearing out of the past and their falling in love all over again. She'd invented several scenarios for Madeleine: sudden – but painless – death, a lover for whom she'd abandoned Jake, or even a simple breakdown of the marriage, which left them amicable but indifferent. She hadn't, however, made any allowances for the four little girls. Jake did not speak about them but they presented more of a difficulty. He did not discuss his marriage nor did he show any signs of weariness with his family life. It was as if, for this moment in time, they had simply ceased to exist.

She remembered that Jake had always been capable of this; of living in the moment, accepting what came to pass.

Kit thought: but what about me? There has to be more to it than this.

Perhaps she had been less encouraging than she'd imagined. Although it was obvious that she wasn't married she'd allowed him to believe that there was no lack of men and that she had a very busy social diary. Maybe she should make it clear that she was willing to take him back into her life without making conditions or rocking any boats. After all, Paris wasn't very far away. Now that they'd met again it wouldn't be too difficult to maintain a relationship – despite Madeleine and the four little girls. That evening one of her clients was giving a party to celebrate the opening of his wine bar and she'd persuaded Jake to escort her. This time she must make more of an effort to convince him that they mustn't lose each other again. She'd made that mistake once already.

Now, sitting in Mungo's courtyard, she remembers how the telephone rang in her study all those years ago, making her jump. It was Jake. He'd broken straight through her delighted greeting, coming directly to the point.

'I'm at the airport,' he said. 'There's been an emergency. Gabrielle has been taken ill. Madeleine took her home to Paris and she's in hospital. I'm booked on the next flight.'

'Oh, but, Jake . . .' She hesitated, confused, bitterly disappointed, not wishing to sound heartless. 'But what shall we do?'

'Do?' he sounded puzzled.

'We can't just leave it at that.' She tried to say it lightly. 'Not after meeting up again after all these years.'

'Darling Kit,' he said gently, 'it's been such fun. But what else can we do? We can't go back, you know. Life isn't like that.'

'Not back,' she said quickly. 'Of course not. But can't we go forward?'

'I don't think we can.' He sounded sad but quite firm. 'I have a wife and four children whom I love. Forgive me, Kit, but there can't be any future for us. How could there be?'

She spoke from the heart. 'But I still love you, Jake.'

'I love you, too.' She could hear the smile in his voice. 'But our love has to be put where it belongs. It's been fun remembering the way we were. But that's what it is. A memory. We have to live in the real world, Kit.'

'I can't bear it,' she said flatly – but she knew that he was no longer hearing her. She could tell that all his attention was strained away from her, concentrating on the quacking voice that echoed in the background. Suddenly he was back with her again.

'They're calling my flight, Kit,' he said. 'I must go.'

'Wait,' she said urgently. 'Jake. Don't go. Please. Just give me a second.'

'You have the locket,' he said. 'I know that you still wear it. You were my first real love, Kit. Nothing's changed that. But the locket should be a delightful keepsake, not an icon. Don't let it blind you to other kinds of love. I must go. Goodbye, my darling. God bless.'

All these years later she can still hear the particular tone of his voice – the tenderness and regret – and then Mopsa comes bustling out into the courtyard, shattering her reverie.

'Could you take her out, sweetie?' calls Mungo. 'I'm just getting the supper organized.'

Kit gets up, glad of the distraction, and opens the gate into the lane. And here, nearly at the gate, is a small boy riding a little silver scooter. He jumps off quickly, gazing at Kit in alarm, turning to look over his shoulder as if for reassurance. Some way behind him a young woman strolls, pushing a buggy. Kit seizes her chance.

'Hello,' she says. 'Something tells me that you're Joe.'

She can tell by his expression that his conviction that she is a witch has deepened. He nods silently and she smiles at him.

'My name's Kit. I saw you at the Dandelion Café. Did you see me?'

He nods again. 'And the dog,' he says cautiously, indicating Mopsa. 'You had the dog with you, sitting on the sofa.'

'That's right. And Mungo was with us, too. You met Mungo earlier, didn't you?'

'Yes.' He looks more comfortable now. 'He came to lunch with Camilla and Mummy.'

Kit glances along the lane. Emma is catching up. 'And Mummy was at the café too. But your daddy is away, isn't he? He wasn't at the café.'

A shake of the head this time. 'He's in Af. But Marcus was there. He's Daddy's friend.'

'Oh, that's nice.'

'Mmm.' He's lost interest in Marcus and is making a fuss of Mopsa. 'What's his name?'

'It's a her. Her name's Mopsa.'

'Mopsa.' He tries it out, chuckling. 'It's a funny name.'

'Isn't it? It's from a play.' Emma has caught up with them now and Kit smiles at her. 'Hello. I'm Kit Chadwick. I'm staying with Mungo. He told me that he met you all at lunch with Camilla.'

'And the dog is called Mopsa,' cries Joe. 'I told you I saw them in the lane, Mummy. And at the café when we met Marcus. I told you.'

Emma flushes brightly – she is completely taken off guard – and Kit quickly bends over the buggy to cover the younger woman's embarrassment.

'And this is your sister?' she asks Joe, trying to remember if Mungo has mentioned the baby's name.

'This is Dora,' says Joe. He is excited by the encounter, now, and ready to show off. 'You were wearing a long dress when I saw you in the lane,' he tells Kit.

'And you thought I was a witch,' she says mischievously.

He looks taken aback for a moment, and then he laughs. 'Or a princess,' he says.

'And so which am I?' she asks teasingly. 'Be careful or I might turn you into a caterpillar.'

He gives a great shout of laughter, though he still watches her as if she might be more than a mere mortal. Mopsa trots away down the lane and Joe scoots after her, calling her name. Kit looks at Emma at last, hoping that she's had the time to recover her sang-froid.

'What a sweetie he is,' she says lightly. 'I feel rather flattered to be called a witch or a princess.'

They walk along together and Kit begins to understand what Mungo means; there is tension in Emma's whole demeanour, a kind of wariness. Kit talks casually about Camilla and Archie, about Mungo, and her relationship with them all. From the corner of her eye she sees that Emma is beginning to relax but she remains distracted, as if there is something occupying her thoughts that she can't shake off.

'Come back and have a drink,' Kit says impulsively. 'Mungo would love it.'

Emma looks at her and, just for a moment, there is a great longing in her eyes for company, chatter, distraction. Kit feels a huge sympathy for her, recognizing a desperate need not to be alone, and she wants to put her arms round the younger woman and hug her.

'It sounds wonderful,' says Emma wistfully, 'but I must get them back for supper and bed. It's a bit late now, actually, but I love it out in the lane at this time of the evening. Everything smells so wonderful after the heat of the day, and it's so quiet.'

'It must be a bit lonely,' ventures Kit, 'once Joe and Dora are in bed, with all the evening stretching ahead.'

Emma nods. 'It's great to have some peace and quiet,' she admits, 'but it would be heaven to have someone adult to talk to sometimes. Just to gossip with. You know?'

'Oh, I know!' says Kit feelingly. 'My oldest friend and her husband live in the flat above me in London and sometimes I have to restrain myself from rushing up and hammering on their door, screaming, "Talk to me. Talk to me!" It's one of the reasons I come down here and inflict myself on Mungo. I know he feels the same from time to time. We're alike, which is a real bonus. It's rare to find someone who truly understands you.'

Emma is looking at her with real interest, as if she no longer feels a requirement to be polite.

'Oh, it is,' she says eagerly. 'It's special, isn't it? I used to feel like that with Rob . . .'

She looks away, her eagerness fading, biting her lips as if she wishes she hadn't been drawn into the admission.

'Rob?' asks Kit idly. 'Is that your husband? It's more difficult to keep that special quality going in a marriage, I suspect,
with children and all the hurly-burly of daily life together. I
wouldn't know. I've never tried it.'

'Rob was like it to begin with,' says Emma slowly, almost
reluctantly. 'He'd just qualified as a doctor when we met and
he was very idealistic and so was I. I'd trained as a nurse.
Then he decided to join the navy, and not long after that he
decided to try for the Commandos. It was very tough but he
got his green beret and he was just so proud. Well, so was I.
But he seemed to change a bit.'

'I know what you mean,' says Kit. 'My brother was in the
navy. They can get a bit obsessive, can't they? He's retired
now, of course, but he made admiral so we were all proud of
him, too, but we had to sit on him from time to time to keep
him in his place.'

Mopsa and Joe are coming back towards them and Emma
stops and waits for them.

'I think we ought to go home,' she says – and Kit can
see that the moment of confidence is over. Perhaps it was a
mistake to mention Hal and the navy connection.

'Come and see us,' she says, 'when you've got a minute.'

Emma nods. 'Thanks. I'd like that.' The mobile in her
pocket rings and she takes it out, looks at it and snaps it shut
quickly. Her cheeks flush bright red and her eyes are miserable. 'Nothing important,' she says, trying to sound cheerful,
and turns to Joe. 'Come on. Time for baths. See how quick
you can go. We'll race you, won't we, Dora?'

Joe hesitates, as if he might protest, but then speeds away
along the lane, glancing back to see if Emma and Dora are

catching up. Emma waves to Kit, calls a farewell, and begins to hurry after him. Kit follows more slowly with Mopsa. She is beginning to believe that Mungo has a point: Emma is in some kind of trouble.

'You're right,' she says to Mungo, finding him sitting at the table finishing his gin and tonic, telling him about the encounter. 'I see exactly what you mean about her feeling guilty. She was embarrassed when Joe said they'd been with Marcus at the café, and again when her mobile rang. I'm sure it was him. She looked utterly miserable. I still don't see what we can do about it, though. It's up to Emma to tell him to back off – assuming that she wants to.'

'You haven't seen him, sweetie,' says Mungo with a kind of gloomy relish. 'He doesn't look like a man who takes no for an answer. He's a real tough.'

'You clearly studied him closely,' says Kit, grinning at him. 'But even so, it's got to be her call.'

'I hear what you say and I know it's right but I still feel worried about her. Maybe it's crazy but there was a lot of emotion going on when I saw them together.'

'Then the important thing is that she knows she's got people around her who are looking out for her,' says Kit. 'I wonder why she moved here.'

'She said at lunch that she was simply tired of the military goldfish-bowl life and that it would be good for them all to be in the country. Camilla and Emma's mum are friends, and she heard that the cottage was up for letting and decided to give it a go. Sounds reasonable.'

'Mmm,' says Kit, 'and if she'd just begun to have a bit of a flirtation with this Marcus she probably thought it might be better conducted off the base, so the cottage was an added attraction.'

'And now she's changed her mind and is feeling vulnerable?'

Kit nods. 'The children make good chaperones, of course, but she's probably wishing she'd stayed put. Joe said Marcus is "Daddy's friend" so he's probably another commando.'

'He certainly looked tough enough. In which case let's hope he gets recalled to duty.'

'I'll drink to that,' says Kit.

Mungo stands up and goes inside to check on the supper, and she reaches out to touch the petals of the sweet peas: delicate pink and mauve and white. Bridesmaids' colours. She is seized with a sudden fit of depression, a sense of inadequacy, and when Mungo calls that supper is ready she gets up with relief to go to join him.

James sits on the doorstep of the cottage, looking out into the lane, missing Sally. It's been a productive day; driving around has refreshed his ideas, got a few new threads up and running. Tomorrow he will go back to Totnes. Sitting in the sun watching the market traders and the local people is both relaxing and stimulating, and he can see his own characters moving amongst them; coming out of a shop, sitting in a café, hovering at one of the stalls. He's beginning to get a plan of the town in his mind, which will be necessary when he starts to write. He'll remember what it was like to be there, to walk in the narrow streets, look up at the castle, have a pint in the Bay Horse. It will give him confidence knowing that he's been there, doing what they will be doing, seeing what they see:

the sound of the gulls from the river, the smells of incense and fresh flowers. The trouble is, he knows by experience that it's this part of the creative process that he really loves: sitting in bars with his laptop open, jotting down ideas; walking around new places; watching people and inventing little scenarios for them. It's rather depressing that, when the time comes to sit down and actually write the story, his enthusiasm wanes. It's not nearly so much fun sitting in their tiny spare bedroom on his own, trying to hammer the story into shape, trying to fit it in around all the administration that has to be done for school. Of course, when he's made it as a novelist he'll actually be able to spend the time writing in bars or cafés. Other writers do it. It's rather fun talking to the barman or the girl behind the counter and telling them he's a writer. They're always so impressed, even though nobody's heard of him yet. He longs for acclaim: to touch people's lives; to make a difference. It's great to have this cottage, of course, and the time and space to work in it, but if he's honest, it's being out and about that he's really enjoying. Now, walking around Totnes, driving in the lanes, sitting in wine bars, he sees the book as a real possibility. He doesn't want to think about the long slog ahead; just at the moment he's excited by the fun of it all and he would like to have Sally here now to talk about the story, flesh out one or two ideas, try out a bit of the plot on her.

He goes inside and sits down to write to her.

It's going well, Sal. Feeling confident. I saw the two old boys from the farm this afternoon, Philip and Billy. Brothers, both widowed. Lovely blokes with that wonderful Devon drawl and a real twinkle in the eyes. Not the sharpest knives in the drawer but easy to be with. Billy's had a stroke but he's on the mend. I had a cup of tea with them in their orchard. So peaceful and full of good vibes. Their family has lived here for ever and you get that amazing sense of continuity. It's like you've really stepped out of time and that nothing bad could ever happen here. You felt that when we were here before, didn't you? The Land that Time Forgot and all that stuff. Personally, I think I need a bit more going on. Real life. You know what I mean. It's great with these long summer days, but what happens when it gets dark at four o'clock and there's nothing to do until bedtime except watch telly and get drunk? Still, they're used to it, I suppose.

Went back to Totnes this morning. Chap offered me his parking ticket with a couple of hours left on it but you know me when I get absorbed in the book. I never know how long I'll be wandering about or sitting in some café with my laptop so I refused. Odd-looking man, actually. Weird eyes. Very cold and grey, but tough-looking. A bit like one of those no-mates fitness freaks you get at the gym. Clearly a loner that spends his spare time in his room playing video games or working out. As you well know, Sal, I love people-watching, sizing them up and wondering how to fit them into the books, and I do rather pride myself on my judgement. Perhaps I'll put my loner in the book. I had my lunch in a wine bar called Rumour. Perfect for illicit meetings! Lots of corners where my lovers can sit and be hidden away.

Still trying to decide how the husband kills the lover. Deliberate stabbing, hit-and-run – don't really like that one

– or an accident. And then there's the question of the body! I must admit that I'm really enjoying sitting in cafés or pubs, watching people and letting the ideas come and go. It's kind of exciting and I just wish that this could be my full-time job. Beats teaching any time, I can tell you. I get really twitchy about losing my laptop or someone pinching it and I've decided to let this happen to my lover character. Probably the husband pinches it, having seen some emails on his wife's, or maybe her mobile phone or something. I need to work this out but I'm quite excited by it at the moment.

Shall have a stroll to try and unwind before I go to bed. It was good to have a chat this morning and I'm glad you're OK and not too stressed out. Just wait till I've won the Booker and you never have to work again. Night-night. J xx

He pings off the email, leans back in his chair and stretches mightily and decides to wander out into the twilight. As he approaches the farm he can see the headlights of a car flickering towards him, still some distance away. He decides to wait in the farm gateway. The lane is narrow and he's not that visible in this deep twilight. The car comes cautiously round the curve, slowing at the sight of James waiting by the gate. The driver's window is down and James looks in at him, a hand raised in acknowledgement – and is jolted by surprise. The driver is the man he saw in the car park in Totnes who offered him his ticket; the man with those weird, light-coloured eyes. He and James stare at each other just for a second before the car accelerates away.

Must be a local, thinks James. It's a bit late, though, for

driving round these lanes. Perhaps he *is* a bit of a nutter; a loner.

He shrugs and turns back. But for some reason he hurries along the lane, peering ahead to see if the car is parked up anywhere and, when he gets inside the cottage, he makes certain that all the doors are locked and the ground-floor windows fastened securely.

Marcus drives back towards Ashburton, strangely affected by the sight of the nerdy guy he'd seen earlier in Totnes. What the hell is he doing walking in a lane miles from anywhere at this time of the evening? He's surprised at how it's unsettled him. And then it occurs to him that it must be Emma's neighbour. The man who arrived last week: who comes and goes and is a bit elusive. Odd that he should have turned up just now.

Once he's well beyond the cottages – he daren't stop now to see what Emma's doing, why she isn't answering her phone – Marcus pulls in at the verge and switches off the engine. It's silly to get rattled, but he feels the least bit edgy. Was it nerdy guy who was watching him that night from the shadows of the garden? And had he just arrived in the car park in Totnes by coincidence or had he been waiting for Marcus to come back to his car? Just when he was thinking how easy it was to follow someone, too. Perhaps he was in Rumour, watching Marcus watching Emma . . .

He gives a shout of derisive laughter – complete rubbish – but he still feels edgy. He's got a lot to lose: if he's seen to be stalking a fellow officer's wife, his promotion, for a start. He'd lost Brownie points when Tasha insisted on this trial separation, he knows that. And then there's the Mountain

Leader course. He really wants to go to California, to work with the US Marines. He most certainly wants to be a part of that . . . Marcus shakes his head, deriding his ludicrous notion that nerdy guy might be following him. Suddenly he frowns. Could Tasha have found out about Emma? Might she have mentioned it to one of their friends, who tipped off a senior officer so that they've decided to keep tabs on him?

'Get a grip, mate,' Marcus tells himself as he starts up the engine and pulls away – but as he drives back to his B and B in Ashburton he feels kind of twitchy; can't get nerdy guy out of his head. 'Losing touch with reality', Tasha calls it. Wants him to see the MO; go to counselling. He snorts with contempt; like he's going to admit that he's . . . what? Paranoid? Not bloody likely. Anyway, he's fine. He just gets frustrated when things go wrong and Emma won't answer his texts. He can see why she doesn't want him turning up at the cottage – too many nosy parkers around – but it stresses him when he can't contact her; when he's not in control.

But she's promised next time she'll see him alone; without the kids. That's when he'll really get his chance. It'll be fine.

CHAPTER ELEVEN

Jake hesitates in the doorway of Salago, keeping back in the shadows, his eyes fixed in amazement on Kit, who sits at a little table at the edge of the pavement outside The Brioche. When he drew a blank in London Jake's instinct brought him to the West Country; to The Keep, where the Chadwicks have lived for centuries. He booked a room at the Royal Seven Stars Hotel in Totnes.

Way back, Kit always drove him from London to The Keep in that crazy little car she called Eppyjay because the number plate was EPJ: a Morris Minor convertible. She always preferred to drive than to go by train and he was surprised that, after all these years, he remembered the journey so clearly, though he was more cautious once he turned off into the lanes around Staverton and headed towards The Keep.

Finding nobody at home he decided to go back to Totnes; to explore the town the Chadwicks loved so much and which he'd visited with Kit all those years ago. He drove slowly in the narrow lane, his window down, observing the cows crowded together in the shade of a huge oak tree, tails swishing at the tormenting flies; a family of swallows balancing on an overhead wire; a tangle of creamy-pink dog roses in the hedge. The lane was rutted with dry pink earth, ditches choked with bleached feathery grasses and tall purple loosestrife, the air was hot and shimmering blue. The scents drifting through his window were rich and sweet, and evocative of summers long past.

Jake let the engine dawdle. He had only to close his eyes to see them all, that great extended Chadwick family – and Kit, his love, his friend, his soul mate. Yet they'd lost each other. Had they been too laid-back, enjoying their relationship whilst wondering if there might be something more, something better, further on? Perhaps they'd both believed, deep down, that they would finish up together but they'd pushed their luck too far. He'd been afraid to drop the mask of light-heartedness that hid his very real love for her lest it should frighten her off and Kit – despite his regular proposals of marriage – had been unwilling to commit until it was too late.

And now, coming upon her unexpectedly, he stands in the shadows watching her as she laughs and talks with her companion. She is showing him something she has bought from one of the stalls in the market across the street: a scarf, which she throws around her neck with a flourish whilst he smiles his approval. Jake recognizes him: Sir Mungo Kerslake, actor and director, sixties theatre and film icon. It is such a shock to see her there, as if his thoughts and memories have given her life, brought her into being. A shock, too, that though many years have passed she is still so like the Kit of his heart. Perhaps it is because he has been looking for her, hoping to see her, that he sees through the changes that time has made, but it is still a shock to find her so quickly, so easily; sitting with the pretty scarf thrown around her neck, clasping the mug of coffee, smiling at Sir Mungo. There is an ease between them, a casual give and take that indicates a comfortable friendship. Jake's instinct and experience tells him that they are not lovers, but this scene has taken him by surprise. He wonders if she is staying with Sir Mungo rather than at The Keep, and he realizes that he knows very little about her private life. They exchange birthday cards each year, which sometimes contain small news items, but nothing has indicated that she has ever been deeply involved with another man.

Suddenly he feels nervous. The impulse that drove him to write to her, and that has buoyed up his spirits for so long, shrivels in his gut. He should have waited for a response to his letter instead of acting on his instinct that it was foolish to waste time; to come to find her. As Jake hesitates, Mungo gets to his feet and strides off down the street. Kit picks up her cup and leans back in her chair, relaxed, watching the market traders. Hoisting up his flagging confidence, pulling on a mask of light-heartedness he is far from feeling, Jake moves out of the shadows and into the sunlight at the edge of the pavement beside her table. She glances up at him idly, the mug halfway to her lips, and freezes into immobility as she stares at him.

'Jake?'

He sees the word form, rather than hears it, and he smiles at her and slips into the chair that Mungo vacated. She puts the mug down, still staring at him – in horror? In disbelief? He can't quite decide, but knows he must seize the moment before his courage utterly deserts him.

'I love the scarf,' he says. 'And I recognized Sir Mungo Kerslake. What exalted company you keep.'

It's as if this casual approach disarms her because she relaxes back into her seat and picks up the cup again and begins to laugh.

'I simply don't believe this,' she says. 'It's crazy. Impossible. I was hiding from you, for God's sake.'

And now he laughs too, though his heart is pumping violently and she will never guess at the depths of his relief.

'I couldn't find you in London so I came down to see if you might be at The Keep. May I join you?'

'Of course,' she says. 'Pull up another chair for Mungo and go in and order some coffee. They'll bring it out for you.'

He gets up, hesitates. 'You won't disappear while I'm gone, will you?'

She stares at him, and for the moment they are both quite serious. 'Of course I won't,' she says. 'I promise. Go and order the coffee, Jake, while I recover from the shock.'

He pulls another chair across from a nearby table and goes into the café, looking back at her, before joining the little queue at the counter.

'What's the matter?' Mungo drops a bag on to the third chair and sits down. 'You look like you've seen a ghost.'

'I have,' she says. 'You won't believe this. Jake's here. In there,' she jerks her head sideways, 'ordering coffee.'

'No!' Mungo turns to peer into the interior of the café. 'Don't tell me he just walked up and said "Hi"?'

'You don't have to look so pleased about it,' she says,

irritated by his insouciance. 'You look positively gleeful. I was supposed to be in hiding, remember?'

'But it was never going to last, was it, sweetie? You've had time to think, we've talked it all over, but you were always going to want to see him.' He leans forward. 'Did you recognize him at once? What does he look like?'

'You are impossible, Mungo,' she exclaims. 'This is not a movie set. This is my life.'

'Of course it is.' He settles back. 'But you have to admit that it's rather fun. Now come on. First reactions.'

She shakes her head, begins to laugh. 'I give up. Perhaps it *is* a movie set. I can't believe this is happening. He was just standing there . . . Here he comes. Oh God . . .'

Mungo stands up as a tall man in jeans and an open-neck shirt comes out of the café. He looks like an academic; iron-grey hair, dark brown eyes – rather George Clooney-ish.

'Very nice, sweetie,' Mungo murmurs appreciatively to Kit, before holding out a hand to the newcomer.

'Come and sit down,' he says. 'Kit tells me that you're Jake. I'm Mungo Kerslake.'

'I know who you are,' says Jake. 'It's a great honour to meet you, Sir Mungo.'

'Oh, don't do that,' says Mungo, pretending embarrassment but really rather pleased. 'Kit's in shock at you suddenly appearing like the Demon King in the pantomime, but I'm not going to be tactful and disappear in a puff of smoke. I'm much too interested.'

He moves his shopping from the chair and Jake sits down, glancing at Kit, who rolls her eyes and shakes her head as if disassociating herself from the proceedings. But Mungo can see that Jake is quite pleased to have a third party at this reunion. It takes the pressure off and lends an air of celebration.

'It's tremendous luck,' Jake is saying, with another cautious glance at Kit, 'to meet right here, so unexpectedly. I went to Kit's flat in London first but then decided to try her family.'

'Ah, so you've been to The Keep,' says Mungo approvingly. 'Good detective work but, you see, she's staying with me. You'd never have found us, tucked away in our valley, so you're right. It's a great stroke of luck that we should all be here today. It must be fate.'

'Mungo,' mutters Kit. 'Shut up.'

Jake laughs. 'No, no. Don't stop him. It's good to see the great impresario at work. I suspect he's taking notes.'

'To the creative mind nothing is ever wasted,' says Mungo with satisfaction. 'Ah, here's your coffee, Jake.' He waits whilst cups are cleared and then beams upon them both. 'Now then, where shall we have lunch? My place?' He raises an eyebrow at Kit, who gives a barely discernible nod. 'Or do you have other plans, Jake?'

'No.' Jake looks startled. 'That would be extraordinarily kind. Are you quite sure? I must admit I had no plans.'

'That's settled then. You have a car?'

'It's in the car park of the Seven Stars Hotel. I'm staying there for a few days.'

'Then we can pick you up as we come past and you can follow us out.'

'I can't believe my luck,' says Jake, smiling at Kit.

'He's even a good cook,' says Kit drily. 'Which, as you will probably remember, I am not.'

'Oh, I remember all sorts of things,' he answers, smiling a little secret smile.

Disconcerted, Kit bites her lip and Mungo beams delightedly upon them. His Machiavellian tendencies have come to the fore again and he's decided to encourage this second-time-around love affair. If Kit doesn't want this gorgeous man she must be crazy; meanwhile it will be fun watching things develop.

'I suppose you know what you're doing?' asks Kit later, as she drives her bright yellow drop-head Volkswagen Beetle through The Plains towards the hotel. 'I don't remember this being in the script.'

'We hadn't got as far as the script, sweetie,' says Mungo. 'We were just considering the options. I like your Jake. Look, there he is, hovering in the gateway there. I'll wave to him. That's it. Onward. Keep him in sight.'

Confused, nervous, Kit drives on, glancing from time to time in her rear-view mirror to make certain that Jake is behind them. She's unprepared for this feeling of joy that has engulfed her at the sight of him – and at the odd sensation that they have met again after a few short weeks instead of twenty years. It's crazy to feel like this. And Mungo, sitting beside her, humming happily, isn't encouraging her to behave sensibly.

'We'll have a *ménage à trois* at the smithy,' he'd said, as they'd walked back through the market to the car park while Jake headed off to the hotel. 'You and Jake can move into the barn. What fun!'

'You are impossible,' she cried. 'You're supposed to be on my side.'

'Oh, I am, sweetie,' he said. 'Not many people get a second chance, you know. You should grab it with both hands.'

'And who would you like a second chance with?' she asked sharply. But he simply shook his head.

Now she can see him peering in the wing mirror, keeping an eye on Jake's car, and she laughs.

'I think you've fallen for him yourself,' she says.

'It wouldn't take much,' he agrees. 'He doesn't sound very French, does he? I imagined someone more Gallic.'

'His mother was English and he was brought up in England. He went to Ampleforth and the LSE. His family are bankers. Actually, one of the things I was imagining was that he'd have become much more foreign, a stranger, which would have made it so much easier, of course. But he's just the same. Older, of course, but still utterly Jake. Gosh, it was a shock to see him standing there.'

Actually, she's relieved that Mungo is here. She can't imagine how she would have handled that scene outside the café without him. Mungo has managed to turn it into something rather fun, something quite natural, whilst giving her a breathing space. At the same time, he makes her feel nervous. She can feel the vibes coming off him; she can see the excitement of it sparkling in his eyes at the prospect of this new production.

'For heaven's sake,' she says, 'don't invite him to stay at the smithy. Not yet, Mungo. Promise me.'

'It seems a pity,' he answers, rather reluctantly. 'It would be such fun. Though you might be right. Mustn't rush things.'

'If you do, I shall go straight back to London,' she warns him, 'and I shall never speak to you again.'

'Indicate early,' he advises, ignoring this, 'so he knows you're turning right. Give him plenty of warning.'

Feeling irritated, excited and anxious all at once, she drives across the bridge and turns towards Ashburton.

'He's still with us,' says Mungo. 'Good. I give him full marks for coming to find you. I do so approve of that. I like a man who knows what he wants. Let's face it, left to you, you'd have just sat and talked about it. He's got up and put himself out on a limb. And he really has, you know. It must have cost quite a bit of courage to confront you like that after all these years. Don't underestimate it.'

'I'm not,' replies Kit rather crossly. She's torn between being irritated at his criticism of her cowardice and flattered by Jake's determination. 'But I still have to feel right about it, don't I? It's not just to do with how brave Jake is.'

'No, of course not,' says Mungo, rather contritely. 'I just don't want you to miss out on something good. Better a sin of commission than a sin of omission.'

'You always say that.'

'Well, think of a situation where it isn't true. Aren't most of your regrets for things you didn't do rather than for things you did?'

'Oh, shut up, Mungo. I can't concentrate on that now,' she says, her eyes darting to the mirror to check that Jake is still there and then signalling left. 'I'm in an advanced state of shock, can't you see? Stop nagging at me and tell me how to play the next scene.'

Following them, Jake is also in shock. He has an odd desire to burst out laughing with the sheer relief and joy of it all. To see

Kit sitting there, so much like herself, her greeting and then Mungo's arrival have all combined to make him feel almost euphoric. It is eight months since Madeleine died. He misses her gentle presence but it was never a marriage of real fusion. Her hero-worship for him quickly morphed into strong maternal care for her four daughters, and then for their children. She was most herself when she was pregnant, with her little brood around her, and then as a devoted grandmother. They were happy enough but they never shared the fun, the closeness, the passion, he'd known with Kit. It was as if an essential part of him had withered. Yet in London, in the West Country, that once vital essence began to stir again. Driving back from The Keep, the memories returned, fresh and vivid, and when he saw her at the little table he felt reconnected with that Jake of the past; the Jake who loved Kit.

He was faithful to Madeleine in his fashion; he loves his children, and their children, and nothing can change that. Surely now, though, there might be a chance for him to be complete, to be whole again, without disloyalty and damage.

He follows the little yellow Beetle – how typical of Kit to have a yellow Beetle – as if his life depends on it. Weaving through the town of Ashburton, diving down narrow lanes, he feels as though he is plunged into adventure. Mungo has added an extra dimension, given them the opportunity to renew connections within a secure framework, and Jake is very grateful for it. He knows, though, that he must go carefully. Kit's reluctance to commit might still be a real problem. He hardly dares believe that it is her love for him that has prevented her from making any other lasting attachment.

Yet at the end, she offered to go with him to Paris, to marry him. He remembers his pain, the disbelief.

'Twelve bloody years,' he said to her, 'and you're three months too late.'

He closed down on the pain; put it away. He was able to compartmentalize his life so that those years in London became a part of his past that he rarely visited. Remembering, he wonders how he and Kit managed to survive so long back then as lovers without any proper conclusion to the relationship. Of course, Kit had been sharing a flat with Cynthia – nicknamed Sin – since student days and neither of them seemed to have any inclination to disturb the status quo: Sin working as an archivist at the British Museum; Kit at the art gallery in Kensington Church Street. Kit often spent nights at his flat and Sin was never short of boyfriends. The three of them were content to keep a measure of independence, have fun, share outings; he and Sin were regular guests at The Keep. To an outsider it must have looked as if they were having the best of all worlds, and then Kit met Mark. He was giving her advice about starting her own business and she was clearly attracted to him.

Now, Jake wonders why that was the breaking point: the last straw. Immersed in his own anger and jealousy, back in Paris for his grandmother's funeral, he allowed himself to be comforted by Madeleine who'd loved him since she was a child. She knew Kit, had met her, knew Jake loved her. Later, Madeleine told him: 'I saw my chance and took it' and occasionally he wonders if she hoped that a child might be the outcome. He is still capable of a twinge of guilt when he thinks about it – he was so much more experienced and he should have known better – but it comforts him that she had so much joy from her children and grandchildren, that they shared many happy family moments. But now he is alone and free to follow his heart – and his heart has brought him back to England and to Kit.

The yellow Beetle passes a cottage, indicates left and slows down. Mungo is clambering out and coming towards him, showing him where to park. He has arrived.

CHAPTER TWELVE

Camilla sits at the table on the veranda surrounded by the paraphernalia of a morning spent writing a letter, choosing a present from a catalogue, searching for a recipe. The ornamental vine that grows over the roof casts delicate patterns across the flagstones and the table; its crimson and gold leaves tremble in a sudden warm movement of air and its shadow flickers in response. A sparrowhawk hurtles round the side of the house, a feathered missile, lethal as a bullet. It stalls, drops like a weight and jinks over the hedge, hoping to light upon some unsuspecting prey on the other side.

Camilla waits for the scuffle, the flutter of feathers, distracted from writing a birthday card to one of her grand-children. She misses them; wishes they were with her helping her to cook, to garden, to draw and paint. She is so proud of them, her heart so full of love, yet she is firm with them and likes to teach them skills and encourage them to learn. She's not very happy with the way they are becoming addicted to iPads and mobile phones; they are beginning to grow away from the happy domestic tasks she creates for them and she feels sad and frustrated.

It's been fun to have little Joe playing on the tractor and helping her make cakes. He enjoyed it, too, and now Emma has phoned to ask if Camilla could look after both the children, just for a couple of hours tomorrow, so that she can visit a friend. Morning might be better, Emma said, because Dora has a sleep mid-morning, which means she shouldn't be too much trouble. Camilla never thinks children are too much trouble; it is simply a question of organization. She agreed at once, says she will give them lunch so that Emma has plenty of time with her friend, and is already thinking carefully about this unexpected treat with all the attention to detail of a field marshal planning a campaign.

The sparrowhawk has been denied its kill and is back again, watching its opportunity. It alights briefly on the branches of the vine: beautiful and deadly, iron talons gripping, silken wings folded. Camilla watches it, holding her breath, not moving. Quite suddenly it soars upward, tilts sideways and speeds away out of sight. Camilla picks up her pen again. She wants to enclose a photograph with the birthday card; a memory of the earlier summer holiday. Photographs are so important, evoking happy moments caught for ever by that press of a button; the flash of a bulb. She has photographs of her children, and their children, in almost every room: formal in frames, carefully chosen for montages, pinned haphazard on notice boards. There is a selection now before her on the table and she sifts them, studying them, remembering this occasion and that.

How precious they are, these children. She thinks of them

with tenderness, feeling again the weight of a baby in her arms; the warmth of a child sprawled against her, thumb in mouth, as she reads a story; the strangling hug of strong little arms. She sees the beam of a smile, the droop of a mouth, the beauty of childish limbs dancing, playing.

For some reason there are tears in her eyes and her heart aches. She wants to hold life in her control, keep the children safe from harm. Camilla shakes her head at her foolishness, selects a photograph, and begins to write in the card.

Archie, back from his walk, calls out from the kitchen, comes on to the veranda leaving the dogs gratefully lapping at their water bowls. He sees Camilla's expression, notes the birthday card and the photographs, and guesses that she's having one of her maternal moments.

'How about coffee?' he suggests. Eating and drinking is a cheerful occupation and he offers it as a kind of comfort. 'And some of those biscuits you made? Shall I put the kettle on?'

She nods, smiling at him, and he goes back inside feeling slightly relieved: the dangerous moment might be past by the time he's made the coffee if he's lucky. Poor old Camilla has been a bit down since the holidays, missing the children, upset that neither of their boys or their wives seem interested in keeping the house once he and Camilla have gone. Of course, he understands how they feel — neither couple could be expected to give up their jobs to live here and it would be ludicrously extravagant trying to keep the place on as a bolt-hole — nevertheless it's a very sad prospect and Camilla is taking it badly.

For himself, the on-going nightmare of living on a

shoestring whilst he tries to hold the estate together is getting too much. With the proceeds from the sale of his share of the partnership he was able to refurbish one cottage to a standard where it could be let out again but the second cottage down by the farm needs a complete overhaul, the farm is run down and, even here, the house needs replumbing, new window frames, and the roof is looking fragile.

Archie grimaces to himself as he waits for the kettle to boil. He tells himself that he would be glad to sell, move on, enjoy a bit more sailing. At present he is gardener, navvy, odd-job man, and he'd be very pleased to let it all go. Of *course* it's sad; of *course* he'd miss the old place. But he's tired of years of ducking and diving, making ends meet, organizing holiday lets for the cottages and placating tenants.

'And what would happen to Philip and Billy if we sold?' demands Camilla when they have these fruitless and fractious conversations. 'They wouldn't be covered by their agricultural tenancy now they've stopped farming properly, would they? They'd hate it if they were turned out.'

And that's the trouble. He knows they'd hate any kind of change. They'll put up with damp, rotting window frames, old-fashioned plumbing, rather than move – and he doesn't blame them. This valley has been their lives; their livelihood. Archie reaches for the cafetiere. Sometimes he thinks he'd be very happy in a small, sunny, modern flat on The Plains in Totnes, with his boat nearby on a mooring . . .

'And,' Camilla reminds him at regular intervals, 'I will never live in a place where the children can't come to stay with us. Never, Archie.'

Yes, well, that's it. Finish. End of, as his grandsons say.

Mungo has offered to contribute. After all, he says, his nephews will inherit everything he has, so why not let him help to restore some of the property? It's all the same in the end. But Archie feels it's rather unfair to allow Mungo to shell out on the estate that their father so ruthlessly withheld from his younger son.

'You might need your money later on,' Archie said. 'You can't tell. What would you do, Mungo, if Camilla and I sold it all up and moved?'

Mungo was clearly shocked at the prospect; much more upset than Archie would have imagined. After all, Mungo spent half the year at his flat in London.

'Is that likely?' he asked. 'Is it really that bad? Surely Camilla would chew off her own arm rather than leave? I can't imagine being here without you just up the lane. Look, I wish you'd let me help you.'

Archie loads up the tray, thinks about the estimates for repairs, renewals, replacements, lying on his desk, and he closes his eyes briefly in despair. Today he feels old and tired and ill.

The dogs nudge at his knees, tongues dripping, eyes bright, and he looks down at them and his heart eases a little.

'You want your biccies,' he murmurs. 'Good boys, then. Good fellows.'

He rummages in a cupboard and gives Bozzy and Sam their treats and strokes their smooth coats while they wag their tails appreciatively and crunch up their biscuits.

Archie sighs. He wouldn't be able to keep the dogs in that nice small sunny flat by the river in Totnes. Picking up the tray, he carries the coffee out to Camilla.

*

Later, Mungo walks with Mopsa in the lane. He has decided that it would be tactful now to leave Kit and Jake alone. They are relaxed, they've had a good lunch, they need to have a moment to themselves. He feels confident that he has directed the scene to a perfect moment; a delightful conclusion for their first meeting.

He walks slowly, hands in his jeans pockets, his thoughts drifting from Kit and Jake back to his conversation with Billy yesterday afternoon in the parlour at the farm. Well, it was hardly a conversation but it was still faintly disturbing. The old fellow had been in a cheerful mood, his wheezy chuckle escaping in breathy bursts from his distorted lips. They talked of old times, of how he would soon be up and about, of how he could still manage a little walk in the orchard.

'I like my walk in the orchard,' Billy said. He winked at Mungo. 'Remember? First he walked all over her and then she walked all over him.'

And he began his disgraceful old chuckle again, leaning forward in his chair until he was breathless, and Mungo stood up and bent over him anxiously. Philip came in then, looking preoccupied, as if he'd been on some distant mental journey, and hurried forward when he saw his brother gasping for air.

'Daft old bugger,' he said. 'What's he been saying? Come on, Billy. Stop it now or you'll choke to death.'

They eased the old man upright and Philip pushed his wheelchair out of the parlour with Star running at his side.

'We'll walk you home,' he said to Mungo. 'Give him some air. What was he saying?'

Mungo shrugged. 'We were talking about old times. Nothing much.'

'Ah. Old times,' said Philip thoughtfully. He glanced side-ways at Mungo; an odd, almost hopeful look. 'Perhaps it's best to forget old times.'

Mungo turns along the track beside the stream. How is it possible to forget old times? Clearly Kit and Jake haven't. It's as if their shared past has been deep frozen all these years and has now resurfaced, bursting out of the cold, sealed ground; fresh and green and full of possibilities. Their memories are not withered and decayed but are blossoming with renewed hope; they see in each other those young people that shared so much, that talked and danced and laughed and made love.

Perhaps, thinks Mungo, that's why the friends of our youth are so dear to us. To each other we aren't grey and old and dull. We remember times when we took chances, acted courageously, rescued each other and gave each other support. These things remain. In their company we are the people we've always been: viable and strong.

The stream ripples over round brown river stones, trickles down miniature waterfalls, flows under the crumbling bank where the water rat has its home. In the shadows beneath the willows the heron waits: motionless, watchful. As Mopsa comes in view it rises with a few elegant flaps of its great wings and heads upstream to more solitary fishing grounds. As boys they fished the stream for trout. Philip and Archie, silent, patient, were best at it. He and Billy would get bored; slip away to find the kingfisher's nest or to watch the dipper bobbing on its stone and then plunging into the rushing water to collect beakfuls of grubs for its young. Later, Archie tried to teach Izzy the art of fly-fishing, wading out mid-stream with her, showing her how to back-cast beneath the canopy of trees. Slipping on the stony bed, laughing, clumsy with the rod, poor Izzy did her best but even Archie's patience began to wear thin.

Mungo remembers how he and Camilla watched from the bank, Camilla large with her second child, whilst small Henry dozed in his pushchair.

'He's loving every minute of it,' said Camilla, her eyes on the pair in the river.

Mungo glanced at her, hearing an odd kind of bleakness in her voice, and hastened to reassure her.

'It's just some silly fun. She'd drive him mad after a while, you know that, Millie. He's getting a bit fed up now, actually, isn't he?'

'She's so sexy.' Camilla put her hands to her bump. 'And she's so damned thin. Archie fancies her, I can see that. She plays up to him.'

'That's just how she is. Izzy doesn't mean to make trouble. She's like this with everyone. She just loves people to be happy, to make them laugh. Then she can feel safe.'

'Safe?'

'She doesn't have your kind of security, Millie. Izzy needs constant reassurance that she's worth anything.'

'Oh, don't you start on all that stuff about her losing her parents and being brought up by some old aunt or cousin and how brave she is. Archie tells me often enough.'

'Izzy's just novelty value. Archie adores you,' Mungo said firmly. 'You're having a prenatal wobble, Millie. This isn't like you.'

She smiled, slipping her hand within his arm, holding it tightly.

'I may not be an actor,' she said, 'but I'm allowed to have a dramatic moment occasionally. You have no idea what it's like to be very fat and unwieldy and dull, and have to watch your husband being chatted up by a girl like Izzy Trent.'

'But I do know what it's like to be jealous,' he said, squeezing her hand with his arm, 'and it's hell. Let's leave them to it and go back and have some tea. Archie will soon get bored, I promise you, and Izzy won't enjoy it so much without an audience.'

Now, as Mungo turns to go home, he remembers that later, back at the smithy, he asked Izzy if she fancied Archie. She gazed at him in amazement.

'Fancy him?' She shook her head. 'I love him, though. He's so kind, isn't he? You feel safe with him.'

How important it was to her: to be safe. Her self-esteem was so low that she imagined any act of kindness or attention was so undeserved, so valuable, that it needed rewarding, acknowledgement. Nothing could be taken lightly or easily. She so longed to be loved that she was prey to any man who wanted to get her into bed, mistaking any show of affection for a declaration of love. It was almost a relief when she fell in love with Ralph and they became lovers. At least, then, Mungo only had to worry about one man – though he wished it could have been anyone else rather than Ralph. In an odd way, Ralph kept her safe – but only for a few years.

'The baby's come too early, Mungo,' she said, phoning him on that cold March morning from her flat in London. 'He's hardly a baby at all. He's so small I can hold him in the palm of my hand. I'm all alone with him here. Can you come?'

By the time he arrived she'd wrapped the tiny form in soft

wool and put him into her grandmother's pretty mahogany tea-caddy with a few keepsakes: one of Ralph's silk handkerchiefs, a miniature teddy bear she'd had from childhood and a scattering of sweet-scented potpourri.

'I couldn't just throw him away, darling, could I? I want him to have a proper burial place. Take him and find somewhere you and I can remember him. Somewhere nobody else knows. Promise?'

Now, Mungo pauses beside the old Herm. He crouches down to push aside the dreadlocks of faded grasses and yellow vetch that frame the ancient stone face. His finger traces the rim of beard, the faintly smiling lips, and he is filled with a terrible sadness.

There is a toot of a horn, the roar of an engine, and young Andy, Philip's grandson, raises his hand from the quad bike. Mungo stands up and moves to one side, waving back as Andy sweeps past. Mopsa is well ahead now and Mungo hurries to catch her up. Perhaps Philip is right and it's best to forget the past. But at the turn in the lane Mungo glances back at the old Herm, standing at the crossroads, still guarding the secrets of a thousand years.

CHAPTER THIRTEEN

There is silence in the kitchen after Mungo and Mopsa depart: an awkward silence during which neither Jake nor Kit can think of anything to say.

'Well, that was excellent,' says Jake eventually. 'You were right. Mungo is a very good cook.'

Kit agrees brightly: too brightly. She feels embarrassed and constrained, yet while Mungo and Mopsa were with them everything was so easy; such fun.

It's crazy, she thinks. I don't know what to say to him now. I just sound banal and he knows exactly how I'm feeling and he doesn't know what to say either. Blast Mungo. Why did he have to go?

'It's odd to see Mungo here in this cottage,' Jake is saying. 'From what you read about him you imagine him happiest among the fleshpots, not in a tiny rural hamlet.'

Kit knows that Jake is trying to slice his way through the barrier that has suddenly grown up between them with casual conversation but it hurts her that she and Jake of all people need to use this device. She wants to recapture the ease, the old familiarity of friendship, which was so quickly resumed earlier. The pain and resentments of the past dissipated in the face of Mungo's humour, his delight in the situation and his generous hospitality. His approving presence gave them the freedom to accept each other; to feel young again: conversation, like Mungo's wine, flowing freely, jokes being made, the old affection springing up so naturally.

'Mungo tends to send himself up in public,' she answers, 'and, of course, the media love it. They respect him, though, and leave his private life alone.'

'No scandals?'

Kit shakes her head. 'None. Well, there was a time in the sixties when the nation thought that he and Isobel Trent were the great romantic couple of all time but Mungo and Izzy managed to keep everyone guessing until it died a natural death. Mungo's very clever.'

'He must be,' says Jake, smiling a little. 'Now that I've met him I'd say that he is what my maternal grandmother would have called "other". Back then the media could have had a field day.'

'Versatile,' says Kit primly. 'That's how Mungo describes himself.'

Jake laughs out loud. 'Love it,' he says. 'So then, Kit. What happens next?'

She stares at him in alarm. This switch throws her off balance and she doesn't know how to answer him. She just wants to go on sitting in Mungo's kitchen without having to think about what happens next, and she curses herself for her inadequacy. Why should it be that she, who has spent her working life confidently deciding what her clients should sit on, eat from, cook with, look at on their walls, should be so inept at making decisions about her own life?

'Do we think we can move on?' he's asking. He leans forward, his hands clasped on Mungo's beautiful old French farmhouse table. 'It seems specious to say "carry on where we left off" because it's too long ago and too much has happened, but now, here, it almost feels as if we could. Do you want to try, Kit?'

'Yes,' she says quickly, her own hands clutched together on her knees, out of sight beneath the table. 'Yes, I do.'

He sits back with a great sigh of relief. They look at each other and the old, familiar ease begins to creep between them again.

'But not here?' he suggests, amused. 'You know that Mungo has invited me to stay in the barn?'

'Well, he shouldn't have,' she says crossly. 'I told him he wasn't to do that. It's completely out of order.'

'I agree,' says Jake, grinning. 'I think he sees himself as a dear old nanny looking after two wayward toddlers.'

'Hmm,' says Kit sceptically. 'I think he just wants to keep you nearby in case I turn you down. I adore Mungo but I wouldn't trust him an inch.'

They both laugh, completely at one again.

'I'm very grateful to him,' admits Jake. 'This has just been a perfect way to reconnect.'

'I agree,' says Kit, 'I just don't want us to be regarded as Mungo's next production. Seriously, though, he's a fantastic friend and I can't bear to hurt his feelings either. I can't just walk out on him now that you've turned up. What are your plans?'

'I shall go back to the hotel,' says Jake. 'I booked three nights to give me a chance to find you if you were around but I've no immediate commitments. Come and have dinner with me this evening?'

She hesitates, nods. 'And Mungo? Or just me?'

He thinks about it. 'Invite him,' he says at last. 'I think his answer will be very revealing as to how we play the next few days.'

'You can't be serious,' says Mungo indignantly, when she poses the question later, when Jake has gone. 'Being a gooseberry isn't my line at all, sweetie. Lunch was quite different, and I'm glad it got you both off to a good start, but I'm not good at being an extra. Leading man or nothing, that's me. You can invite him here, of course, whenever you like.'

Kit feels huge relief but guilt, too. She knows she's trying to have her cake and eat it: she wants to have Jake nearby, to have time to test her feelings about him, whilst keeping Mungo's support. She goes and puts her arms around him.

'You are such a mate, Mungo,' she says.

He gives her a hug, pats her shoulder blade. 'Silly moo. I suppose this means you'll be going back to London?'

She can hear the disappointment in his voice and hastens to reassure him.

'Oh, not just yet. I think we can have quite a lot of fun here before we take the next step. I think Jake will enjoy seeing the old familiar places and I want you to get to know him.'

'That's good then.' Mungo brightens at the prospect. 'I have to say he's gorgeous. I'm rather sorry that he didn't take me up on my offer of the barn.'

'Well, I'm not,' says Kit firmly. 'I need space. You said you wouldn't ask him. You promised.'

'Couldn't resist,' he sighs. 'My baser instincts got the better of me. But I agree you need your own space. You must do whatever is best for you, sweetie.'

'I'll stay for a few more days, if that's OK,' she says. 'I'd really like that.'

Now that Mungo has stepped back Kit feels quite happy to remain here with him. She's not ready to be on her own with Jake in London; she'd rather take things slowly surrounded by old friends on neutral territory.

'That's settled then,' he says contentedly. 'So what will you wear this evening? I hope you've brought something pretty with you. You can't go to dinner with an old flame in those tatty jeans.'

Jake drives carefully, repeating Mungo's directions under his breath. 'Turn right at the end of the lane. First left, then follow the directions for Ashburton . . .'

He wonders if Mungo will come to dinner, and hopes not, but he's glad that Kit has decided to stay on. He knows that she's not ready for the next step; that back in London on her own patch, she might get an attack of the wobbles and be unwilling to take the risk to change her well-ordered life.

A small boy on a scooter whizzes around the bend in the lane and Jake turns the wheel quickly to avoid him. A pretty girl, pushing a buggy, hurries to his side, waves apologetically at Jake, who waves back miming 'no harm done' and glances in the rear mirror at her. She has a kind of gamine, Audrey Hepburn look; very attractive.

Kit used to call him 'Jake the Rake' when they were young because of his predilection for pretty girls. She didn't seem to mind. It was as if the chemistry between them was much stronger and more important than simple physical attraction. Anyway, she liked to play the field, too, and it was she who resisted his proposals of marriage. He wonders how she would get on with his daughters and their families; whether she would connect with them. He hopes that in time they might be relieved to see him with a companion, someone of his own, and he has no intention of becoming a well-loved but slightly inconvenient parcel to be passed around at Christmas and on his birthday. 'We had him last year, it's your turn this year.' He loves his girls and his grandchildren but he is a pragmatist. They are busy: they have their own hectic lives. He wants his own life, his own agenda, and someone with whom to live it, and he is certain now that he wants that someone to be Kit. She is a huge piece in the puzzle that is Jake; an important piece that was lost for a while, leaving a jagged space; an emptiness. As soon as he saw her sitting with Mungo at the café table it was as if something happened in his heart: he was made whole again.

Earlier, while they were together with Mungo, he believed that she felt the same. Now, as Jake drives back to Totnes, anxiety begins to nibble like a rat at the edge of his confidence. Is it possible that she might still be unable to commit to him? What can he do to show her how good life could be if they were to share it? He must make the most of this evening. Perhaps he should take her somewhere a little more intimate than the hotel full of families on holiday. He wonders if he should check out the local hostelries and then decides that he'll play it by ear. They'll do it together as they always used to; peering through restaurant windows, sitting at the bar having a drink in a bistro, checking out the specials' board. Kit might have a favourite place she'll want to share with him.

The prospect fills him with delight. He drives through Ashburton and heads back towards Totnes.

CHAPTER FOURTEEN

Philip wheels out the rubbish bin ready for collection next morning – recycling and garden waste this week – and stands it by the gate. A small boy is approaching at speed on a scooter and a young woman is following behind him, pushing a buggy. Philip guesses that this is the family who are living at the cottage and he waits to meet them; to say 'hello'. The scooter swerves, bumps up over the rutted verge, tips sideways: the child stumbles, loses his foothold, lands on his knees in the lane.

Philip hastens towards him as he begins to howl, lifts him upright, looks at the scratched knees.

'Not too bad,' he says reassuringly. 'No blood. You'll live.' He brushes some gravel from the thin brown legs and smiles at the young woman as she arrives with a rush. 'He's OK. Fright more than anything else, I reckon.'

She nods gratefully, bending down to look at the damage.

'That's just a graze, Joe,' she says comfortingly. 'You've had much worse than that.'

She gives him a hug, picks up the scooter, and Philip

watches them, considering whether he should make a neigh-bourly gesture and invite them in.

'You must be from the cottage,' he says. 'I'm Philip Judd. Nice to meet you. I've been meaning to come down and intro-duce myself but my brother hasn't been well and things are a bit busy, if you see what I mean.'

He holds out a hand to her and she takes it, smiling at him.

'I'm Emma,' she says, 'and this is Joe. And this is Dora. We're loving it here. Everyone's so friendly.'

'It hurts,' whines Joe, looking at Philip for sympathy, stretching a leg to show them the grazes. Philip bends to pick a dock leaf from the ditch and holds it against Joe's knee.

'There,' he says. 'That feels good, doesn't it? Nice and cool. That'll do the trick. Now you hold it in place for a minute.'

Joe watches, fascinated, and obediently presses the leaf against his knee. It's at this moment that Star appears in the yard, gives a bark and comes to investigate. Joe drops the leaf and hurries to meet her, his woes forgotten, though Emma calls to him to wait.

'She won't hurt him,' Philip says. 'No need to worry about Star. She was raised from a pup with children crawling all over her. Mungo was here earlier. He told me you'd moved in. Let me know if you need logs later on. My grandson's clearing a bit of old woodland further down the valley.'

Joe has now discovered the chickens scratching around in the stables and is calling to Emma to come and see them. Philip takes a chance.

'Like to have a look around?' he offers rather shyly. 'My brother, Billy's, sitting in the orchard. Like I said, he hasn't been too well. He's had a stroke but he's recovering and he loves a bit of company. Come and say "hello" to him.'

Emma hesitates and then nods. 'Thank you. Why not? If you're sure we're not in the way. Have you always lived here?'

'Born here,' he tells her as they cross the yard. 'And my father before that.'

'How lovely,' she says rather wistfully. 'It must be good to feel that you really belong somewhere. I've never known that.'

Suddenly he is struck by her resemblance to Izzy. It's not just the short dark hair, the lovely face, the thin boyish figure. He recognizes that particular warmth, combined with a longing to be loved and accepted, which invoked in him such a sense of protectiveness towards Izzy. He remembers Mungo telling him that Emma's husband is away with the Commandos in Afghanistan and he wonders how much she must miss him and worry about him.

Billy is sitting in his wheelchair amongst the apple trees, watching them approach, and Philip raises a hand to him, indicating that all is well; nothing to be alarmed about. To his intense pleasure Emma goes at once to Billy, kneeling on the grass beside him, showing him the baby. Joe has found an old ball, which he throws for Star, boy and dog running in and out of the trees. Flickering light and shade, the sweet scent of new-mown grass, small green apples warming and ripening in the sun; Philip watches the little scene, his fingers smoothing the grainy roughness of an overhanging branch. He is oddly moved between tears and a sense of joy. Emma glances up at him, eyebrows raised, as if to say: 'Is this OK?' and he nods encouragingly, as if saying: 'Stay with us. Don't go yet.'

The girl's kneeling figure, the old man stretching unsteady hands to the baby, the small boy bending to stroke the dog – they transform the orchard into something special: a painting or a scene from a play. Then, all in a moment, the ball is thrown too wildly and hits Billy's chair, Emma starts back in alarm and shouts at Joe, and the baby begins to cry. The scene breaks and reforms, and Philip moves forward.

'No harm done,' he says. 'Nothing to get upset about.'

But Emma is on her feet, apologizing to Billy, consoling Dora, calling to Joe.

'We must be going,' she says. 'It's tea-time. I hope we haven't tired Billy.'

'You'll have done him good,' he tells her. 'I hope you'll come again.'

'I'd really like that,' she says – and he knows she means it.

They all walk to the gate together and he watches the little family set off down the lane. Joe turns and waves and Philip raises his hand in return, and then Emma turns and waves, too, and he's filled with that old unreasoning sense of joy.

He goes back to Billy, wanting to make sure he's all right, to prime him before Mags turns up for the evening shift. He doesn't want old ferret woman asking questions about their visitors; judging them with her green-glass, glinty eyes, mouth pursed.

'Nice little maid,' Billy says. He cocks an eye up at his brother. 'Remind you of someone?'

Philip nods. He wonders if Mungo has seen Emma's likeness to Izzy.

'Keep it to ourselves,' he says. 'Don't want Mags getting in on the act.'

Billy laughs his silent, wheezy laugh. 'Don't worry, boy,' he says. 'I shan't say nort.'

As Emma opens the kitchen door the telephone is ringing and she hurries to answer it. She has no fear of the telephone. Marcus has only her mobile number. It is Camilla.

'Now, Emma,' she says. 'About tomorrow. All my grand-children are well out of the nappies-and-baby-food stage so don't forget to bring what I shall need for Dora.'

She talks on for a while and Emma listens, still feeling strangely cheered by her meeting with Philip and his brother. Presently, when Camilla is satisfied that she will have every-thing she needs for the next morning, Emma tells her about them.

'They were so sweet,' she said. 'So kind.' She wants to add that Philip must have been a real looker when young, and how she had the oddest desire to fling herself on his chest and ask him to look after them all, but she knows Camilla won't understand such weird emotions and that it might actually worry her. She is quite certain that Camilla would never be prey to insecurities and anxiety attacks. 'Philip has said he'll get me logs when the winter comes,' she says instead.

'Philip is the most useful man,' says Camilla. 'Archie always said he was the brightest of all the boys around here, streets ahead of old Billy. He passed the eleven-plus and he had a first-class grammar school education. Philip's one of the most practical men I know. He's run that logging business since he was not much more than a boy and he'll always help you out if you have a problem. You'll be quite safe with him or with his grandson, Andy.'

Safe, thinks Emma, as she puts down the phone. How wonderful it must be to feel safe.

She wonders if it is because her father left her mother and their two small children for his mistress that she's always had a tendency to look to older people to shore up her confidence or confirm her decisions. Her mother is neither strong nor capable, she bounces from one disastrous relationship to another, and sometimes Emma is anxious that she herself is rather like her. Take this madness with Marcus, for instance; surely this is the same kind of instability from which her mother suffers? Emma loves her mother, who is cheerful, funny, generous, but she shows that same insecurity that Emma felt earlier when she responded to Philip's calm strength. Perhaps this is what her mother looks for in her relationships but never quite finds.

Joe has switched on the television and Dora is gurning quietly in her chair so that, just for a moment, Emma can relax and remember that odd moment in the orchard when she felt surrounded by love; by peace. With those two old boys, the sunlight slanting down between the branches of the apple trees, the warm late summer scents, she felt peaceful for the first time for months. She wanted to cling to Philip's muscular suntanned arm and cry: 'Tell me what to do.'

She's seen Andy astride his quad bike, with his corn-yellow hair and cornflower-blue eyes, the height and the strength of him, and she knows exactly what Philip must have looked like as a young man.

'Awesome,' she says to herself, perching for a moment on the arm of the sofa, and Joe glances at her sideways, frowning.

'What?' he asks. 'What's awesome?'

'Nothing,' she says. She feels stronger, surrounded by friends, and her anxiety about meeting Marcus tomorrow morning fades a little. Maybe she will be able to be firm with him: to tell him that things have got out of hand and it's best that it all stops now. She imagines herself saying this to him and her heart quails a little. In her mind's eye she sees his focused grey stare, the intensity of his body. Marcus won't give up easily. Yet there's not much to give up on, after all: a few significant eye-meets to begin with, some silly light-hearted exchanges with a sexy undertow, then a few 'accidental' meetings. He's behaving as if there has been something really special between them for a long time, which now, at last, has been allowed to surface – but this isn't so. She admits to a kind of long-term flirtation that often happens between a woman and her husband's close friend, but nothing that Rob isn't fully aware of and perfectly happy with. So what tipped that flirtation into this intense relationship? On her part it was to do with feeling low in spirits after Dora's birth, Rob's grumpiness, a sense of being unappreciated. Marcus' attention was the equivalent of a tonic but she doesn't require it as permanent medication. The really stupid thing is that she's gone along with it; let him believe that there might be some future in it.

Emma gets up and goes out into the kitchen. She needs to move about, to try to walk away from the thought of Marcus and those silly texts on his mobile phone that would be so difficult to explain to Rob. Suppose somebody were to see them together and tell Rob? Mungo and Kit saw them; who else might? The foolishness of this silly affair forcibly reveals itself with a clarity that has been dimmed and disguised by her vanity and immaturity. She's seen it as a romantic fling to which she is entitled because life hasn't been quite as kind as she deserves. She is putting her marriage and her children at risk for a few moments of self-gratification. Emma folds both arms across her ribcage and groans with mortification.

Tomorrow she will end it. She will see Marcus this one last time and explain how she feels – and if he tells Rob then she will have to do her best to make him understand the real truth of it. Thinking of Rob far away, surrounded by danger and hardship, fills her with misery and her eyes brim with tears.

'Are you all right, Mummy?'

Joe is at the door, watching her, and she quickly straightens up and smiles at him.

'I was missing Daddy,' she says truthfully and, rather to her surprise, he looks almost relieved; as if he is glad.

A new terror grips her: supposing Joe were to guess, to suspect? How foolish and blind she's been in imagining that he is too young to understand.

'Come and watch *Shaun the Sheep*,' he says sympathetically, taking her hand, towing her back into the sitting-room. 'It's really funny. Come on, Mummy. You'll be all right.'

She's touched by his care, by his love for her, and they sit close together on the sofa with Dora beside them whilst Emma stares unseeingly at the television screen and prays that she can put things right.

By the time Mags turns up Philip has wheeled Billy back into the kitchen and is peeling potatoes for supper.

'I could have done that,' she says, just like he knew she would. How she would love for him to be more dependent:

to need her. 'I got the steak and kidney pie out of the freezer. Did you see it?'

Off she goes, ferreting about, peering into the fridge. He glances at Billy and gives him a wink. Old Billy sits placidly, one hand tremblingly smoothing Star's head, smiling to himself.

'I saw Archie,' she says, bringing out the pie. 'In the lane with those dogs of his. He's looking a bit frail, if you ask me.'

But they're not asking her and Philip remains silent, washing the potatoes under the tap, slicing them on the board.

'Have you thought what you'd do if him and Camilla couldn't manage the estate any longer? Supposing they wanted to downsize? They'd sell it all up and then what? Where would you go?'

Philip hides the flicker of fear, the sinking of his gut, beneath a shrug.

'Why should he?' He feels angry because suddenly he's frightened – and he doesn't want Billy to be upset. 'Archie's not going anywhere.'

She makes a face – smug, knowing – and he wants to slap it.

'You hope,' she says. 'Anyway, it might suit him to sell up. It must cost a packet trying to keep it all together. Or he could do a bit of development, convert the stables. Or the orchard. You'd get quite a few houses in the orchard the way they pack them in these days.'

Philip's hands are stilled; he thinks of the diggers moving in, turning the earth, the cries of discovery and the inevitable scandal.

'It'll never happen,' he says, but his voice is uncertain.

She stands beside him, peering up at him, pleased that she's unsettled him.

'You were always soft about that old orchard,' she says.

He looks at Billy, ready to warn him in case he bursts out with something, but Billy is dozing. Mags follows his glance.

'You didn't expect him to have a stroke, did you?' she mutters, almost triumphantly. 'But it happened. You can't tell what's round the next corner.'

'Oh, stop your croaking,' he says angrily, keeping his voice down. 'Go home, Mags. We don't need you here any more. He's doing all right, Billy is. We've got the community nurse coming in regular now. Just leave us alone.'

'How d'you know he won't have another stroke?' she says. 'I know you've got family just up the lane but they won't be much help if Billy has another stroke or if Archie decides to sell up. Always so cocky, you and Billy, weren't you? Well, he isn't so cocky now, is he?'

'That's enough.'

He's very angry now and she hesitates, knowing she's gone too far, unwilling to back down. He puts his face close to hers, so that she flinches.

'Get out,' he says, 'and don't come back.'

She grabs her bag, flounces out to the car, while he watches from the kitchen window.

'Got rid of her, boy?' says Billy. He's wide awake, eyes bright. 'I didn't say nort.'

'No.' Philip sits down at the table. 'She's right, though, isn't she?' He looks to Billy for the reassurance he's had from him since he was a tiny boy. 'Archie's getting old like the rest of us and it's possible that he might decide to develop the orchard. What shall we do?'

'Only one thing we can do,' Billy answers. 'Told you before but you wouldn't have it.'

'Tell Mungo?'

Billy nods. 'Can't leave it to chance any longer. Time's right.'

Philip sits in silence. He feels sick. Deep down, though, he knows Billy's right. Earlier, talking to Mungo about the past, he wanted to share the burden. He looked at him, almost hoping that Mungo might have guessed, had some suspicion. Sometimes, when they've been talking about Izzy and Ralph, he's believed that Mungo has always known the truth – an odd expression in Mungo's eyes, a kind of wariness – and has gone along with it in silence. This hope has enabled Philip to push it out of sight but he can't count on it much longer. Mags has dragged it into the open and forced him to look at the truth.

Philip stares at his clasped hands, imagining ways that he can explain to Mungo that Ralph Stead's body is buried in the orchard. He thinks of telling Archie, and puts his head in his hands.

'Don't get ahead of yourself,' Billy advises. 'Step at a time. You tell Mungo I did it.'

Philip shakes his head. 'No. If I tell him anything I shall tell him the truth. Exactly as it happened.'

'And can you remember?' asks Billy softly. 'Can you remember exactly how it happened? All those years ago?'

Oh, yes. He can remember. He can remember the icy cold of that February day: snow on the moor, ice in the lanes, snowdrops smelling of honey growing under the garden wall. They went out after breakfast to check the pregnant ewes, to fill the racks with hay, to carry on with the clearing of the orchard where some old trees had been taken out and new were to be planted later in the season.

Mungo drove down to the smithy for the weekend with Izzy and Ralph. He phoned to ask Philip to get some heating going, to light the solid-fuel Rayburn, as he always did in the winter when he made these sudden visits. Philip saw Mungo's car go past and, later, he saw Izzy walking in the lane and went out to talk to her. She looked tired, her small face pinched and pale, her arms wrapped about herself as though to keep herself warm. He wanted to put his own arms round her, to protect her, but stuck his hands in his pockets instead. She smiled at him, such a sweet, tender smile he could almost believe that she loved him. She did love him. Izzy loved everyone. She took his arm.

'Walk back with me,' she said coaxingly, though he needed no encouragement. 'We haven't seen you this time. How are you and Billy? How's Smudgy? Did you find homes for the kittens? I wish I could have had one but I'm not allowed to have pets in my flat.'

She talked to him, clinging to his arm, occasionally slipping on the ice and laughing. But he wasn't fooled by the chatter and the laughter. He bent his head to catch that familiar flowery smell of her and was seized by love and longing.

'And how are you?' he asked at last. He stopped and looked down at her – she was so tiny, so beautiful – and she tried to smile back at him but her mouth went all crooked like a child's about to cry.

'Don't,' she said. 'Don't ask me, Philip. Don't be kind to me. I can't bear it. Come on.'

She made them walk on until they reached the smithy and then she reached up and kissed him, her lips just touching the corner of his mouth.

'We're not going back until tomorrow,' she said. 'We're all going back in the car with Mungo. 'Bye, Philip. Take care of yourself. Give my love to Billy and Smudgy.'

Which was why it was such a surprise when the phone rang later and Mungo asked if he could take Ralph to the train that evening. He sounded angry and when Philip asked what time he wanted him to come up with the Land Rover, Mungo said abruptly: 'The bastard can walk down,' and hung up.

Mungo could be touchy and difficult, but clearly some-thing was really wrong between these three old friends. Philip thought about Izzy's pinched expression, the way she'd talked, and decided to see for himself.

'There's been some kind of row,' he said to Billy. 'Izzy was in a state when I saw her earlier and now Mungo's chucking Ralph out, by the sound of it. He's asked me to drive him into Newton to get the train. I think I'll just take a stroll down and see what's going on.'

It was nearly dark, freezing hard. The cobbles in Mungo's courtyard were like glass under his feet. The light was on in the kitchen and the three of them were framed in the window like a scene in a play. Izzy was facing him and he kept back in the shadows, watching, drawn by the tension that held the three figures. Mungo was leaning forward, his weight resting on his hands, speaking to Ralph, who watched him from the other side of the table, smiling a little, his arms crossed. Izzy stood between them, her face anguished. Suddenly she put both hands to her belly, a tender, protective gesture, and at that moment Philip understood it all.

As if he could hear them speaking he knew that Mungo was reminding Ralph of his responsibilities to Izzy's unborn child and that Ralph was not only rejecting them but scorning Mungo and Izzy in the process. He saw Ralph speak, saw his derisive glance at Izzy; he saw Izzy burst into tears and run from the room; he saw Mungo's fist shoot out and connect with Ralph's jaw.

It was at this point he hurried to the door and went into the kitchen. Ralph was sitting in a chair, his hand to his jaw, and Mungo was standing over him. He turned as Philip came in, his face anxious, but Ralph laughed.

'You'll have to do better than that, Mungo,' he said. 'And here's Gabriel Oak to back you up.'

'What's going on?' Philip asked.

'None of your business,' said Ralph. 'Your business is to get me to the station for the London train.'

Philip was filled with rage and humiliation; he wanted to hit Ralph, too, to smash the grin from his face.

'Find your own way,' he said, turning to leave.

'Wait,' said Mungo. 'Please, Philip. This one last time. I don't want to leave Izzy and I want him out of here.'

Ralph got to his feet, his hand still to his jaw. 'Bring the Land Rover while I get my case,' he said casually to Philip.

'You can walk down,' Mungo said. 'Get a move on.'

Ralph swaggered out and Mungo looked at Philip.

'Sorry,' he said. 'This is awful. Look, I'm really sorry to

drag you in on this. I can't leave Izzy and we'll never get a taxi out here in time. I just want him out of this house.'

'It's OK,' Philip told him. 'I'll take him.' He hesitated. 'Is Izzy . . . ?'

'Pregnant,' muttered Mungo. 'The bastard says he doesn't give a damn. He's been offered a job in America and he's leaving in a few days' time. Izzy's devastated.'

Outside the temperature was dropping, the sky clear and full of stars as Philip walked the half-mile between the smithy and the farm. He could see a light moving in the stable and the dogs came to meet him. He called to Billy: 'I'm taking Ralph to the station,' and swung himself into the Land Rover. He started the engine, switched on the headlights, and drove out into the yard just as Ralph came striding in from the lane. He raised his hand to Philip and began to laugh, his expression full of amused contempt, of triumph. Remembering Izzy's unhappiness, overwhelmed by rage, by frustration and jealousy, Philip swung the steering wheel so that the Land Rover was driving straight at Ralph and, in that brief but glorious moment, he saw Ralph's face change to alarm, to terror. Just for that second he had the upper hand: he was in control. He turned the wheel back again but the Land Rover refused to respond. It began to slide on a patch of ice, hurtling out of control, knocking Ralph to the ground.

He felt the jerk as the wheel passed over Ralph's body and then Billy was beside him, shouting, while he jammed on the brake and swung open the driver's door. They were both kneeling, hauling Ralph from beneath the vehicle, shouting to each other.

Philip stared in fascinated horror at the immobile form,

scrambled up, still unable to look away from it. His breath was uneven and he wanted to flee.

'I'll call an ambulance.'

'Don't be a fool.' Billy kneeled beside Ralph, examining him carefully. 'He's dead.'

Billy got up. The dogs circled, their lips lifted fastidiously as they sniffed cautiously at the body. Philip was rigid with horror.

'Dead?' But he knew that Ralph was dead; he'd known when he felt the wheel pass over the body. He began to tremble. 'What shall we do?'

'We'll get rid of him. Bury him.'

'Bury him?' It was just a whisper. 'Shouldn't we tell some-one?'

Billy bent down and shunted the body sideways, back under the Land Rover out of sight in case someone came by. 'No good telling anyone. He's gonna disappear, that's all. No questions asked. Think of Mungo. And Izzy. You said they'd had a row. Lots of people asking questions, poking their noses in.' Billy shook his head. 'We need a quick drink. I'll get the brandy. You get the wheelbarrow.'

Still trembling, Philip obeyed. Followed by the dogs, he went into the stable to find the wheelbarrow tipped up against the wall. He grasped its handles, stood for a moment trying to control the shivering that shook his whole body, and then pushed it out into the yard. Billy appeared with a bottle and offered it to him silently with a quick nod of the head. Obediently he took a swig, choked, and gave it back. No noise, no sign of anyone. They dragged the body out again and put it into the barrow, covered it with a sack, wheeled it into the stable. Billy went back for Ralph's suitcase and dropped it on the wheelbarrow.

'Now, you and me are going to drive to Newton,' Billy told him, opening the Land Rover door and letting the dogs jump in. 'We're gonna make sure that someone sees us at the station and then we'll come back again and sort him out.'

Billy drove. Philip sat in frightened silence, dazed and shocked. Inside his head he played the scene over and over: Ralph's amusement changing to terror, the sense of shock when the Land Rover refused to respond; that desperate turn of the wheel and his whole frame clenched as he willed the sliding vehicle away from Ralph; the soft jolt as the wheel passed over his body. He knew that it would live with him for ever. He stayed in the Land Rover while Billy disappeared into the station and then reappeared, calling cheerfully to someone over his shoulder, and hoisted himself back into the driving seat.

'Good,' he grunted, starting the engine, swinging out on to the road. 'That's good.'

The nightmare continued. Back at the farm in the icy black night, they wrapped Ralph's body in tarpaulins, wheeled it into the orchard, and began to dig. The spades sliced the frozen earth, striking into the cold ground. Somewhere a vixen screamed.

'Put 'un in deep, boy. Foxes'll get 'un else.'

They hauled the body out between them and tipped it along with the suitcase into the empty space at their feet. Quickly, violently they hurled in spadefuls of heavy earth, filling the hole, covering it again with rough tussocks of grass. Billy stamped them in.

'Our turn to walk all over him for a change,' he said. 'Always treated us like dirt. And that little maid.' He looked at Philip, still shivering with shock. 'Come on. We need another drink.'

Billy is still watching him: compassionate, unrepentant. 'We had no choice, boy,' he says. 'Mungo'll understand.'

'Yes,' says Philip; he feels ill and sick. 'I'm going to phone him now and tell him I want to talk to him.'

CHAPTER FIFTEEN

'Are you seriously trying to tell me,' says Mungo, 'that Ralph Stead is buried in the orchard? Look, I'm sorry, I can't get my head round this.'

He turns away from Philip, hands bunched in his pockets, unable to grasp what Philip has just said. Philip doesn't move. He leans against the dresser, arms folded, waiting. Mopsa watches them from her basket whilst Mungo wrestles with a whole variety of reactions: disbelief, shock – and an odd and reprehensible desire to burst out laughing. This is risible. Ralph, whom he's loved and missed and raged against all these years, is just down the lane in the old orchard.

'So you left here,' he says, repeating Philip's story, 'ran Ralph over when he turned up, drove to Newton Abbot to provide an alibi should it be needed, and then you and Billy came home and planted him in the orchard.'

Just for a minute he can visualize the scene. The vicious twist of the wheel, Ralph's horrified expression caught in the beam of the headlights, the inexorable slide of the Land Rover . . .

'But why didn't he jump clear when you began to skid?' he asks. Surely that's what would happen? He can see it clearly in his head: Ralph leaping to one side, out of the path of the moving vehicle. That's how he would direct it.

'The wheel just wouldn't respond and he seemed to disappear underneath,' says Philip. 'Perhaps he lost his footing, slipped on the ice and was knocked off balance. It just went straight over him.'

Mungo paces, assembling the facts. 'No ambulance?'

'No point,' says Philip bleakly.

'But why didn't you report it? It was clearly an accident.'

'It wasn't that simple. I hated him. When I swung the wheel I was just trying to scare him but somewhere deep down I'd've been glad to see the back of him. The way he treated Izzy. You'd hit him just minutes earlier, damn it! It would all've had to come out, wouldn't it? Izzy and the baby, the way he was walking out on her and going to America. It wasn't just me. It was all of us. Even though it was an accident, it was as if we were all implicated in it and I was afraid. It happened so quick. I kept thinking about Izzy and how she looked that weekend. Like Billy said, there would have been people asking questions, poking their noses in, digging the dirt. You and she were just getting famous by then. It would have been disastrous. That's what it felt like back then. Surely you can remember how it was?'

Oh, he can remember all right. The arguments, the tears, the pleadings. Izzy wanted him there as advocate, friend, persuader: but nothing moved Ralph.

'What shall I do?' Izzy asked desperately. 'Help me, Mungo.'

He invited them down to the smithy as a last resort, a reminder of those happier times when friendships were developing into something much stronger and durable, hoping to soften Ralph, to appeal to his loyalty. It didn't work. Ralph's underlying cruelty, which Mungo found rather exciting to bring out and work on in direction, grew more destructive. He delighted in mocking Izzy's pathetic attempts to resurrect times past, to rekindle the love that had been between them. The weekend slid into disaster.

'I warned you,' Ralph said to Izzy. 'I told you not to plan a future around me. I told you I'm not that kind of guy. It was very silly of you to take such a chance.'

'I didn't plan it.' Izzy's face was pulpy with tears; she was drenched in them. Mungo had never seen such anguish. 'You know I wouldn't. Please, Ralph, don't go. Don't leave us and go so far away. It's not just about our baby. I can't believe you were just going to walk out without telling me.'

His smile was wolfish. 'Well, now you can see why. I get enough theatricals on the stage. I don't need it in my private life. It's over, Izzy.'

'Then you can get out,' Mungo said. 'I'll ask Philip to give you a lift to the train.'

'In that case I'll go and pack,' Ralph said cheerfully. 'And let's try to be civilized with our farewells, shall we?'

But when he came back into the kitchen it all started up again. Izzy pleading, tear-stained; Mungo trying to beat down his own pain in the face of Izzy's desperation. He'd wanted to reach out to Ralph, to hold on to him. Instead, he hit him.

'Anyway,' Ralph said, leaning across the table, 'how do

I know it's my child? It might be Mungo's. After all, you're very versatile, aren't you, old chap?'

There was a freeze-frame of silence; two heartbeats, maybe three. Then Izzy fled from the kitchen and he hit Ralph. It was a long stretch but Mungo's speed and accuracy, and the surprise of the blow, unbalanced Ralph. He staggered backwards with his hand to his jaw, and for the first time that weekend his face wore a genuine expression: shock and admiration.

'I didn't think you had it in you,' he said.

Then Philip came bursting in and it was all over.

'You see?' Philip says. 'It wasn't so simple, was it? The newspapers would have had a field day. Even so, it's my responsibility. I killed him. For years I used to wake up sweating with terror, listening for a knock at the door, terrified at the sight of a police car. But what good would it have done to anybody to know the truth?'

Mungo knows he's right. It would have been a catastrophe.

'But why are you telling me now?' he asks.

'Something Mags said. She saw Archie and said he was looking his age, that he might want to sell up or develop some land. She said if he got planning permission he'd get quite a few houses in the orchard. He could do just that, couldn't he? It's not actually part of the farm.'

Mungo frowns. Archie has spoken to him of selling up, downsizing, though Camilla is fighting it tooth and nail. Supposing he were to decide to do some development to raise some money? So what? The orchard is the obvious choice, of course . . . And then he sees it. He imagines the diggers moving in, turning the earth, the cries of discovery, the scandal.

'It's possible, isn't it?' Philip is saying.

Mungo tries to quieten his heartbeat, to be rational and cool.

'Let me think about it,' he says. 'Give me time to take it all in. It's been a shock.'

'Has it?' Philip's look is quizzical, hopeful.

Mungo stares at him. 'What d'you mean?'

Philip shrugs. 'Dunno. Just always had a feeling that you knew something. Guessed, perhaps.'

'No.' Mungo stands up. 'I promise you, Philip, I had no idea that Ralph Stead was buried in the orchard.'

He feels confused, nervous, but Philip smiles at him complicitly.

'Secrets,' he says. 'Dangerous things, secrets.'

Friendship stretching back for a lifetime flows between them. Mungo holds out his hand and Philip grasps it in a strong grip.

'Billy said you'd understand,' he says simply.

'Billy,' snorts Mungo. 'I bet that old bugger was behind it all, wasn't he? I can see him.' His eyes widen, remembering his last conversation with Billy. 'Is that what he meant? "First he walked all over her and then she walked all over him." My God.'

'He used to enjoy the joke. He was very fond of Izzy. We all were, weren't we?' Philip pauses. 'What happened to the baby?'

'She lost the baby. You know that.'

'Yes. I know that. See you later.'

He goes out, leaving the door open to the warm night air. Mungo stands quite still, grateful that Kit has not yet returned from her date with Jake, thinking about Philip's extraordinary story. How poignant it is, this little history; death coming for Ralph one icy February night, and for his unborn child, a few weeks later on a cold wet March morning with Izzy alone at her flat.

What happened to the baby?

Secrets. Dangerous things, secrets.

CHAPTER SIXTEEN

As she drives Jake from the Sea Trout Inn at Staverton, out through Dartington, along the road beside the river and back to Totnes, Kit begins to feel nervous again. But this time she feels nervous in an excited way because it's been such a good evening. Driving in to meet him, all kinds of terrors raised themselves and she wondered if it would always be like this when she was away from Jake. When she was with him she had more courage; alone, she could see the hazards of embarking on this new adventure, the risks she'd have to take. Jake was a family man, she reminded herself, with a whole life in another country. How could they possibly make it work? She had her work, friends, family here and she couldn't abandon them. It was foolish to imagine that any relationship apart from an ordinary friendship could be managed. During the journey she talked herself into such a state of negativity that by the time she arrived at Jake's hotel she'd convinced herself that the whole thing was impossible. He was waiting for her in the bar, casual and elegant in a linen jacket and cotton chinos, smiling at her with his own particular Jake smile: affection, humour, secret knowledge. She was glad that she'd packed her pretty dress from Monsoon; confident after Mungo's critical praise that she looked good. If Jake noticed her tension he made no mention of it and within minutes she began to relax.

Now, after the delicious food and the one glass of wine she's allowed herself, she's experiencing the familiar euphoria that Jake's company engenders. She feels more confident, able to see around difficulties, and is simply happy to be with him. Kit wonders if he's thought ahead to the rest of the evening or whether she simply drops him off and goes home to Mungo. That seems like a pretty flat idea and she gives a little sideways glance to gauge Jake's mood. He's been a little bit quiet since they left the pub and she wonders if he's feeling nervous. Immediately she feels huge sympathy and love for him; she remembers how she messed things up all those years ago and she's determined to try not to be so feeble now. At the same time it's a tricky one. She can hardly suggest that they go up to his room and she doesn't want to drink any more because of driving home. It would be an anticlimax simply to sit in the hotel bar. Perhaps she'll suggest a stroll along the river. She remembers how natural it was simply to roll into bed together and she yearns for those easy, happy days of their youth.

'Don't forget, sweetie,' Mungo said earlier, 'that when you get old you need a good sense of humour when it comes to sex.'

Somehow this remark isn't particularly comforting at the moment and she wonders if Jake is having the same problem trying to figure out the next move. She touches him lightly on the knee and he glances at her and smiles.

She looks ahead again, changing gear ready for the lights, which are changing, her heart bumping.

I love him, she thinks. I do love him. I wonder if he's thinking the same about me.

Jake fingers his mobile in his jacket pocket and wonders how he can send a text without alerting Kit and so risk breaking their happy, intimate mood. His youngest daughter, Gabrielle, is expecting her first baby in six weeks' time and he is in touch with her regularly. Of all the girls, Gaby misses her mother most. She is heartbroken that Madeleine will never see the baby and Jake has promised that he will be there when the time comes. His eldest daughter, Amélie, has told him that she will watch over Gaby in his absence and make sure that all is well, and Jake has every confidence that she will. Amélie is strong, bossy, practical and loving, and she has always been ready to keep an eye on her younger sisters. He suspects that Amélie will be glad to see him settled with someone, rather than remaining as her own particular responsibility – which is how she sees him – and she will influence the younger girls, who might look askance at a new woman in their mother's place. Gaby will be the most difficult to persuade, he knows that. She adores her papa, and might well see his affection for Kit as a betrayal of her mother. She was a frail child, and she is suffering with this pregnancy, so he is trying to take Madeleine's place by sending Gaby texts and keeping in touch.

He checked his mobile when he was paying the bill, and there was a text from Gaby that had come in much earlier. He'd switched his phone off for the evening but now he wonders if he should try to send a text or wait until Kit has gone back to

Mungo. He doesn't want to spoil this first evening by being too much the family man; Kit has stayed right away from the subject and he's afraid to introduce it. He knows he must at some point, but not now, not when everything has been so perfect. Yet he thinks about Gaby, not wanting her to think he doesn't care because he has found his old love. It's important that all the girls get on with Kit and that there should be no resentment. He's beginning to see now exactly how difficult this balancing act might prove to be.

Kit touches his knee lightly, smiles at him quickly, and he feels a huge rush of affection for her, which briefly displaces his anxiety about Gaby. What should be the next step? If they were in London they could go back to Kit's flat but he can hardly invite her to his hotel room, and it would be rather a letdown to go and sit in the bar. He tries to think of a solution whereby he can keep Kit's company for a little longer and meanwhile send off a very quick text to Gaby.

'I was just wondering,' Kit says casually, 'whether we might have a walk along the river. What d'you think? Unless—'

'Perfect,' he says quickly. This sounds an excellent plan: a stroll in the dusk; an opportunity for an intimate moment. 'I'd love it.'

Suddenly he decides that the text will keep; that he'll send it as soon as he gets back to the hotel. This next precious hour is between him and Kit and his instinct tells him to take no chances with it.

Emma stands in the kitchen staring at the text. Marcus has phoned her mobile several times and has now sent a text asking her to confirm what time she will meet him in the car park in Ashburton. The plan is that he will then drive them somewhere to have a walk and then lunch. She feels panicky; definitely, now, she knows she doesn't want to be in his car with him. Yet how can she change the arrangement without explaining why? She thinks about where they could meet so that she will feel quite safe and won't be tempted to commit herself to anything foolish. She needs to be able to explain to him that this is their last meeting and then be able to get into her own car and drive away. It's odd that she feels so anxious about it: like Marcus might suddenly pull a knife on her or kidnap her. She tries to laugh this idea off but at some level in her consciousness she is beginning to wonder if it might be only too possible. There is the evidence of Joe's crushed spoon to support her anxiety. Each time she looks at it she feels a slightly sick sensation; a visceral curdling of fear.

Earlier she telephoned another service wife, an old friend. They chatted for a while and then very casually she mentioned meeting Marcus by chance, so that if there were any gossip it would be scotched from the beginning.

'He's become a bit odd, don't you think?' the friend said. 'I know he's a brilliant officer, and that's why he's being made up to major much earlier than usual, but he tends to blur the real world with a kind of fantasy. At least that's what Tasha said was beginning to happen and that's why she's insisting on this trial separation, apparently. She wanted him to have counselling because she felt he was too near the edge and that he'd do something silly that might mean he wouldn't get promotion. Personally, I've always found him a bit scary. Sorry, I forgot he's Rob's friend . . .'

Now, with the children in bed, Emma stands indecisively

in the kitchen staring out of the window thinking about this conversation and about the crushed spoon. She is even more determined to be able to get away from Marcus when the time comes but she can't think where they could meet that would enable a safe retreat. Supposing he were simply to follow her home?

Mungo is out in the lane, strolling slowly, Mopsa pottering a little ahead of him and, quite suddenly, an idea occurs to Emma. It's crazy, wild, but she's desperate enough to try it. Quietly she goes out into the hall, opens the front door and steps into the lane. She waits for Mungo to come nearer, waves to him, and then he sees her too and raises his hand in greeting. As he gets closer she sees that he seems preoccupied, deep in thought, but he smiles at her and she dredges up her courage to make her request.

'I need to ask you something,' she says directly. 'It sounds really weird but I need help.'

Mungo raises his eyebrows. 'I promise you,' he says, 'after the news I've just had nothing will ever sound really weird again, but carry on.'

She glances along the lane just to be on the safe side; nobody around.

'You know when you saw me at the Dandelion Café I was with a man? Well, he's an old friend of ours, but to be honest he's becoming a nuisance.' Mungo's eyebrows rise even higher but she hurries on. 'I admit I encouraged him in a silly way but now I'm getting frightened.'

'Yes,' says Mungo. 'I remember him. And I also remember thinking at the time that he looked as though he could be a bit of a thug.'

This slightly disconcerts her. 'Did you?'

'Mmm,' he nods. 'I wondered if you might be getting out of your depth. Very attractive but a bit scary.'

'Yes, that's it exactly.' She hesitates. 'You're going to think I'm seriously mad but can I show you something?'

He follows her into the kitchen looking slightly surprised and waits whilst she rummages in her bag. She takes out the spoon and shows it to him.

'He did this when we were having coffee this morning in Totnes.' Emma hesitates. 'I met a friend and she made me see that I could really be asking for trouble with Marcus. When she left Marcus suddenly appeared out of nowhere.'

'He'd followed you?'

She shrugs; gives a little shiver. 'I suppose he must have done. Anyway, he seemed to guess that I was cooling right off. I could see he was angry but he seemed in control of himself. All the time we were talking he was playing with the spoon but it wasn't until afterwards I saw what he'd done. It's kind of frightened me.'

Mungo takes the spoon, turns it, tries unsuccessfully to straighten it and then hands it back to her.

'Suppressed violence,' he says. 'It's always a frightening thing, isn't it, and this being your child's spoon makes it much worse somehow.'

'Exactly.' Emma is distressed. She stares at the spoon and then puts it back in her bag. 'I'm scared that he might . . . lose control. I feel such a fool. And I sent him texts, you know? It would be so humiliating if he showed them to anyone, especially Rob. Oh God! How could I be so stupid?'

'We've all been there, sweetie,' says Mungo comfortingly.

'How can I help? What do you think I could do? I'm not sure I'm in his league if it comes to the heavy stuff.'

She smiles as she knows he means her to, feeling comforted.

'We're meeting tomorrow,' she tells him. 'He thinks it's the beginning of an affair but I plan to tell him it's the end. He wants to drive me off on our own but I don't want that so I thought I'd arrange to meet him somewhere, have coffee, or even lunch, and then leave. This is the favour. If I were to make it the Dandelion Café could you be there again? You know, just stroll up casually and say "hi" and be around while I get out.'

Mungo is looking really interested now, as if he can imagine the scene already.

'I see what you're getting at,' he says. 'I could cover your retreat.'

'Exactly,' she says eagerly. 'It's an enormous cheek to ask you but I don't know what else to do. I've been a complete idiot. Arranged for Camilla to have the children for the morning. Agreed to meet him in Ashburton car park more or less after breakfast. I don't know how to play it now. I suppose I could just not turn up but I don't want him coming to look for me. I want to draw a definite line under it all.'

Mungo considers the problem. 'First of all you need to be late so as to spend as little time with him as possible. Leave the arrangement as it stands, then you phone or text tomorrow morning and say there's a bit of trouble with the baby, whatever, and you'll meet him at the café about eleven thirty. He won't want to sit about in a car park all morning so that should do the trick. I'll make sure I'm there just before you. You have coffee, and if it works out and you feel up to it you have lunch, and at some point I'll wander over and say "hello" and you can introduce me and make certain that he knows I live practically next door to you. Then when you get up to go, I'll keep an eye and follow you home. Don't worry, I'll try not to make it obvious.'

'It sounds wonderful.' She still feels a little uncertain. 'You don't think he'll guess we've set it up?'

He beams at her. 'Trust me, sweetie. I'm an actor. But you must play your part, too. Amazement when you see me, don't forget. A nice blend of anxiety and embarrassment. Dither a bit. You get the picture?'

She begins to laugh. 'You're amazing. Shall I phone you when I set out?'

'Let me have your mobile number,' he says. 'Just in case there's any kind of crisis with the children. Then we can stay in touch as you go along. I'll aim to be there around eleven.'

'I'll write it down,' she says. 'Then if you phone it when you get home I'll have your number, too.'

After he's gone she feels quite weak with relief. It's clear that Mungo had already guessed that something was going on and is only too ready to help. Instinctively she knows that he's a good friend to have in your corner; that she can trust him. She sends Marcus a text agreeing to meet at ten o'clock in the car park and crosses her fingers.

Please let me get out of this, she prays, and I'll never be so stupid again.

Mungo walks back to the smithy feeling as if he has been knocked on the head. First Philip; then Emma. His stroll was taken in an attempt to straighten out his thoughts about

Ralph, the accident, and Billy's decision to keep the whole affair quiet. Although Mungo knows that this was a drastic and illegal step, for his own part he is simply very grateful when he imagines how it might have been back then. Despite his and Izzy's popularity the press would have been full of it; Archie, Camilla and the children would have been involved, and Philip probably put in prison for manslaughter. The thought of Izzy being questioned makes him shudder; unintentionally she would have destroyed them all. And, after all, Ralph had no family to mourn him. Like Izzy, his parents were dead; he'd been sent away to boarding school by an indifferent but wealthy guardian and then won a place at drama school. Their pasts had been a connection between them; they had no family; no roots.

Even so, it's illegal to bury bodies in orchards, accident or not, and when he thinks of explaining the situation to Archie, Mungo's heart quails. His big brother will take the straight line; he will be horrified. And now there is Emma to worry about and to protect.

Back at the smithy he pours himself a large whisky. He's rather pleased that all his instincts are right; that she is in trouble – danger even, given the evidence of that crushed spoon. The prospect of seeing off such a tough young man gives him a bit of a thrill. Mungo begins to plan his strategy, relieved to be distracted momentarily from his thoughts about Ralph and the prospect of his meeting with Archie.

James turns the television off and wanders over to his laptop to write his evening email to Sally. He's enjoyed his morning in Totnes, has definitely decided to use the wine bar Rumour for one of his pair of lovers' clandestine meetings, and is now thinking about the darker side of his plot. He likes to sit in Rumour with his laptop, making notes, sketching out ideas. Several other people do the same and he wonders if they're writers, too. He'd like to tell them that he's published, that he's writing his second book, that he's no wannabe trying to look the part, but he doesn't. He guessed that there would be no copies of his book in the bookshop and he's left a copy with the guy there, although he didn't look all that keen, even when he explained to him that the new book will be set in Totnes.

He opens his laptop and begins to type.

It was quite odd this morning, Sal, seeing Sir Mungo and his friends in Totnes; watching them from the market across the road. It was as if they'd turned up in the middle of my story, which is crazy, of course. Mungo was there having coffee outside one of the little cafés, I think it's called The Brioche, with his thesp woman friend, and then he went off and this other guy turned up. Another thesp, by the look of him and by Sir Mungo's reaction to him when he came back. My guess he's one of his ex-lovers. I could just tell by all the body language and stuff. A little bit of drama for a change. I can't quite see them all involved in clandestine love affairs, murder, and worrying where to hide the body, though. I've had this good idea about that, by the way, of dropping it over the side of a boat just out at sea. I mean, what on earth do you do with a body? You can't just bury it in the garden, can you? That trip on the river Dart last week with Archie gave me several ideas and I'm hoping to go out with him again. He was very tactful and asked no questions, though I think he

was dying to ask. Bit of a blimp, old Archie. Hardly possible
to believe that he and Mungo are brothers. I bet they drive
each other up the wall. Frankly, I'm surprised Mungo keeps
a cottage here. After all, he could afford to buy a bolt-hole
almost anywhere, and I simply cannot see him enjoying the
company of our two old boys at the farm or a gung-ho army
wife. I look at my neighbours as we wave to each other and
call out greetings in the lane and wonder how they'd react if
they knew what madness and mayhem was going on in my
mind! I don't think that Billy and Philip have ever been beyond
Newton Abbot in their lives! This valley is another world;
true escapist stuff. Doors left unlocked, car windows down.
They wouldn't survive ten minutes in Oxford. It's great,
though, the sense of innocence and peace. Anyway, I saw
another car parked outside Mungo's cottage earlier so I guess
that the thesp ex-lover I saw in Totnes is now staying with
him and the female thesp. One big happy family, eh!! Archie
and Camilla must be having fits!

I've taken your advice and left a few copies of the book
where they might be picked up and read. Part of me can't
bear the waste but I suppose you're right, and if it leads to
a few people reading them and wanting more then it can be
looked on as a kind of advertising. It was a bit embarrassing
in Rumour because I left a copy on my table but on my way
out the girl came rushing after me, shouting, 'You've left your
book behind.' I'd already explained that I was writing a book,
hyped it up a bit, so I didn't like to say why I'd left a copy
behind. I'd told her my name when I was in a few days ago so
I hope she didn't guess. I just shoved it in my bag. I suppose

I should have brazened it out, asked if I could leave it on the counter. I might do that, actually. What d'you think?

Supper now (and yes, I am eating properly: fish and chips!) and then some work. Actually, it was really strange. I keep seeing this weird guy around. First in Totnes, then driving in the lane here, then in the fish and chip shop earlier this evening. He really stared at me with these very pale eyes but I pretended not to see him. Something scary about him so I didn't hang around! Hope all is quiet at the Radcliffe. Missing you, love J xx

CHAPTER SEVENTEEN

Camilla wakens first. No birdsong; the birds are silent in August. No breeze to disturb her pretty Laura Ashley curtains, though the window is wide open. Camilla turns her head to survey the sleeping Archie. How vulnerable people are when they sleep; how defenceless. Archie's face is crushed into his pillow, his mouth slack, his eyelids jittering as he dreams. She watches him with a mixture of love, irritation, and terror that something might happen to him. He is still fit and strong, but there is also a frailty about him that clutches at her heart.

Yesterday they had a row. Deciding that, with the weather so hot, it might be a good idea to have the playroom ready for action, Camilla spent the afternoon fetching out old toys, dusting off picture books, checking jigsaw puzzles. It was stuffy, stifling, and she went to the window to open it wide and give the room some air. The frame was in a bad way, the window stuck fast, warped with damp despite the hot weather. She gave it a thump and the fragile wood buckled, cracking the glass.

Archie was furious. 'You *know* the state they're in,' he kept saying. 'You *know* all the windows need replacing. Now I shall have to get it sorted out. That'll be four hundred pounds' worth at least.'

For the rest of the day the storm of his wrath grumbled on: the cost of keeping the house in a reasonable state, the problems with it being listed, the difficulties in trying to manage with as little help as possible. Yet Camilla knows that, despite his talk of a flat on the river in Totnes or a bungalow near his mooring at Stoke Gabriel, Archie doesn't really want to leave this valley where he was born and has grown old, and where they've brought up their own children.

She watches him, hoping that the storm will have passed when he wakens; hoping that she can get him back on an even keel. Even so she knows with a sinking of the heart that all he says is true: that they are hanging on by their fingertips. This moment will pass, as others have before it, and they'll soldier on again – but for how long? Perhaps they should jump before they're pushed but how can she bear to leave this house with all its memories? Her whole adult life has been spent within its sheltering walls; her creative instinct has shaped the gardens. It is their home. Everywhere there are memories of her children and their children. Their shadows on the stairs and along the corridors; echoes of their voices from the lawn that stretches down to the Horse Brook. The thousands of books that line the walls of Archie's study and the bookcases along the landing; her collection of blue and white china on the shelves in the kitchen. The toys and books; the paintings and ornaments. How would they fit into Archie's flat by the river?

Camilla wants to weep, but instead she gently pushes back

the sheet – too hot for the duvet – and slides out of bed. She will make tea for Archie, get on his right side before the day properly starts. Then breakfast, and after that the children will be arriving. Her heart rises at the prospect of those little ones and she goes downstairs feeling happier.

Archie stirs. He senses Camilla's absence before he opens his eyes and stretches with a little groan of pain as his aching limbs protest. Thank God that the hot weather has slowed the growing of the grass and weeds and he can concentrate on mending the fence that edges the river path. There's a right of way along the river there and he needs to make sure the dogs can't escape. The old posts are rotten and he's shocked at the price of new ones; but then he's shocked by the price of most things these days. He simply doesn't have enough income to keep ahead. Of course, the rent from the cottage is helping, but there are far too many outgoings – and now the playroom window will need replacing.

Archie's irritation rises again at the thought of this com-pletely unnecessary expenditure and he wants to pull the sheet over his head and groan with despair. Instead he pushes himself up, hauls his pillows behind his head and tries to take a more reasonable view. After all, it wasn't Camilla's fault; it's a perfectly natural act, to open a window. Yet his irritation still bubbles at a deeper level, fuelled by his fear. His life seems to be spent in doing sums, dreading letters from the bank and his accountant, juggling incomings and outgoings. His whole body aches from the physical effort required to keep the place from falling down.

He hears Camilla on the stairs and wonders whether to

remain grumpy; make her suffer for her thoughtless action. She comes in, carrying the tray, smiling hopefully, and he remembers that Emma's children are coming today and that Camilla will be anxious that all will be well with them. His self-pity melts in the face of her wary but determinedly cheerful expression – Is he still in a bad mood? How can I jolly him along? – and he begins to laugh. Her face smooths out into relief, surprise.

'I was thinking of my old dad,' he says. 'Do you remember how he used to say, "Start the day with a smile. Get it over with"?'

She laughs with him; the tricky moment has passed and the day lies open before them.

Joe eats his breakfast with enthusiasm. He can't wait to be with Camilla, to play with the unfamiliar toys, ride the tractor, walk with the dogs.

'Where will you go, though, Mummy?' he asks, pausing in the middle of spooning up his Cheerios. 'Where are you meeting Naomi?'

She frowns, biting her lip, as if he has said something upsetting, but next moment she's smiling again as she makes up a bottle for Dora.

'We shall go to the Dandelion Café again,' she says firmly. 'Coffee first and then lunch, then home to fetch you and Dora.'

Joe pushes his spoon round and round his bowl. He wonders if he ought to say that he wants to go with her – and a part of him does want to; he doesn't really like her to be too far away. He decides to test her.

'I want to come with you,' he says. He makes his voice a bit whiny to show that he means it and she looks really surprised, even frightened, so that he begins to feel anxious again. But very quickly she's laughing.

'No you don't,' she says. 'You want to go and play with all those lovely toys and see Bozzy and Sam. I nearly believed you for a moment but I don't now. You don't want to sit in a boring old café when you could be riding that tractor.'

She puts his smoothie next to his plate and bends to kiss his cheek. He still senses that something isn't quite right but the prospect of the tractor and the dogs sounds much more fun than sitting with Naomi and Mummy while they talk and drink coffee.

'Camilla said something about a tent,' Mummy says. 'What fun. I shall dash back after lunch so that I can have a go in it.'

He feels excited again; happy.

'You might not be able to fit in it,' he warns her. 'It might be just for children.'

Mummy pulls a funny face showing that she'll be sad if she can't get in the tent and he makes a face back at her and waves his spoon.

'Dora can go in the tent with Bozzy and Sam,' he says.

Dora lets out a great yell, as if she's understood him and wants to go in the tent with the dogs, and he and Mummy laugh and laugh and everything is good.

Mungo arrives first. He goes down the steps and puts his newspaper on the table next to the window beside the bar. The other tables are occupied and he has a sudden misgiving: supposing Marcus arrives and is obliged to share his table? This wouldn't be quite the scenario he's planned. He goes to the bar, orders coffee and carries it back to his table. Several people are finishing their drinks, almost ready to go, and he unfolds his newspaper whilst keeping an eye on them.

It's a shock when Marcus walks in, almost as if until now it were all just a game; something that wouldn't really happen. But he's here, pausing just inside the door, giving a lightning glance around as if he's mentally noting everyone who's there. He goes to the bar, waiting his turn, leaning against the bar, surveying the room. A family gets up to leave and he moves across, speaks to them, makes a little joke, puts his jacket on the chair. All his actions are quick and controlled, packed with energy. He goes to fetch his coffee and then sits, half-turned, with his back to the wall, his eyes on the door. Every so often he checks his mobile for messages and then puts it back on the table impatiently.

Watching him from behind his newspaper Mungo can gauge the exact moment that Emma enters the bar. Marcus' expression changes from watchfulness to a kind of relieved triumph; his pale eyes widen and his thin lips curve upwards. Then he is on his feet, going to meet her, taking both her hands in his. Emma is tense; conscious of her surroundings, pulling her hands away quickly after that first greeting.

Mungo is fascinated. He notes all their tiny reactions, their body language: Emma's nervousness, Marcus' intensity. There is no way, he thinks, that this can last right through lunch, and he prepares himself for action. Emma sits down with her back to him but, as Marcus goes to the bar to order coffee for her, she glances round and he lowers his newspaper to let her see where he is. By the time Marcus looks back to smile at her Mungo is bent over the crossword, pen in hand.

*

When she sees Mungo in his corner by the bar Emma almost collapses with relief. She has become more and more nervous during the drive to Haytor and now she feels quite weak. She presses her trembling hands between her knees and gets ready to tell Marcus exactly how things are. There is no way that she can sustain a long friendly lunch with him.

He puts the mug down in front of her and slides in opposite. She sees that he is ready to behave as though there is no longer any doubt that there is to be a relationship between them; that by turning up she has agreed; accepted this. Emma fumbles with the paper packet of sugar, her hands are shaking, and he puts his own out and holds them over hers, squeezing them. His hands are warm and strong. She can barely look at him but knows she has to; that she has to hold it together.

'Don't worry, Ems,' he says. 'It's going to be so good. Trust me. It's going to work out, you'll see.'

She withdraws her hands, puts the sugar into the mug, not able to look into those pale, mesmerizing eyes. Lifting the cup in both hands, she sips the scalding coffee and is filled briefly with a kind of strength. She puts the cup on the table, still holding it, and finally looks at him properly.

'No, Marcus,' she says. 'No, you've got it wrong.'

Still he smiles; at least his mouth smiles, but his eyes grow wary. Her hands tighten on the mug but she keeps calm.

'Wrong?' he says lightly, very quietly.

'Mmm.' She nods. Suddenly she is resolute. She remembers how she has lied to Joe and she sits back a little, distancing herself from Marcus but still looking at him. 'It's not going to work between us, Marcus. I haven't been thinking clearly and I apologize for misleading you, but I love Rob and my children and I'm not going to risk my marriage. I'm sorry, Marcus.'

He sits back, too, and his eyes are very bright and very angry.

'I'm sorry, too, Ems,' he says, 'because you're making a big mistake. You can't give up on this now. I shan't let you.'

Emma takes a very deep breath. 'But you can't stop me,' she says gently. 'Can you? I'm married to Rob. Please, Marcus, be reasonable.'

He laughs, a short, violent burst of laughter that makes her flinch back from him, afraid again, for suddenly now she can see all sorts of ways in which he might destroy her life. She thinks of her children and of Rob and she is swamped with fear. Marcus leans forward, begins to speak but he is forestalled.

'Good grief, is it Emma?' cries Mungo in a ringing voice trained to reach the back of the gallery. 'Yes, it is. I thought I recognized you. Hello again.'

She jumps violently, staring up at him with all the amazement he could have wished. Just briefly she'd forgotten all about him.

'Mungo,' she stammers. 'How . . . how nice to see you. I didn't notice you.'

'Ah, but I noticed you.' He beams upon them. 'And is this your husband? How do you do?'

'No, no,' says Emma awkwardly. She hadn't realized how very easy it would be to play the part so convincingly; she feels utterly confused and totally embarrassed but deeply relieved that Mungo has made his move. 'This is Captain

Marcus Roper. He's a commando, like Rob. They're very old friends. This is Sir Mungo Kerslake,' she says to Marcus. 'He lives next door to me. It's wonderful,' she adds, pulling herself together as he and Mungo shake hands, 'to have such a famous actor as a neighbour.' She glances round the bar quite casually. 'Are you alone? Would you like to join us?'

She feels Marcus' fury like a lick of flame across the table but she ignores him, smiling at Mungo, who sits down on the chair beside her and looks at their coffee mugs.

'Thank you very much,' he says warmly, 'I should love to. Now what are you drinking? Shall I get you more coffee?'

He looks at Marcus enquiringly, the benevolent old uncle, and Marcus is obliged to offer Mungo coffee and stand up and go to the bar to order it.

'Didn't like the look of things,' murmurs Mungo, beaming all the while. 'We'll go out together when you're ready. Make sure you get away before I do.'

Emma doesn't know whether to laugh or weep so she beams back at him to pretend they're having a jolly conversation, and by the time Marcus comes back she's relaxed; she's safe.

'Marcus is off to California soon,' she tells Mungo, 'to join up with the US Marines on an exercise.'

And then Mungo starts a conversation about filming in California and tells a long and rambling anecdote that includes several famous names. Marcus maintains a polite expression but Emma knows that he's simply waiting for a moment to suggest that he and she make a move. As Mungo finishes his anecdote and his coffee she gets in quickly.

'Marcus, I'm sorry about this but I have to go. I told you earlier that Dora's not very well and she's playing up so I promised Camilla I'd get back as soon as I can. I'm glad we've been able to see each other to say goodbye. I hope the course goes well.'

She picks up her bag and Mungo gets to his feet. 'I must be off, too. So nice to meet you, my dear fellow.'

He puts his newspaper on the table, knocking his spectacle case to the floor so that Marcus is obliged to scrabble about under the chair for it. Apologizing, continuing to talk to them both as they walk out together, Mungo takes Emma's arm, gestures to something, commenting about the weather. Marcus only has a short opportunity to get close to her as she fishes her keys out of her bag and unlocks the car door.

'Please, Ems, we can't just finish like this. For God's sake—'

'I'm so sorry,' she says quickly, very quietly. 'Forgive me if you can. It was just a midsummer madness. Take care, Marcus. Goodbye, Mungo.' She raises her voice. 'Great to see you.'

He lifts his hand to her. 'Race you home,' he cries jokingly.

Emma drives away, heart thumping, looking back in her mirror at them standing together watching her go. Just for a moment she regrets the excitement, the fun of having a secret, and the satisfaction of seeing Marcus' desire for her. But she shakes her head, repudiating it, remembering how she'd felt when she lied to Joe, telling him she was meeting Naomi. It's a false happiness; shadow not substance.

She drives fast but carefully, wanting to be home, back with her children.

*

Marcus watches her go. He is so angry that he can barely be polite to the old queen beside him, with his pretty silk scarf and his tight jeans. Just for a moment he wondered back there in the café if he'd been set up, but Emma looked so shocked, so disconcerted, that he dismissed the idea. Anyway, this old luvvie wouldn't have the bollocks to try to cross him.

He's getting into his car, saying goodbye, and Marcus nods to him and strides away. He needs to walk, to climb, to work off his frustration in physical activity. Haytor hardly rates as a climb but it's better than nothing – and it's there.

So what's the next move? He passes the holiday-makers, toiling up as if they're climbing Everest, and perches on an outcrop amongst the heather and the gorse, staring out towards the sea. It's not just that he'd like to get Emma into bed. Of course he wants to, but he also wants to prove that he's capable of a relationship, that Tasha was wrong when she called him an emotional retard. Emma makes him feel warm and loving; he knows he can make it with Emma. He'll text her, insist on one more try. She owes him that. This morning has been a complete farce.

He reaches into his jeans pocket but his phone isn't there. He stands up and digs his hands into his jacket pockets: nothing. He looks around him on the rocks. Where the hell . . . ? He must have left it in the café, on the table. He was so anxious to get a moment alone with Emma before she went that he'd forgotten it.

Cursing, he begins to descend, half running, half sliding and slipping, leaping down the slopes of the tor, dodging the holiday-makers and their dogs and children. He crosses the road, hurries back into the bar. There's a group of teenagers at the table now and they stare at him as he asks if they've seen his phone, shrugging, glancing at one another with silly grins and raised eyebrows. He wants to slap them about a bit, teach them to show respect, but they continue to look blankly at him and shake their heads.

He goes to the bar and asks if anyone has handed in his phone; more checking, more head shaking. His anger is rising. Someone's taken it but there's nothing he can do about it. He goes outside and gets into his car, trying to calm himself down. There's no real harm done: the phone is purely for private use, though a few of Emma's texts might have caused her a bit of embarrassment if he'd wanted to hype up the action. Even so, he feels that one way and another he's been completely rolled over and he's not used to it.

And no, Tasha, he shouts silently inside his head, I am not a control freak nor am I an emotional retard.

Suddenly he remembers the multimedia photo she sent him yesterday of their two boys in the garden, beaming out at him. The message read: 'See you on Saturday, Dad. Love you xx'.

Suddenly, shockingly, his eyes are full of tears. Angrily he swipes at them; he wants to see that picture again. An idea occurs to him: could Emma have picked up the phone by mistake? He sits in his car thinking about the possibilities this offers. He can't text, he can't ring, but what's to stop him dropping in and asking the question? Perfectly reasonable. He looks at his watch. It's a bit early. She's bound to be home with the kids around tea-time. He'll make a recce. Meanwhile he'll find a pub and have a pint and a sandwich.

Suddenly he thinks of the nerdy guy in the fish and chip shop last evening. Just as he was getting over his paranoia about being followed, there he was again. He'd wanted to grab him, question him, but nerdy guy slipped past him and hurried out while the woman behind the counter was asking him what he wanted and by the time he'd got out nerdy guy was long gone. And, though he might tell himself that if nerdy guy was following him then he was rubbish at it, something else was just nagging at the back of his mind, wondering if this was the whole point: that he wanted to be seen, as a kind of warning. As if he might be saying: stop now and it'll be OK. We're on to you but it's not too late. You could stop stalking Emma, go back and make it up with Tasha and your kids, celebrate being made up to major next year. It's all still there waiting for you.

Marcus hesitates but then the thought of being rolled over by that old queen fills his gut with rage and bile and he knows, he just knows he's got to give it one last go. Anyway, there's a possibility that Emma might have picked his phone up by mistake. It's a long shot but it's a good enough reason to make one last bid.

CHAPTER EIGHTEEN

'I cannot *believe* that you stole his phone,' Kit says. 'Honestly, Mungo! How could you *do* that?'

She and Jake have been waiting for Mungo's return and now they sit at his kitchen table eating fresh rolls with cheese and olives whilst he tells them what happened.

'Well, do you know it was easier than I believed it would be.' Mungo is still pumped up by his part in the action. 'He'd been checking it, you see, and he just left it there, lying on the table beside his coffee mug. I remembered poor Emma saying that she was worried about a few indiscreet texts so I decided to remove it. First, I just casually put the newspaper on top of it and then I did that sort of dithery old codger thing. You know? Drop my specs case on the floor and then emit cries of distress while he grovels about under the chair for it and I trouser the phone. By this time Emma was heading off, so naturally he dashed after her. Went like a dream. Take One. A wrap.' He sighs with contentment. 'I hadn't realized, though, just how difficult it would be to play the part of a rather dotty old man.'

Jake bursts out laughing. 'A true professional,' he says, and Kit glares quellingly at him.

'You *are* a dotty old man, Mungo,' she says severely. 'Stealing people's mobiles just isn't done. It's theft. A criminal offence. What have you done with it?'

He shrugs. 'Nothing yet.' He takes it out of his pocket and puts it on the table. 'I might chuck it in the Horse Brook.'

'You haven't by any chance looked at those messages?' says Kit suspiciously. 'I wouldn't put it past you.'

'Certainly not,' he says indignantly. 'What do you take me for?'

'A common thief,' answers Kit. 'Suppose he guesses and comes after you?'

Mungo purses his lips. 'Could be rather fun.'

To be honest, Kit has to admit that she is enjoying herself, and she can see that Jake is, too. It's good that all this is happening to add to the excitement of their reunion, rather than it being just a normal, dull, daily round. It's good that he can see that she has wacky friends with lots of jollity going on, and that she hasn't simply grown old and boring and lonely.

'Even so,' she says, 'you should ditch it. Not in the Horse Brook. It's not running very fast after all this hot weather. It'll just lie there.'

'Take out the SIM card,' suggests Jake, 'and drop the phone in very deep water with nobody watching. The SIM card's rather a different proposition. It's very difficult to destroy a SIM card. Perhaps we could bury it somewhere remote and inaccessible.'

They look at him with respect.

'He's a banker,' Kit says to Mungo. 'He knows about these things. Let's have a jaunt this afternoon and do just that.'

'You and Jake can do it,' says Mungo, 'since he's full of such good ideas. I've got to see Archie.'

He looks sober, suddenly, as if he's remembered something rather serious and worrying, and Kit feels a little thrill of anxiety. After all, it was rather brave of him to take on Emma's commando, and clever to think of grabbing the phone to protect her, even if it's such a risky thing to do. Mungo's a good friend and she doesn't like to see that shadow of disquiet in his eyes.

'Sure you're OK?' she asks casually.

He nods. 'Go off and have fun. But you're very welcome to come back for supper.'

'Sounds good to me,' answers Jake. 'Kit?'

'Yes,' she says, 'and then we can tell you how we've incriminated ourselves in your interests. Has it occurred to you that he might be with MI5 and that phone could be bugged?'

'If he's with MI5 he wouldn't be stupid enough to leave his phone on the table but he might try to get it traced. Do you want to take Mopsa on this mission?'

'Shall we? Would you like a jaunt?' Kit leans from her chair to stroke Mopsa, who is stretched out on the slates. 'One wag for yes, two for no.' Mopsa's tail lifts slowly and thumps the floor once. 'There. We'll take that as a yes. We'll go in my car. Jake's always been a terrible driver. He drives on the wrong side of the road half the time.'

'You don't have sides of the road in these lanes,' retorts Jake. 'Everyone drives straight down the middle. But that's fine with me. I like being a passenger and you know all the best places to go.'

'Leave the clearing up to me,' says Mungo, as they get up, 'and don't forget the phone.'

Kit takes it rather gingerly. She imagines what her brother, Hal, would have to say about such felonious behaviour and feels even more anxious. 'I still don't feel right about having this,' she says.

'Then the quicker you lose it the better,' says Mungo.

'Give it to me,' says Jake. He prises open the phone, takes out the SIM card and tucks it into his wallet, then puts the phone in the pocket of his jeans. 'Mungo's right. Let's go and lose them somewhere.'

After they've gone, and he's finished clearing up, Mungo looks at his watch. By this time lunch should be over and Archie will either be in his study catching up with his paperwork or out in the grounds somewhere. He's been replacing the posts down by the river so that might be the first place to try. Mungo draws a deep, steadying breath, jams his old straw hat on his head and sets out.

It's quiet in the lane, and it's odd without Mopsa at his heels. He doesn't quite know why he suggested that Mopsa should go on the jaunt, except as a kind of moral support for Kit in case she were to have one of those moments of panic about Jake. Having Mopsa there will distract her, give her time to regroup. Dogs are useful like that. By the look of things, however, it seems an unnecessary precaution. Despite Kit's terrors, she and Jake are very much at ease together; they have reconnected remarkably quickly. He wonders how they will take the next crucial step but, at the same time, he knows that he is thinking about them to distract himself from the forthcoming meeting with Archie. He's planned what he's going to say but he has no confidence that Archie will accept his suggestion.

Mungo salutes the old Herm and turns on to the track that leads down to the stream. He walks slowly. His morning with Emma and her commando has tired him a little. He's pleased with his performance, however; that touch of the old, gay, actor-manager with his pretty silk scarf and his long, rather racy anecdote was effective. Taking the phone was, perhaps, going just a tad too far; his sense of theatre overcame him at that point and he couldn't resist the gesture. Nevertheless, Emma will be safe now from the texts being shown to her husband if Marcus decides to be difficult.

The track tips and twists down to the stream between high banks of scrubby thorn and holly bushes. He pauses on the bridle path to watch a group of mallards cruising close to the bank beneath the overhanging boughs of willow and alder. A grey wagtail struts on a granite boulder in the middle of the stream; flitting up in a flurry of gold to snatch at an insect, landing again to patrol the pitted stony surface.

Above the splash and rush of the water Mungo can hear that rhythmical thud of metal on wood and as he rounds the bend of the stream he sees Archie, driving a post into the ground. At this distance, with his sleeves rolled up, Archie looks vigorous and strong, but Mungo wonders if he should be doing quite such heavy work at his age. He wishes he had Mopsa with him. It looks odd to be walking on his own along the bridle path and he thinks how to begin the conversation.

230

Archie stops, drops the sledgehammer, stretches, and Mungo calls to him.

'Hot work,' he says. 'Can't you get young Andy to help you with it?'

'Harvest,' Archie answers briefly. 'Rain forecast for the weekend. He'll come and help as soon as he can. How are you doing?'

'Fine. Just felt like stretching my legs. Kit's gone off with Mopsa and an old friend over from Paris.'

There's a little pause while Archie swigs some water from a bottle. Come on, Mungo tells himself, just get to the point.

'Look, I've been thinking, Arch, trying to find ways to spread the load a bit, and I had an idea last night. What if you were to sell me the farm? No, wait. Hear me out. I buy the farm. We leave Philip and Billy *in situ*, of course. After I die, it'll come to your boys anyway, you know that, but meanwhile you've got some cash to do the repairs to the house and the other cottage and put another tenant in, like you have with Emma. And it leaves you in a much more comfortable situation financially. You could afford to bring in more help. The farm's upkeep becomes my responsibility. You know I can afford it, so why not?'

Archie is staring at him, working it out, thinking it through. 'And what do you get out of it?'

Mungo shrugs. His heartbeat quickens. Could it really be this easy? 'I get the satisfaction of seeing you slowing down a bit, taking things easy, not killing yourself.'

Still Archie stands, frowning. Suddenly he shakes his head. 'It's not quite that simple. For a start, I'm not sure how long Camilla and I can manage, even without the responsibility of the farm, and I think the place would sell better as a whole. It could become an equestrian property. They are getting very popular round here now and I've been advised that it would be sensible to keep the house and the farm with its stabling together.'

Mungo's heart sinks; not only at the rejection of his idea but at the thought that Archie has been taking advice to sell.

'Think about it, though,' he says. 'It would break Camilla's heart to leave the valley and yours, too, if you're honest. If you had that money, life would be much easier and more comfortable for you both.'

'Thanks for the offer,' says Archie, slightly awkwardly. 'I don't mean to sound ungrateful but I want to do what's best all round. I'll think about it, though. Did you come down here just to talk about that?'

'I wanted to have a private moment with you. Will you tell Camilla?'

Archie thinks about it. 'Probably not until I've really thought it through. She's very twitchy about the subject and I don't want to raise her hopes.'

'You admit that she'd approve, then?'

Archie picks up the sledgehammer. 'Probably. But I still want time to think about it. Thanks, though, for not mentioning it in front of her. Bring Kit and the friend up for drinks later.'

Mungo hesitates, wondering if Kit is ready to expose Jake to Camilla's attention.

'Thanks. I'll see what time they get back.'

Archie nods, Mungo raises a hand, and they part.

*

Emma picks up her bag ready to go to get Joe and Dora. For the last hour she's been prepared for Marcus to come after her but there's no sign of him. Mungo arrived back very soon after she got home from Haytor and stayed with her for a little while, just in case. They were both hyped up; still running on adrenalin. He showed her Marcus' mobile and she stared at it in disbelief.

'No need to worry now,' he said. 'I'll lose it somewhere. Trust me.'

'You were brilliant,' she told him. 'I can never thank you enough.'

She could see he was pleased. 'It was rather fun,' he admitted, 'but you're well out of it, sweetie. He's a very tough cookie. Please don't be tempted to give it another go.'

She shook her head. 'I shan't. It was like some kind of madness, like a terrible illness, but I'm cured now. Would you like some lunch? I feel I've rather rotted up your morning.'

'I've got Kit and a friend of hers at the smithy,' he said. 'You're welcome to join us if you feel up to it.'

Under the circumstance the thought of Kit and a friend was rather daunting. She couldn't imagine making polite conversation just yet.

'Honestly, I'm fine,' she told him. 'I'll make myself a sandwich and then go up to Camilla after lunch to fetch the children. I don't want to mess her around by appearing unexpectedly early.'

'OK, but if Marcus turns up you know where I am.'

Quite suddenly she put her arms round him and hugged him.

'I feel such a fool,' she muttered. 'Thanks, Mungo.'

'Join the club,' he said, returning her hug. 'Welcome to the human race.'

It's odd, she thinks, how ready she's been to trust him; how quickly he's become a friend. It was amazing to see how he slightly camped himself up for Marcus' benefit so as to make himself appear unthreatening. It was a brilliant performance but she still feels slightly on edge, wondering what Marcus will do next. How could she explain these last few days to Rob? It's so strange how quickly this foolish passion for Marcus has subsided. It's been like having a fever that's distorted her outlook and muddled her feelings. She misses Rob: wishes he were here so that if Marcus were to try to make trouble she would be able to talk to Rob about it face to face. Though she feels panicky at the prospect, a part of her knows that he would understand; that he would remember how difficult and unsatisfactory the last leave was after Dora was born and be able to make allowances. She remembers how upset he was when she told him about the meeting at Haytor and the prospective visit to the zoo and suddenly she is wrenched with misery at the idea of him so far away and feeling jealous and insecure. Tonight they will Skype at the arranged time and she will make certain that Rob feels completely reassured. Another idea occurs to her: she will invite his mother for a visit. This will certainly allay any fears he has and Joe will love to see Granny. Emma is very fond of her mother-in-law who, rather like Camilla, is a wonderful cook, does a great deal of charity work since she was widowed, and will love to see the children and the new cottage. Trips will be made, perhaps a little party planned for all these lovely neighbours, and Rob will be happy.

Emma steps out into the lane, glances quickly up and down, and sets off for the house. She can hear shouts of glee, Joe playing on the tractor, perhaps, or in the tent. Her heart lifts and she hurries up the drive towards her children.

Kit and Jake journey slowly through deep, secret lanes, across the bleak, high moors, beside fast-flowing rivers, and they talk gently and quietly together. Each new conversation begins with: 'Do you remember when . . . ?' or 'What was the name of . . . ?' or 'This seems so weird . . .' Their past is recalled, relived, shared; their reuniting is discussed, the odd coincidence of their meeting again marvelled over. The mobile phone is forgotten and they are hardly aware of the country through which they are travelling.

With the roof down, they are reminded of long-ago jaunts in Kit's Morris Minor convertible when their youth stretched endlessly into the future and life was uncomplicated.

'Of course, these days we would have simply lived to-gether,' Kit says. 'It was so much more important making a commitment, back then.'

'Possibly,' Jake answers. 'Though I think you'll always have a problem about any kind of emotional commitment. You're such a coward, Kit.'

'I know.' She isn't in the least resentful. It is absolutely true. 'I took you for granted and thought I could have it all. Sin warned me how it would end but I didn't believe her. In some ways we were like an old married couple without being married or a couple, weren't we? I felt totally secure without actually having to give anything up. I was a selfish cow.'

'And I was a fool,' he admits. 'I was afraid of frightening you right off and so I just allowed us to drift along.'

She puts out a hand to him, without taking her eyes from the moorland road, and he holds it tightly.

'Thank God for Mungo,' she says. 'He's taken all the stress out of it, hasn't he?'

Jake nods. 'He's great. How on earth did you meet him?'

'I was supplying the props for one of his productions. But actually I first met him way back when I was working for the Old Vic in Bristol in my school holidays. I was about sixteen and he was very young, very minor roles and understudies, but it was a point of contact. Something to talk about; reminisce about. Then he introduced me to Isobel Trent, the actress, and we just clicked at once. She was such huge fun. Completely over the top but with an odd humility that was very touching. She loved doing this, actually. Just driving in the car. We'd come down from London to stay with Mungo and I'd bring her up here and drive her around and she'd sing.'

'Sing?'

'She was really a musical theatre person. It was her first love and when she was older she did cabaret. She was utterly brilliant. She could make you laugh until it hurt and then weep and be absolutely lacerated with her pain. I suppose because I knew her so well it made it more poignant somehow. It was like she had a skin missing and things were more painful or more wonderful for her than for the rest of us.'

Kit falls silent; just for a moment it's as if it's Izzy with her in the car, crying out with joy at miraculous sights: thickets of golden flowering gorse; a small, heavy-headed foal pressed against its mother's flank; deep blue water glimpsed between tall dark pine trees. Leaning to peer from the window at a peaty moorland stream falling in a noisy rush over stones and boulders and vanishing beneath an ancient clapper bridge; staring in awe at the stony magnificence of tumbled granite rocks, thrusting and bunching up into the pale blue sky, Izzy would be transported by such magic. Kit can hear her voice, poignant and intimate, singing Joni Mitchell's 'Both Sides Now'.

'That song just about sums me up,' she'd say. 'I want it at my funeral, Kit. Don't forget.'

Remembering that day, the silence into which those words were sung, Kit wants to weep.

'So you all became good friends?' asks Jake gently, after a moment.

Kit nods. 'We just hit it off straight away. It was a bit like you and me and Sin, actually. Just a perfect mix. Well, you've met Mungo. You can imagine.'

'I can. I feel he sees us from his own particular point of view, don't you? What would he call this production, I ask myself? *The Revenant? Second Chances?*'

'Mungo is a complete one-off. He so enjoyed his morning saving Emma, didn't he? It was going too far, taking the phone, though. And how on earth shall we lose it?'

Each bridge and river has, so far, been crammed with the great British public on holiday: children, canoeists, picnickers, and their dogs, all of whom might rescue or retrieve the phone or the card if it were tossed from the car.

'The crucial thing is to get rid of the SIM card,' Jake says. 'After all, there could be state secrets on it, never mind Emma's indiscretions.'

'Maybe we could feed it to a sheep,' suggests Kit, 'or a pony?'

Jake takes the mobile out of his pocket and looks at it.

'I must admit I never thought how impossible it would be to find a deserted part of Dartmoor to commit a crime. The place is heaving.'

'I wish you'd stop using the word crime,' she complains. 'Hal would have a fit if he could see us.'

'Dear old Hal,' says Jake reminiscently. 'So completely the naval officer. His reactions were always so utterly predictable. So how will he and Fliss react to my turning up?'

'They'll be thrilled,' says Kit. 'As long as I don't start panicking around again. After all, it's not as if we'd just met on the internet or something.'

She begins to laugh, remembering one or two unsatisfactory encounters – and Hal's outspoken reactions.

'What?' asks Jake.

Kit shakes her head. 'I've had a brilliant idea. We'll drive to Venford Reservoir and throw the phone and the SIM card into the lake. And then I'll buy you an ice cream. We shall pretend we're holiday-makers.'

He shudders. 'No, no. I remember your British ice cream. Awful. And on such a hot day, too. It'll melt and drip and be horribly glutinous.'

'You sound like Mungo. OK. I'll buy you a cup of tea at the dear little community café in Holne. Earl Grey and delicious home-made cakes. How does that sound?'

'It sounds as if I've come home,' he says.

CHAPTER NINETEEN

After Emma and the children have gone Camilla sits on the veranda, her feet up on another chair, her eyes closed. She is exhausted. It's a while now since she had two small children in her care and she'd forgotten how tiring lifting and carrying a baby can be. Her back and legs ache and she is very glad to sit down. She can hear the thud of Archie's sledgehammer down by the stream and feels sympathy for him. He'll come back with all sorts of aches and pains, too, but part of him will know the satisfaction of having achieved something necessary.

We need to remain viable, she thinks. We mustn't just close down so that in the end we're just staring at daytime television and living for the next meal. Better to be stretched than to be bored.

Even so, she knows that the kind of strain Archie is under isn't good for him. It's one thing to be busy and quite another to be stressed. He's always been an active, energetic man; ready to take on challenges. He inherited just after they were married and they entered with great enthusiasm into the work necessary to bring the house up to date.

Camilla makes a little face, remembering how their arms and backs had ached from rubbing down, scraping, painting walls and ceilings. When Archie's father was alive, Philip's mother helped in the house, cleaned and cooked, and Billy and Philip looked after the grounds between them. They continued to assist the young married couple, though not to such a great extent, and even now Philip is always at hand to put in some work in the garden whilst Philip's daughter-in-law, young Andy's mother, comes to help Camilla in the house.

They worked hard, back then; refreshing the house with clean bright paint, making new curtains, reshaping the garden. Each morning Archie would dash off to the law practice in Exeter and when he returned he would change into old clothes and cheerfully continue the work in hand.

It seems to Camilla, looking back, that they were never idle for a moment. They took the dog – Archie's father's amiable if slow-witted golden Labrador – for long walks on the moor and Archie still found time to go sailing. In those days he had a little racing Merlin Rocket, which he kept on a trailer in Coronation Park by the Higher Ferry slip in Dartmouth. The children slowed them down for a while whilst they were toddlers: unable to walk too far and a liability on the boat. Pretty soon, though, they were managing longer and longer walks and she was able to let them go off sailing with Archie without living in terror of their falling overboard or being knocked unconscious by a swinging boom. Archie was quite tough with his boys, allowing them to take risks whilst watching at a sensible distance: what these days might be called loving neglect. He expected them to take part, reach beyond themselves, seize opportunities, so that they were able to experience freedom and challenge within the boundaries of his love for them.

He was strict, yes, careful with expenditure, but so was she. Their biggest extravagance was entertaining. Both of them loved to have friends to dinner, to stay weekends; to invite the boys' friends for exeats and during the holidays; taking them all up on the moor, to the beach, out sailing. How lucky they've been to live in this idyllic valley, between the moor and the sea, to bring up their children here, and now to watch their grandchildren enjoying the same privileges; and how hard it is to feel the constraints of age, the closing in of the bars, the threat to freedom. Archie fights against his stiffening muscles, his increasing deafness, the weakness of his body, but she can see that this is one battle he can't win.

Camilla turns her mind from the problem, listening to the sounds of high summer: the faint trickle of the stream; the sighing shift of the weighty canopy of shabby leaves. August is a silent month. Birds no longer sing their love songs, no longer protect territory with warning cries. Only the distant monotonous three notes of the collared dove, 'coo-*coo* coo', and the nearby drone of a bee amongst the tangle of sweet peas scrambling up a wigwam of willow in a big wooden pot at the end of the veranda.

Camilla's mind drifts to her garden — what to harvest, what to plant — and presently she dozes.

Archie raises a hand to her as he climbs the lawn from the stream but even at this distance he can see that she is asleep.

Her neck will ache when she wakes up. He pauses to look at her, thinking of Mungo's proposition, knowing how it will hurt her to leave. Yet, if something were to happen to him, how could she manage here alone? Wouldn't it be best to make the move whilst they're both still young enough to cope with it?

Archie thinks of the crammed attics, the bulging cupboards, and his heart fails him. Would they even survive a move? And would Camilla be able to deal with the huge task alone? Of course, the boys would help; the family would rally round. They are lucky to have the boys and their families within easy driving distance, Henry in London and Tim in Gloucestershire, not too far away in case of emergency. He'd hoped that one of them – Henry, perhaps – might have followed in his footsteps, continued the family tradition, but Henry studied medicine and Tim qualified as a vet. They still love to come back to the valley but they have their own lives, their wives have jobs, the children are settled in school. As the grandchildren grow older they, too, begin to have their own schedules: clubs, parties, friends. They enjoy a few days here but they are beginning to outgrow the simple country pleasures; they demand trips to Exeter, to Plymouth, to more sophisticated entertainment. He can understand that but it's not so simple for Camilla. She misses them and gets hurt when the children grow bored with the activities that once enchanted them. At least he and Camilla are blessed with good friends who are having the same experiences with their own families. The crucial thing is to keep going; to have something to get up for; to be happily occupied.

Archie skirts the veranda and goes quietly into the kitchen.

The dogs, who are stretched out on the cold slates, barely move as he comes in. They, too, are exhausted after their busy morning with Joe and Dora. He washes his hands, pours a glass of water and swallows it down, thinking of Mungo's proposal. It seems unfair that Mungo should sink his money into a property he doesn't want and will never live in: it's a crazy – if very generous – offer. And, in a worst-case scenario, if Mungo were to die, the farm would revert to the boys, who would simply sell it anyway. They've already suggested that a short-term solution is to apply for planning permission to build in the orchard. There is good access and it will raise some ready cash. On the face of it, the plan certainly solves the immediate financial problem. Archie shakes his head. He can't think straight and he's too tired to make proper sense of it all.

Camilla comes in behind him, dazed and dishevelled.

'I didn't hear you come back. I was out for the count, I'm afraid.'

'I could hear you snoring halfway up,' he tells her. 'I saw Mungo and invited him for drinks with Kit and a friend of hers that's over from Paris.'

'A friend?' Camilla looks interested. 'What kind of friend? Male or female?'

'I didn't think to ask. Sorry. Does it matter?'

Camilla purses her lips. 'It might. What time?'

'He didn't know. They've gone off for the afternoon so we left it open. I'm going up to have a shower.'

'We'll have some tea when you come down. Joe and I made Smartie fairy cakes.'

Archie goes along the passage to the hall, feeling the

warmth of the house, its familiarity all around him. How could he ever bear to leave it?

'Camilla and I made Smartie fairy cakes,' says Joe, loading his treasures out of his knapsack on to the kitchen table. 'Camilla put them in a tin for us to have at tea-time. And I did a drawing of the dogs and I planted some seeds in this flowerpot. I have to remember to water them.'

'Goodness.' Emma is impressed by all this industry. 'And what about Madam Dora while you were doing all this?'

'She cried quite a lot,' says Joe with a certain amount of indifference. 'But Camilla carried her about and sang to her. So she was OK.'

Dora has fallen asleep on the walk home and lies peacefully in her buggy.

'Let's leave her there,' suggests Emma, 'and have a Smartie cake, shall we? They look very good.'

Joe tries not to beam with pride. 'If you like,' he says nonchalantly. 'They were really easy. Camilla asked if we did cooking but I said no. You're always too busy so we buy our cakes.'

Emma is washed with shame: Camilla would never be too busy to cook and she certainly would never buy a shop cake.

'We could try,' she offers, 'if you enjoyed it.'

'If you like,' he says again. He is buoyed up by his morning's achievements, still bursting with energy.

Emma prepares tea with the sense of someone who has been on the brink of losing something very precious. She feels weak with relief and gratitude that she has not destroyed it.

If only Rob were here to eat a Smartie cake and to be part of their little celebration.

'We can have a Skype with Daddy later,' she says. 'It's Skype night. You can tell him about your cooking and show him the picture of the dogs.'

Joe does a little dance round the table, punching the air and shouting, 'Skype night. Skype night,' though very quietly so as not to waken Dora. He scrambles on to a chair and examines his picture of Bozzy and Sam and plans what he will say to Daddy.

He feels happy, as if some danger has passed, though he doesn't quite know what the danger might have been. And then, through the window, he sees Philip pushing old Billy in his wheelchair in the lane and he goes running out, flinging open the door, calling to them.

'Come and have some tea,' he shouts. 'Mummy's just making it. And I've made some Smartie cakes.'

Behind him, Emma waves to Philip, beckoning them in.

'The more the merrier,' she says. 'Would you like a cup of tea?'

Star dances at Joe's knees, jumping to attract attention. Philip bends to see if Billy is happy to join the party and they turn in from the lane.

'Let's go round the side to the patio,' Emma suggests. 'It'll be easier for Billy in his chair where it's all paved. I'll bring the tea out. Take them round there, Joe.'

Joe can see that she's pleased that they are there to share this odd little celebration. Importantly he leads Philip, old Billy and Star round to the back of the cottage and drags up the green plastic chairs to the wooden table ready for the party.

Emma comes out with the tray of plates and cakes and mugs of tea. She looks a question at Philip who shakes his head: Billy can't manage a mug; he will dribble. Philip places one of the little cakes on a plate on Billy's lap and he crumbles it with his good hand and puts the pieces carefully into his mouth.

'I wish it was someone's birthday,' says Joe longingly. 'Then we could sing and it would be a real party.'

'Never mind,' says Emma. 'It's lovely anyway. And the cakes are delicious.'

'As it happens,' says Philip, 'it *is* someone's birthday.'

Joe stares at him. He and Billy look much too old to have birthdays. 'Is it your birthday?' he asks.

Philip shakes his head. 'It's Star's birthday.'

'How old is she?' asks Joe eagerly.

'Twelve,' answers Philip. 'She's twelve today.'

Emma looks at him quizzically and he meets her eyes with a guileless blue stare that makes her want to burst out laughing.

'Twelve,' says Joe, looking at Star with respect. 'Shall we sing to her?'

'She'd like that,' says Philip. 'Loves a bit of a singsong, Star does.'

So they sing to Star, who watches them with her ears pricked and her eyes darting between them all in the hope of falling crumbs.

Marcus can hear the singing. He knocks at the door but there's no answer and then he hears the voices: 'Happy birthday to you' followed by a little cheer. Silently he treads along the paving at the side of the cottage, edges up to the corner and looks at the group on the patio. He can hardly believe what he sees: Emma and the children, yes, but two old chaps are with her, one in a wheelchair and the other with that lean tough look of the countryman. It's he who spots Marcus and who straightens up to stare at him. Emma notices his distraction and turns to look over her shoulder.

Marcus smiles easily, though he is full of rage and frustration, but Emma's reaction – fear and distress – is very clear, and not only to him. She turns back to the old fellow, says something quick and low to him, and now he is getting up as if he owns the place, as if he is the host, and is coming towards him.

'Can we help you?' he asks. 'Is this a friend of yours, Emma?'

'Yes,' she says, all foolish and helpless and embarrassed. 'Yes. This is Captain Marcus Roper. He's a friend of Rob's. They work together.'

Silly cow. Friend of Rob's. He'll show her.

'I couldn't phone,' he says, stepping past the old man, smiling down at her. 'When we were having coffee together this morning I lost my mobile. I wanted to check that you hadn't picked it up by mistake.'

He watches her blush. That's dropped her right in it.

'No,' she says. 'No, I didn't see it. Sorry.'

The old man stands like a rock beside her, immovable, and it is Joe who offers him a cake.

'I made them,' he says proudly. 'They're Smartie cakes.'

Marcus stares down at the small face, beaming up at him. He thinks of his own boys and suddenly he is confused; angry. He wants to take the cake, to squeeze it into crumbs and hurl it on the ground; to grab Emma and crush her in his arms; to do some violent, destructive act. The old boy moves in closer but as Marcus turns on him, ready to lash out, he receives a shock. Beyond the wall, half-screened by the branches of a cherry tree, nerdy guy is watching him. His expression seems to hold some kind of secret knowledge – a warning even – and at the sight of him Marcus is utterly disorientated, even frightened. Perhaps, after all, he *is* being watched. Perhaps nerdy guy is actually MI5 – and now promotion, California, his whole future could be on the line.

All the fight suddenly drains away and he feels weak. His arm is taken, not gently, by the old man. His fingers bite into the bone and, though he smiles at Marcus, his eyes are as steely as his fingers.

'Time you were going, boy,' he says softly. 'I'll see you to your car.'

He allows the old man to lead him round the side of the cottage, to the car, and swing open the door. To his shame Marcus is aware that he is trembling; he feels sick. He slides into the driver's seat, picks up his bottle of water and drinks from it. The old man crouches by the open door watching him. His expression is gentle, the blue eyes, on a level with his own, almost kindly.

'You don't look well,' he says. 'You want to get back home now as soon as you can.'

'Home?' asks Marcus bleakly. 'Where the hell's that?'

The old man shakes his head. 'Wherever it is, boy, it isn't here. Get on with you now and don't come back.'

He slams the door and stands watching while Marcus starts the engine and drives away. He feels utterly defeated.

Driving slowly, carefully, he reaches Ashburton. Just outside the town, opposite the Peartree Cross garage, he pulls into the side of the road and sits quite still. He wills himself to be calm, to think clearly, though he feels humiliated and very depressed. He knows now that there's nowhere to go with Emma: twice he's been outwitted. How can he go back? What would he say? She's made it plain that she's changed her mind. It's over and he might as well face it. And as for nerdy guy . . . Marcus shakes his head. It seems utterly crazy that back there he actually thought nerdy guy might be MI5 but, in an uncharacteristic moment of self-awareness, Marcus suddenly sees that this small, insignificant man has become a symbol. It is as if he is being followed and watched by his conscience: reminded of how life could be if he faced up to certain weaknesses, sought help and took proper control of himself again.

He sits slumped at the wheel. So what now? Perhaps, after all, he will go home. He'll be a day early but the boys will welcome him. They'll be pleased to see him. They'll clamber on him and hug him, not old enough to understand anything except that he's Daddy, and they love him and he's come home to see them. And maybe Tasha will be like her old self: sarcastic and bossy, yes, but with that old affectionate way of seeing him as he is, and understanding, and still loving him. Perhaps he can pull the relationship back into some kind of shape; agree to seek help and persuade her to give it another go.

Marcus checks the mirror, pulls out and turns on to the A38; heading east towards Sidbury.

*

As they drive down from the moor, back into signal range, Jake's mobile pings and then pings again. Two messages.

'Somebody loves you,' says Kit, backing the car close to an unforgiving stone wall so that a nervous tourist can edge past.

Jake smiles and snaps open his phone: both messages are from Gaby. Perhaps now is the moment to bring his family into this relationship with Kit. It has to happen sooner or later and she seems so relaxed and confident; all is so good between them.

'They're from Gaby,' he tells her, keeping his voice quite casual.

'Gaby?'

'My youngest daughter, Gabrielle. She's expecting a baby at the end of next month. It's her first so she's getting a bit nervous. Understandable, I suppose. She's missing Madeleine.'

Kit says nothing and he talks on for a moment, outlining a thumbnail sketch of his daughters and their families. The tourist has driven gingerly past now, and Kit pulls back out into the lane but still she doesn't speak. There is something odd about her silence, as if a mental switch has been thrown and the current of happiness flowing between them has been suddenly switched off.

'We have to talk about them some time, Kit,' he says mildly. 'They're my family. We can't pretend they don't exist. Once they've had time to adjust I know they will be pleased.'

Out of the corner of his eye he sees her disbelieving expression, the quick sceptical lift of the brows, and he wonders how to move forward. He can understand how it must seem to Kit – that now Madeleine is dead she can be picked up again, dusted off and their friendship resumed – but she needs to remember that it isn't quite like that. She refused his proposals of marriage, gave the impression that she wanted to remain free, and then – when she changed her mind – it was too late. It's because of that he has a family to take into consideration. It's crucial that she accepts the present situation as it is and that they both behave truthfully.

Always aware of Kit's lifelong reluctance to commit, however, Jake fears he might have moved too quickly but all the same he's disappointed. It's been such a good afternoon, full of such wonderful memories, of reconnections. But they can't talk only of themselves and their shared past whilst ignoring the more recent years altogether. He can see that he must expect a few setbacks, a few unexpected wobbles, but at the same time he knows that he mustn't back down altogether. He is beginning to feel confident and he must be confident for both of them.

'I'm sure that they will be pleased,' he says gently, 'but not nearly so pleased as I was to find you so quickly. I think it's very amusing that you ran away to Mungo to hide from me and the first thing I see in Totnes is both of you having coffee together.'

She's smiling now, unable to repress the happy memory of that meeting, and he settles back in his seat with relief. He wonders if she is simply jealous of the girls, or if she sees them as a threat, or – most likely – that she doesn't think of them at all but has simply blanked them out. He is back in England; they are together again. She would prefer to remain in complete denial about his life and his family in Paris. Kit has always managed to hold the usual drudgeries of life at bay, to make interesting and original friends – he isn't the least surprised to find her in the company of Sir Mungo Kerslake – to get involved with crazy schemes. Only with Kit would he be trying to think of a way of losing somebody's SIM card from a stolen mobile phone. He thinks of Madeleine, tries to imagine her in the scene that he has witnessed today, and wants to burst out laughing. He has stepped through the looking-glass and is loving every minute of it.

Kit senses that Jake's decided to give up on the family theme for the moment and takes a breath of relief. She's not ready to go there yet. Odd, and really worrying, how the mention of Gabrielle's name threw her into such a panic. It was because of Gabrielle, all those years ago, that Jake cancelled their dinner together and flew back to Paris. He won't remember that, of course, but it is as if Gabrielle is the synonym for his life and family. The scene rewinds itself, fresh and painful . . .

'I'm at the airport,' he said. 'There's been an emergency. Gabrielle has been taken ill. Madeleine took her home to Paris and she's in hospital. I'm booked on the next flight.'

No future for us, he said back then, she thinks. But now they have another chance. She tries to imagine herself meeting Jake's family, submitting to their scrutiny, their judgement. She tries to visualize Jake the Rake as the family man, dandling babies on his knee and playing with his grandchildren. This is not the Jake she knows. How would she fit into this family; the outsider, the foreigner, the new stepmother? Even if she had the least inclination to do so they would surely resent any attempt on her part to take Madeleine's place. So how is it to be done? She needs Jake to be part of her life, she wants it to be the way it was; she has no desire to be the new add-on to a big foreign family.

Misery threatens to engulf her and she feels resentment for the unknown Gabrielle, who has once again threatened to destroy a new beginning in their relationship. Kit wonders what the texts were about. Did they question him? 'Have you found her yet?' Were they calling him home, telling him how she missed him?

Jake is talking again, and Kit makes a very great effort to raise her spirits. Gradually a measure of ease between them is resumed as Kit tries to push her fears to one side, to block them out, but she knows that sooner or later she is going to have to confront the fact of Jake's family. Somehow a mode of living must be created that can embrace them all whilst leaving her able to be sure of Jake; to trust him absolutely. He's been back for such a very short while that she needs to feel more secure but, at the same time, she doesn't want to make the same mistakes again. At the moment it's all great fun, rather like a game, but what happens when reality sets in?

The joy of the afternoon has evaporated. Fear of her own inadequacies is looming larger than her faith in Jake's love.

CHAPTER TWENTY

When they get back to the smithy, Jake wanders around the courtyard and Mungo watches appreciatively whilst leaning on the bottom half of the stable door.

'You are a very lucky girl,' he tells Kit, who sits in the kitchen behind him. 'He's gorgeous. I can't imagine why you wanted to run away from him.'

'Yes, you can,' she answers. 'You know very well why I wanted to hide. Part of me still does. How on earth is it going to work, Mungo?'

He is silent for a moment, well aware that Kit is working up to one of her panic attacks.

'I mean,' she continues, 'let's face it, I'm not cut out for family life. I don't have the necessary unselfishness for it. I like things my way and I'm worried in case I'm too old to change now.'

'Well, I do sympathize, sweetie,' he answers. 'Jesus wanted me for a sunbeam but we could never agree the job spec. I really do think that it's going to have to be a compromise.'

He doesn't turn round but he can imagine the expression on Kit's face.

'After all,' he goes on, 'Jake's got a family. He loves them. You can't just pretend they aren't there. But you don't have to try to be a second mother, either. They won't want that, anyway. They're not babies. His daughters are grown-up women. Has it occurred to you that they might be very pleased to see him with someone who takes some of the burden from their shoulders? Parents can get to be a bit of a worry, can't they? They're probably thrilled to think he'll be somebody else's responsibility.'

Another silence.

'So what's brought this on?' he asks. 'It was all wonderful when you set off after lunch.'

'Texts,' says Kit. 'Texts from Gaby. She's the youngest one, about to have her first baby, missing Papa.'

'Of course she is,' protests Mungo. 'Come on, sweetie. Use your imagination. Her mother's dead. First child due. Of course she's missing her father. What's the matter with you?'

'I don't know. I think part of it was that it was Gaby who was ill that time when Jake and I were just getting it back together and he went off without a backward look. It hurt, Mungo. It was weird how it kind of resonated when he mentioned her.'

Staring out into the courtyard Mungo is beginning to see more problems than he'd first envisaged. All Kit's insecurities are resurfacing and she and Jake haven't had long enough together to establish a solid new relationship.

'He loves you,' he says strongly. 'That's what really matters. He really loves you, Kit. Please don't be foolish and throw it away for a second time. You told me that you were the one who wouldn't commit, not Jake. OK, so he moved on and now he's got a family out there. But at the first opportunity he's come back to find you. For God's sake, sweetie, don't be a complete idiot all your life. Take a day off occasionally and behave like a grown-up.'

To his relief she laughs.

'Thanks, Mungo!'

'I know, I know,' he says. 'Pots and kettles . . . I just don't want you to miss out. You're so right together, and it's going to be such fun. Trust your uncle Mungo. Oh, and by the way, Archie has invited us all up for drinks this evening.'

'What! Oh God. It'll be so embarrassing. They have no idea about Jake.'

'They've got to find out some time. Do get a grip.' Mungo straightens up. 'He's coming in.'

He opens the lower half of the door and Jake comes into the kitchen. Mungo glances at Kit, who has a rather dazed expression. Clearly she is anticipating the forthcoming drinks party.

'*Courage, ma brave,*' he mutters. 'You've got to practise on someone. I can't wait to see Camilla's face.'

'I still think you might have asked,' Camilla is saying, as she carries glasses and nibbles out to the veranda.

'I can't see that it makes the least bit of difference whether it's a man or a woman,' answers Archie impatiently. 'Honestly, darling, do stop fussing about it. You should have phoned Mungo and asked him if you're that worried.'

Camilla lights the candles. She'd already thought of that but it seemed rather foolish, especially if Kit happened to be near at hand when he answered. It's simply that she likes to be prepared, to know what form the evening might take. 'A friend from Paris,' Archie said – which could mean all sorts of things.

'They're here,' Archie says, as Mungo's familiar call rings out and he hurries through to meet them, and now she can hear Kit's voice and another male voice greeting Archie and she experiences a slight sense of relief that it isn't going to be a smart sophisticated Frenchwoman who might make her feel dowdy. A Frenchman can be relied upon to be polite.

And indeed, this handsome, very sexy Frenchman doesn't make her feel the least bit dowdy. *Au contraire*, as he takes her hand and smiles at her she feels rather flustered, in a good way, and pleased that she changed into a clean shirt and put a silk scarf around her neck. At the very least it will hide the scraggy dinosaur effect she notices when she looks in the mirror. But this very good-looking Jake seems oblivious of the negative aspects of growing older and concentrates on her, laughing at her little witticisms and flattering her with his attention. Camilla finds that she is responding to him, even flirting with him, and she looks round for Kit lest she might misunderstand and be upset. But no; Kit is beaming at her, lifting her glass as though she thoroughly understands the effect that a man like Jake must have upon someone who lives with Archie and two springer spaniels and doesn't get out much.

Camilla pushes her blond hair – slightly assisted these days but still blond – behind her ears and refills Jake's glass.

Archie watches with amusement. Camilla is really enjoying herself and he is filled with an enormous affection for her.

When she tucks her hair behind her ears like that she reminds him of the young Camilla he fell in love with all those years ago. Suddenly he feels stronger, more able, and filled with courage. All in an instant he makes up his mind. He decides he isn't ready to leave the place where he and Camilla have lived all their married lives, where they brought up their children and have been so happy.

Kit is now talking to Camilla and Jake, whilst Mungo is selecting a nibble and fending off the dogs. Archie moves to stand beside him.

'I've been thinking about what you were saying earlier,' he says, keeping his voice down. 'Thanks for your offer, Mungo, I really appreciate it but I've decided to put in for planning permission to build in the orchard. It will bring in money without splitting up the estate and it gives us a breathing space.'

He's aware that Mungo is staring at him rather oddly, almost in alarm, and he frowns enquiringly at him.

'You mustn't worry about Philip and Billy,' he says. 'It'll be a bit noisy, and I know they love the old orchard, but it's not the end of the world.'

'But will you get planning permission?' asks Mungo. 'Honestly, I wish you'd just let me help you.'

'I'm sure we will.' Archie is faintly irritated by Mungo's lack of enthusiasm. After all, this maintains the status quo and doesn't require anyone to fork out. 'The orchard has its own access. It's the obvious thing to do. No, I've made up my mind. Let's drink to it.'

But before he can fill Mungo's glass, Camilla calls to him, suggesting that everyone stays for supper, and the moment passes.

*

'Are you OK?' Kit asks Mungo. He looks odd, a bit shell-shocked, and she's anxious about him. Everyone's having such a wonderful time and she's feeling confident again; happy. It's as if Camilla's response to Jake has made her see him as other women do. She sees anew his warmth and quirkiness; his ability to relate, and it's as if she's falling in love with him all over again. She wants Mungo to be pleased about it; to be happy for her. Instead he looks abstracted, rather as if he's bracing himself to do something he's dreading.

'Jake's going to have to stay overnight in the barn,' she tells Mungo. 'Is that OK? He's had too much to drink to be able to drive. You did say it might be a possibility.'

She waits for Mungo to make a joke about it, as he did earlier, to say that Jake had better lock his door, but Mungo just nods and says it's OK so that Kit feels even more anxious and her high spirits subside a little.

Camilla is beside her and Mungo moves away. 'I like your Jake, Kit,' she murmurs in her ear. 'He is so dishy. I suppose we couldn't share him, could we? Come and help me get some supper. I want to hear all about it.'

Kit glances up, catches Jake's eye and he gives her a little wink. Smiling back at him, she follows Camilla into the kitchen.

Mungo leans against a pillar at the edge of the veranda, staring out into the dusk, and Jake moves to stand beside him.

'Did I pass?' he murmurs. 'How many marks out of ten?'

He sees Mungo smile almost unwillingly, as if his thoughts are far away, and he looks very sad.

'Oh, full marks, I think,' he answers. 'You've certainly made a hit with Camilla.'

Jake feels the weight of Mungo's spirits, the effort he is making to be cheerful, and wonders what has cast him down.

'I was trying to make Kit jealous,' he jokes, hoping to make him laugh.

Mungo shakes his head. 'That won't work. It's your daughters you have to watch out for there. You're not out of the wood yet, you know.'

'I'm well aware of it but I don't know how to play it. What would you do?'

'I'd marry Kit at the earliest opportunity, present it to your daughters as a *fait accompli* and then settle down to making it work. Kit will feel secure and your daughters will soon see that nothing has really changed. She won't want to interfere but you simply mustn't give her time to dither.'

Jake looks at him, impressed. 'You make it sound so easy.'

'It can be if you put your mind to it. I hear you're staying the night.'

'You did say that it would be OK.'

'Oh, it is. I was just wondering . . .'

'What?' Jake stares at him suspiciously. 'If you're wondering what I think you are, Mungo, you can forget it. Apart from anything else I wouldn't be able to face you over the eggs and bacon tomorrow morning.'

'That's the trouble with you Frogs,' says Mungo. 'So sensitive. But perhaps you're right.'

Jake remembers Kit saying, 'I just don't want us to be his next production,' and he smiles to himself.

'I can manage my own seduction scene, thanks,' he says. 'Not that I'm questioning your director's skills, of course, Sir Mungo.'

'I shall watch and learn,' says Mungo drily. 'It's always good to see an expert at work. Only, for all our sakes, do get on with it.'

Philip sits on the bench outside the back door, waiting for Star, who is having her late night run in the orchard. Billy has been in bed awhile, contented with his day: physio in the morning and the tea party in the afternoon.

They both enjoyed the tea party, were invigorated by the company of Emma and the children, and then that young officer turned up. Sharp, he looked, ready for trouble. It was clear that Emma was frightened of him in some way. She leaned forward and spoke very low and quickly. 'Don't go,' she said. 'Don't leave us alone with him.'

Just for a moment he thought that the young fellow, Marcus, was going to do something silly. When Philip gripped his arm he felt him trembling; the rage in him burning like a flame. Then, just for a brief moment, he remembered Ralph, his own spasm of fury and the fatal twist of the wheel, and he held on tighter, pulling the younger man away. And suddenly the fight went out of him, he almost collapsed, and allowed himself to be led away like a child.

When he went back to the party little Joe was showing Billy his trains and Emma was watching, though her thoughts were far away.

'He's on his way home,' he told her. 'He won't be back.'

'I hope not,' she said. She looked like Izzy then; that same old look of despair, humiliation and regret. 'I've been such a fool, Philip.'

He felt the familiar sensations of helpless love, of protectiveness. How strange it was that Izzy should come back to him through this girl.

'We're all fools sometimes,' he said, not knowing how to comfort her. 'Part of being human.'

She smiled then, rather sadly but a smile all the same. 'You sound like Mungo,' she said.

'Well, then.' He watched Billy examining one of Joe's engines, turning it carefully in his good hand while Joe stood at his knee, talking.

'Don't go just yet,' Emma said. 'Or – is Billy OK? Should you be getting him home?'

'Reckon he'll do a while yet,' he answered comfortably. 'How about another cup of tea?'

Now, sitting on the bench, he remembers the glow of pleasure, even triumph, he felt at seeing her smile of gratitude: an old lion defending his territory, his family. And he hopes that Marcus has reached home safely – wherever home is.

'Nice little maid,' Billy said contentedly, as Philip wheeled him home. 'Nice little family. You did well there, boy. Chancing his arm, was he?'

'Trying it on,' Philip said. 'Showed him up. He won't be back.'

Odd how he felt confident about that. No young man likes to be humiliated in front of a young woman by an older man. He still felt strong; invigorated by the encounter. And then, just after they got back inside, young Andy arrived with a proposition. He sat at the kitchen table, eager and strong and young, and told his grandfather his hopes and dreams.

'I've been thinking about stuff, Granddad. I'd like to make a start on my own and I was talking to Dad about whether I could, you know, move down here with you and Uncle Billy, and get the farm up and working again. Get some stock back in. I'd still keep up my contract work and the logging, but then later, if I made a go of it and Archie agreed, and you were OK with it, I could take over the farm tenancy after you.'

He talked sensibly, seeing the need to diversify, but his love for the place was clear and his enthusiasm was catching. Philip promised to think about it, said he'd have a word with Archie, and now he sits wondering how Mungo is planning to work out the problem in the orchard. If Andy were to take over the farm it might never arise – but the risk would always be there.

Star appears out of the shadows and pushes her head against his knee. He fondles her ears and murmurs to her: 'Good girl, then. Good girl.' She presses close to him and together they watch the moon rise beyond the hedge, sailing up above the ash trees, pouring its light into this valley where Judds have farmed for generations.

Supposing Mags were to be right and Archie were to build houses in the orchard so that, instead of this deep silence and velvet darkness, there were to be the noise of televisions, the blaze of lights, cars coming and going? For the moment even the discovery of Ralph's body and the scandal that might follow seem as nothing when set against the destruction of his own small piece of this ancient valley.

Philip gets up and, with Star close beside him, goes inside.

*

James is packing ready for his weekend back in Oxford. He's looking forward to being at home with Sally, telling her about the progress of the book. Actually he's beginning to wonder if there's much more to be achieved here. The peace and simplicity is magical but he suspects that he needs a bit more action; a touch of city life, the sound of police sirens, a sight of feral youth. Nothing happens here to stimulate his imagination when it comes to the seamier side of life. It's been very useful to drive and walk around the location, and it's a real blessing to have the space to write for as long as he likes whenever the moment strikes, but perhaps he's ready to move on. He needs a bigger canvas, a much wider world, so as to touch the hearts and minds of people; to change even one life for good. This is his secret longing: to make a difference. But it won't happen here in this forgotten valley.

He goes downstairs to write to Sally.

Looking forward to getting home. I've decided to make an early start so I shall definitely be back in time for lunch! I want to get on this evening with some writing while I've got a few more ideas fresh in my mind. You know what it's like! Then I shall be ready for a break. In fact, I'm wondering if you could come down for a couple of days next week just to have some time here together before I finally pack up. You've got a few days' holiday due to you, haven't you? We could have that little party I talked about and invite all the neighbours. I know Camilla would be delighted to see you. I think she's secretly hoping that she might appear in the book but I can't imagine any of them fitting into my character list, let alone being involved in my plot! It's a very stereotypical

little hamlet – apart from Sir Mungo, of course, but I suspect
he spends much of his time in London. I've just had a chat
with Emma next door. They were having a little tea party in
the garden with old Billy and Philip when I got home earlier.
I had a little peek over the wall and you'll never guess who
was there! The weird chap I've been seeing around. All good
mates together, friend of the family, so that's all cleared up. I
couldn't believe my eyes for a moment and just stood there
staring at him in amazement. Hope he didn't think I was
being rude. Anyway, I went round after they'd all gone to
say I was off again and to mention that we might be having
a party when I got back. Emma's very nice, very laid-back,
and the little boy offered me a Smartie cake. You'll like him
and the baby. We'll probably have to have them at the party,
too, if she can't get a babysitter! Still, it'll give them all a
bit of excitement in their quiet lives. They all know about
the books and I think I'm almost as much of a celeb as Sir
Mungo!! Looking forward to hearing all your news.

Back to work. See you soon. J xx

CHAPTER TWENTY-ONE

Emma wakens early, even before Joe or Dora stirs. She goes out quietly, listens for a moment at the bottom of the attic stairs, and creeps down into the kitchen. The cakes have all been eaten but the painting of Bozzy and Sam is fixed by magnets to the fridge. Emma opens the door into the garden and stands outside, breathing in the cool air, seeing the monochrome flicker of a magpie's wing high in the beech tree.

They Skyped Rob last evening; Joe chattering away excitedly about his morning with Camilla and the Smartie cakes, whilst Dora waved her fists and crowed, and then Emma told Rob about Mungo and Philip and the tea party.

'So did you go to the zoo with Marcus?' he asked later – and she was able to dismiss it quite nonchalantly, saying that it had all been a rather silly joke, and then asking whether he thought that his mother might like to come for a visit.

'I'm sure she'd like to see the cottage and I know how much she's missing your dad. What d'you think?'

'She'd love it,' he said. 'That's a brilliant idea, Ems. I only wish I could be there too.'

'So do we,' she said. 'But you will be before too long.'

Then they talked of what they'd do when he came home. Joe showed him the picture he'd painted of Sammy and Boz and then it was over and she had to deal with an overexcited bath-time, and Joe becoming suddenly weepy at bedtime because he wanted Daddy home.

Now, Emma thinks of Marcus, how Philip dealt with him, and she wonders if he is right when he says that Marcus will not be back. She longs to believe it, her instinct tells her that it is true, but she daren't trust it. She almost feels that she doesn't deserve to be let off so lightly. It was such luck that Philip and Billy were with her when he turned up, and amazing that Philip was so ready to come to her defence – rather as Mungo had earlier. He phoned to tell her that Marcus' mobile was now at the bottom of Venford Reservoir and that she could relax.

How angry Marcus must be: how frustrated and humiliated. Two old men, Mungo and Philip, have bested him. She can feel sympathy for Marcus now. After all, she encouraged him with her silly flirtatiousness; she is as much to blame. She wonders where he is, hoping that he will be going to see his boys and Tasha, and praying that perhaps he might be able to have some loving future with them. She can see now that all this has probably been an attempt on his part to restore his wounded pride; to show that he is still love-worthy.

As she stands in the garden, in the early morning peace, she regrets her foolishness and knows it is only because of

Mungo's support and Philip's quick reactions that she has got away with it. She's been let off the hook. Now, she and Rob and the children will be able to be happy here in this cottage, surrounded by their new friends. She is safe and free.

Kit is awake, too. She lies in bed, thinking about Jake and how the three of them and Mopsa walked back home through the late summer evening. They linked arms. Kit, between Mungo and Jake, was aware of the man on each side of her and of their tensions and preoccupations. She could guess at Jake's thoughts, his mental attempts to see a way forward for them both, but she was still unable to detect a reason for Mungo's preoccupation.

Back at the smithy he took Jake to inspect his quarters in the barn and then went off to bed, leaving Kit and Jake feeling awkward and embarrassed. Kit found it utterly impossible to be natural and easy in Mungo's kitchen. It was out of the question either to invite Jake upstairs or to follow him into the barn.

Instead, she muttered something silly, kissed his cheek and went upstairs with Mopsa trailing her, leaving Jake to find his way to his room.

Now, after a restless night, she makes a decision. If she wants a future with Jake she must stop allowing her nerves to get the better of her: she must take a risk. The next step needs to be taken, not in her London flat or in Jake's Paris apartment, but on neutral ground. It needs to be taken spontaneously and with generosity, and she wants to be the one to make the first move: to make the commitment.

Kit remembers Mungo's comment: 'When you get old you

need a good sense of humour when it comes to sex.'

She gets out of bed and stares at herself in the mirror, picking up her brush to smooth out the tangles in her fine, feathery hair. She stares a bit longer, makes an encouraging face at herself, and turns away. Pulling on her dressing gown, Kit goes downstairs, leaving Mopsa still asleep on the bed. Quietly she slips into the kitchen and passes through the inter-connecting door to the barn. Outside Jake's bedroom door she hesitates, then she turns the handle and goes in. He is sitting propped against the pillows, a mug of coffee in his hand, and he begins to laugh as she shuts the door behind her.

'What kept you?' he asks, putting down the mug.

And she laughs, too, as she gets in beside him and huddles into his arms.

Mungo sees Kit's bedroom door is open and Mopsa curled on the empty bed. He calls to her and she raises her head and then jumps off the bed and follows him downstairs. There is no sign of Kit or Jake, and Mungo opens the back door for Mopsa and makes coffee, which he drinks standing up. Part of him thinks of Kit and Jake in the barn with relief that the next difficult step has probably been taken, but uppermost in his mind is the interview he must have with Archie. He has spent most of the night rehearsing the scene, just as Philip described it to him, but he knows that he must speak to Archie quickly now before he makes his move and applies for planning permission, and he is overcome with dread.

He knows where he will find him, though. Archie will take the dogs up on to the moor for their morning walk and Mungo has every intention of being there to intercept him so that they can talk in private. He also has some idea that being outside will be advantageous; that out there, on the moor, Archie will be more open to a forgiving and understanding approach than in their father's study with his stern, unbending influence all around them.

He swallows down his coffee, picks up Mopsa's lead and goes out into the lane, passing the old Herm, turning up the track that leads on to the open moor.

Archie stands in the heather, staring at his younger brother, too shocked to speak. The dogs run together, higher up on the ancient sheep tracks, barking for the sheer joy of it.

'I knew nothing about it,' Mungo repeats. 'Nothing at all until Philip told me the day before yesterday. It was an accident, Archie. I'm not condoning it, for God's sake, but try to see it in the right context. Philip panicked and Billy took control. And you have to admit that Philip's right when he says the media would have had a field day and all of us would have been involved. Me, you, Camilla and the boys. Once they started asking questions Izzy would have completely buckled. It would all have come out. The baby, the rows, me hitting Ralph.'

'But why were there no questions asked at the time? How was he just allowed to vanish?'

Mungo takes a deep breath. Archie is very angry and he must tread warily.

'First, remember, Ralph had no family. Second, the whole point was that he was leaving to go to America the following week. Izzy told him about the baby just when he'd been invited to audition for some show in New York. Clearly he decided to leave her to it and go, but he didn't tell anyone until the very last minute. He and I were rehearsing in Manchester and Izzy was in Bristol, staying with a friend, when he broke the news. She phoned in floods of tears, absolutely desperate, pleading with me to make Ralph change his mind. I decided to chance one last throw. Ralph was all set to leave for London so I drove him down here, picking Izzy up on the way through Bristol. He told me it was pointless, that he had no intention of acknowledging the child, but I suppose he felt he had nothing to lose. I think it almost amused him. Ralph could be very cruel. Well, it didn't work. In fact, it made things worse. He was brutal to Izzy and in the end I told him to get out. I've told you the rest, but the point was that Ralph was leaving us. He had his case with him. Nobody expected to see him again. Not for a bit, anyway. Of course we all wondered what had happened when he dropped so completely out of sight but America's a big place and we didn't expect him back. Well, Izzy did. She hoped he'd change his mind and come home. And then she lost the baby a few weeks later.

'The point is we all believed he'd gone. Taken the train to London, caught the plane and was out in America. Yes, we all said from time to time that it was a bit hurtful that he never sent so much as a card, but none of us imagined he was dead.'

Archie still stares angrily at him. 'But what the hell do we do?'

'I've been thinking about it ever since Philip told me and I come back to my original offer. If we want to prevent any future scandal I suggest that I buy the farm from you at open-market value and you put a restrictive covenant on the orchard that forbids any kind of development. If I die your boys will inherit but the covenant remains in place.'

'Are you serious? And that's it? Put a covenant on the orchard and quietly forget that Ralph's buried on my land?'

Mungo watches his elder brother. He's seen Archie like this before: he hates anything illegal, underhand. It will be a terrible thing for him to let this remain unresolved.

'What's to be gained?' Mungo asks quietly. 'Justice for Ralph at the expense of Philip's freedom and my reputation? And what about you and Camilla getting involved? Can you imagine the press crawling all over this valley, Archie? OK, Philip killed Ralph. It was manslaughter. But you might say it was because Ralph left Izzy so brutally and refused to take any responsibility that she lost her child six weeks later. A life for a life. It's forty years ago, Archie. It was an accident; it was freezing cold and the Land Rover slid on the ice, but it would be very difficult to prove that now, wouldn't it? Can you picture Billy and Philip in court? And then, of course, there would be other people who would remember the rows Ralph and Izzy had, and how closely connected I was to them both. The media would embellish the whole story with lies and lurid speculation. To what end?'

He can see Archie struggling with it: his heart telling him one thing, his head another.

'But what am I supposed to say to Philip?'

There is a little silence. 'Perhaps nothing to begin with,' suggests Mungo. 'Until you've come to terms with it. That's assuming you agree with my idea.'

'I have no choice,' mutters Archie angrily. 'I can't risk Camilla. Or you.'

'I started it all,' Mungo said. 'Bringing them down here, getting so closely involved with them.'

Archie shakes his head impatiently. 'Don't be a fool. We loved seeing your friends, especially Izzy. I have to say I never cared much for Ralph.' He looks quickly at Mungo, guiltily. 'Not that I'd have wished that on him, poor devil.'

'Of course not. Are we agreed then? I buy the farm and when we do the legal stuff you put the covenant in place. You know about all that better than I do. It will give you some ready cash to make up for what you might have got from developing the orchard, and to do the work you need to do and take some pressure off.'

Still Archie hesitates. Mungo waits as his brother tries to deal with his conscience.

'I don't want Camilla to know, though,' he says.

And Mungo sighs inwardly with relief and knows the battle is won.

'I agree. It's very hard having a secret like this but the fewer people know, the better. I wish it hadn't been necessary for either of us to know.'

'Tough for Philip,' says Archie unexpectedly. 'He's been living with it all these years, poor devil. Trust Billy to get him into trouble.'

'I think that Billy thought he was protecting us all. He could see just what a disaster it could be and that's why he stopped Philip calling for help. Not that it would have done Ralph any good. It was too late.'

He can see that Archie is nearly convinced. They turn and begin to walk back to the house together, the dogs running ahead.

'The old valley's seen worse than this,' Mungo says. 'At least it was an accident. Can you imagine how many bodies must be buried around here from way back? The feuds. The battles.' He glances at his brother. 'Will you be OK – you know what I mean – having to go back to Camilla and be ordinary?'

'I don't have much choice,' replies Archie grumpily. 'Look, come up later on and we'll discuss the details about you buying the farm.' He hesitates. 'And thanks, Mungo. It's very generous of you. From that point of view Camilla will be delighted. She was dreading the thought of leaving.'

'It was very generous of you to give me the smithy all those years ago. I just wish it hadn't finished like this.'

Archie nods, aware of Mungo's concern. 'It's OK. I'll get over it. I just need time to come to terms with it. See you later.'

When Mungo gets back to the smithy, Jake and Kit are sitting at the table eating breakfast. They look at him with expressions of self-conscious contentment and amusement. He grins at them: it's as if several weights have been lifted from his heart at once.

'All well, my little love-birds?' he asks. 'Do I deduce that my humble barn has been hallowed in my absence?'

'Mind your own business,' answers Jake, grinning back at him, remembering the conversation from last evening as he leans to pat Mopsa.

'Where have you been?' asks Kit. 'You don't usually take Mopsa out this early. What are you up to?'

'Mind your own business,' Mungo says. 'You're not the only one who can have a secret assignation, you know. Pour me some coffee and tell me when and where the wedding will be taking place.'

*

James locks the cottage door and puts his laptop and his case into the car. As he drives past the farm he sees Philip in the yard and slows, opening the window.

'Just off for the weekend,' he calls. 'Back Monday morning. I'm hoping Sally will come down with me for a few days.'

Philip comes across to the car, smiles at him.

'Finished your book, have you?'

James laughs at the idea of writing a book in a matter of weeks. 'I wish. No, but all the important notes are down. Lots of stuff about the location. It's a good place to work. So tranquil. You have no idea how lucky you are to be out of all the strife and noise and disputes of city life.'

Philip still smiles his slow, sweet smile but his eyes narrow as if he is amused by something James can't quite guess at. James begins to feel faintly uncomfortable though he doesn't know why.

'Sal and I thought we might have a little party,' he says. 'Just to see you all before we go. Everyone's been so kind.'

'That'll be good,' agrees Philip. 'Nice to have a bit of excitement for a change.'

'Yes,' says James awkwardly. 'That's all good then. See you next week.'

He puts the car in gear and drives away, glancing in the mirror. Philip is still standing in the lane, his hand raised in farewell, and he seems to be laughing. James shakes his head. Local yokels. Still, he's a lovely guy and the party will be fun. He slows at the junction, turns right and drives away towards Oxford and to Sally.

CHAPTER TWENTY-TWO

In the laundry cupboard, after breakfast, Camilla hums to herself as she sorts sheets and pillowcases, preparing for another family invasion at the weekend. Mentally she plans menus, makes shopping lists, devises entertainment, and underneath all this joy is the contentment that Archie and Mungo have come to an arrangement that means that Mungo will buy the farm and Archie will be able to refurbish the cottage, to let it out – perhaps to another family – and do some repairs on the house. He seems a little preoccupied, rather quiet, but this is probably because it's hard to let go of the reins and also that he feels guilty about Mungo paying out for something he doesn't really need.

After all the anxieties about where the money will come from to make necessary repairs, the arguments about down-sizing, she's so relieved at this outcome that she's able to feel a bit selfish about Mungo's generosity.

'You gave him the smithy,' she reminded Archie, 'and we know that he's not short of a penny, darling, and he'll be getting the rent from the farm. Why not just accept his offer gratefully? It's probably good for him to feel an equal part of it all at last. It wasn't fair of your father to cut him out so completely. You've worked very hard to keep things going all these years and now Mungo can feel that he's doing his bit, too.'

Archie nodded, agreed with her, but she could see that there was something on his mind that he wasn't prepared to talk about.

She knows Archie of old and she's decided to back off and let him sort it out for himself. Just at the moment, with the family coming, she has enough to think about; not least the prospect of Kit's new man.

'What do you think of him?' she asked Archie, after Kit and Jake and Mungo had gone back to the smithy after supper.

'Bit of a surprise,' he answered. 'I like him.' He grinned at her. 'You were obviously taken with him.'

She couldn't deny it; she thought he was gorgeous.

'Much, much better than Awful Michael,' she said. 'Lucky old Kit. Apparently she and Jake had quite a serious thing going when they were young and then something went wrong. His wife died earlier this year and he came back to find Kit. It's rather sweet, isn't it? Perhaps Jake is why she never got married. We always wondered, didn't we? I think it's lovely.'

She also wondered if Archie might be a bit put out that Kit would no longer be available for days out on the river, that he would have to share her in the future, but Archie was in good spirits. They stood together on the veranda watching the dogs running down across the lawn, following a scent beneath the moonlight, and Archie had put an arm around her shoulder.

'I was thinking tonight,' he said. 'We can't leave the old place just yet. We'll stick it out a bit longer.'

It was the next day he told her about Mungo's plan, but his high spirits had subsided and he was preoccupied, though he wouldn't admit to it.

Now, as Camilla passes the landing window, her arms full of sheets, she looks down on the veranda and across the lawn to the stream. Soon the children will be here. There will be games, delicious meals, walks along the river and in the woods. They will want to go sailing and this will distract Archie from his preoccupation. She goes to prepare the bedrooms, to make the house ready for her family, and her heart is full of happy anticipation.

Billy sits dreaming in the late afternoon sunshine in the orchard. His thoughts merge and then flow apart like river water around the stones of his memories; future and past and present seem all one to him.

Mungo's buying the farm from Archie, Philip tells him, with a covenant that prevents any building in the orchard. All their problems solved in one go. Billy isn't surprised: he knew Mungo would have a plan. Mungo always has a plan. Way back, when they were all young, it was Mungo who could be counted on to think of some clever little trick to get them out of a mess. For himself, he'd never avoided trouble, liked a bit of action, but Mungo was always there to back him up. Still is: he's got a lot of respect for Mungo. That's why he didn't want any trouble over Ralph. It was an accident, Philip was in no state to deal with it, and Billy knew that the best way was to bury the evidence. And he was right: nobody was going to benefit by the law sticking their noses in; the newspapers turning up. It wasn't only Philip who would have paid so heavily, but Mungo, too. Perhaps Philip should have been punished for that wild, black moment of rage, for losing it, but it was still an accident and the ones who would have suffered most would have been Mungo and Izzy. Mungo gay, Izzy pregnant with Ralph's child. Their public would never have forgiven them: they'd have been crucified. Of course Philip's had a problem dealing with his conscience all these years – his guilt has seen to it that he's suffered – but at least now he can be safe in the knowledge that Ralph can't harm anybody else.

Then, just when they were enjoying the knowledge that their secret was safe with Archie and Mungo, young Andy arrived, full of eagerness with his plans for the future, looking just like Philip when he was a boy and they were planning to take over the farm from their father.

They had a cup of tea to celebrate, decided which room Andy should use as his bedroom, pulled his leg about how hard he was going to have to work. Then Billy left them to it, discussing how it was to be done, Philip looking just as excited as the boy. Philip pushed him in his wheelchair into the orchard and left him with Star for company, then went back to Andy while Billy dozed in the sunshine.

And at some point, later, Mungo appeared and sat with him and he said to Mungo: 'I didn't say nort.'

Mungo took his hand and held it and said: 'I know you didn't, Billy. You were always a mate.'

And now Billy sighs, remembering how they struggled with the old Herm, that long ago March evening; digging down amongst the loosened roots of the ash tree that thrust deep into the ancient Devon bank, burying the small oilskin-wrapped bundle, and then dragging the old Herm back into its place. The tree was rotten, dangerous, and Philip had taken it down earlier in the week, dislodging the stones in the bank so that it needed rebuilding.

They kneeled side by side, silent for a moment, in the cold, wet spring evening.

'Not a word, remember,' Mungo said. 'I promised Izzy. She trusts you and Philip completely, but even Philip doesn't know about this.'

'I shan't say nort.'

Mungo leaned forward and brushed some crumbs of earth from the old Herm's face.

'She wanted a burial place and a memorial stone for her baby, Billy. You can't blame her for that, can you? I promised we'd see to it. I wouldn't let her travel down – she's not well enough – but it had to be done quickly.'

They scrambled up together. Mungo looked tired and Billy laid an arm along his shoulders.

'Nobody's fault, boy, that the baby came early.'

Mungo shook his head. 'Probably not, though she's been distraught ever since Ralph left. There's been no word from him.'

'She's best out of that,' he answered, thinking of Ralph lying in the orchard. 'You, too.'

'You're probably right.' Mungo bent down again to touch the old Herm, rubbing his thumb along the smiling lips. 'We'll plant some wild flowers along here, Billy, once the wall's finished. Violets and primroses and vetch.'

A thrush began to sing, poignant and beautiful amongst the blackthorn, and Billy pretended not to see the tears in Mungo's eyes. They walked back to the smithy together, his arm still round Mungo's shoulders, feeling his grief, remaining silent.

Now, Billy dreams in the afternoon sunshine amongst the ripening fruit, with Star curled at his feet: all will be well.

In the early evening, Mungo walks beside the stream with Mopsa. Kit and Jake have driven away to London, full of plans for the future. They intend to get married as quickly and as privately as possible and then they will be dividing their time between Paris and London.

'And coming down here to see you, of course,' said Kit. 'Though we'll all be together in London, too. It's going to be such fun, Mungo.'

'And you must come to Paris,' added Jake. 'How proud I shall be to introduce Sir Mungo Kerslake to my friends and family.'

'It seems to be the best solution to begin with,' said Kit. 'To try to decide what works best for us. We both have our own families to consider.'

Mungo was seized with a great sense of relief to hear Kit talk so calmly about families.

'Well, there you are,' he said to Jake. 'How does it feel to be bringing so much joy to us all?'

'Scary,' Jake answered promptly. 'I'm relying on your support.'

Mungo waved them off cheerfully but he's sad to lose Kit; that particular, close relationship he's had with her for so long.

It will be different from now on, but he is happy for her, and for Jake.

There is change in the air. Mist rises, curls and drifts above the water. The rowan berries glow like tiny lamps and the rosebay willowherb that grows along the river bank is beginning to fade. Mungo thinks of Izzy, and of Ralph and their child, but now at last he can think of them with some measure of peace. He scattered Izzy's ashes in the lane, close to the old Herm, and now it is as if the three of them are all together in death as they never were in life. The bitterness that has remained with him all these years, when he never heard from Ralph – not a postcard, not a telephone call – has vanished. If he'd lived, Ralph might have repented, returned to them; who can tell?

Mopsa gives a little bark of welcome and Bozzy and Sam come running round the bend in the path. Archie follows, hands in pockets, his face sombre.

'I was thinking about Ralph,' Mungo says, charging in where angels fear to tread, seeing his brother's mood and deciding to tackle him head on. 'We all felt rather cross, didn't we, that he just walked out on us after all those years? I feel happier now, knowing that he might have regretted his departure, missed us. You know?'

'You mean you'd rather Philip had run him over and buried him in the orchard than think badly of him?' asks Archie irritably.

Mungo bursts out laughing. 'I suppose so, yes.'

Archie shakes his head. 'You're hopeless. You always were, even as a boy. You and old Billy. You lived your whole childhood in a different world; no proper morals, no sense of responsibility, and then, dammit, you went and made a lucrative career out of it.'

Mungo claps him on the shoulder. 'I know. Terrible, isn't it? I cry all the way to the bank. Come on. Let's go back to mine and have a drink.'

They stroll along the bank and up the track. Mungo pauses at the crossroads, makes his obeisance to the old Herm, and then he and Archie follow the dogs up the steps, through the gate and into the cobbled courtyard. In the lane silence gathers again, shadows creep beneath twisty boughs of ash and thorn. The old Herm remains, watching the pathways, guarding his secrets.

ABOUT THE AUTHOR

Marcia Willett was born in Somerset and lives in deepest Devon with her husband. A former ballet dancer and teacher, she is the author of many bestselling novels.